CARRIER

These are the stories of the Carrier Battle Group F——
force including a super ————
cruiser, and destroyer. ————
blistering reality ————
A————

CARRIER ... The sm———— ————
military nightmare: the ———— ————. Intelligence ship.

VIPER STRIKE ... A renegade Chinese fighter group penetrates Thai airspace—and launches a full-scale invasion.

ARMAGEDDON MODE ... With India and Pakistan on the verge of nuclear destruction, the Carrier Battle Group Fourteen must prevent a final showdown.

FLAME-OUT ... The Soviet Union is reborn in a military takeover—and their strike force shows no mercy.

MAELSTROM ... The Soviet occupation of Scandinavia leads the Carrier Battle Group Fourteen into conventional weapons combat—and possible all-out war.

COUNTDOWN ... Carrier Battle Group Fourteen must prevent the deployment of Russian submarines. The problem is: They have nukes.

AFTERBURN ... Carrier Battle Group Fourteen receives orders to enter the Black Sea—in the middle of a Russian civil war.

ALPHA STRIKE ... When American and Chinese interests collide in the South China Sea, the superpowers risk waging a third World War.

continued on next page ...

ARCTIC FIRE . . . A Russian splinter group has occupied the Aleutian Islands off the coast of Alaska—in the ultimate invasion of U.S. soil.

ARSENAL . . . Magruder and his crew are trapped between Cuban revolutionaries . . . and a U.S. power play that's spun wildly out of control.

NUKE ZONE . . . When a nuclear missile is launched against the U.S. Sixth fleet, Magruder must face a frightening question: In an age of computer warfare, how do you tell friends from enemies?

CHAIN OF COMMAND . . . Magruder enters the jungles of Vietnam looking for answers about his missing father. Little does he know that another bloody war is about to be unleashed—with his fleet caught in the crosshairs!

BRINK OF WAR . . . Friendly wargames with the Russians take a deadly turn, and Carrier Battle Group Fourteen must prevent war from erupting in the skies. Little do they know—that's just what someone wants!

TYPHOON . . . An American yacht is attacked by a Chinese helicopter in international waters, and the Carrier team is called to the front lines of what may be the start of a war between the superpowers . . .

ENEMY OF MY ENEMY . . . A Greek pilot unwittingly downs a news chopper, and Magruder must keep the peace between Greece and the breakaway republic of Macedonia. But what no one knows is that it wasn't an accident at all . . .

JOINT OPERATIONS . . . China launches a surprise attack on Hawaii—and the Carrier team can't handle it alone. As Tombstone and his fleet take charge of the air, Lieutenant Murdock and his SEALs are called in to work ashore . . .

book seventeen

CARRIER
The Art of War

KEITH DOUGLASS

JOVE BOOKS, NEW YORK

CARRIER: THE ART OF WAR

A Jove Book / published by arrangement with
the author

PRINTING HISTORY
Jove edition / April 2001

All rights reserved.
Copyright © 2001 by Penguin Putnam Inc.
This book, or parts thereof, may not be reproduced in
any form without permission.
For information address: The Berkley Publishing Group,
a division of Penguin Putnam Inc.,
375 Hudson Street, New York, New York 10014.

The Penguin Putnam Inc. World Wide Web site address is
http://www.penguinputnam.com

ISBN: 0-515-13044-3

A JOVE BOOK®
Jove Books are published by The Berkley Publishing Group,
a division of Penguin Putnam Inc.,
375 Hudson Street, New York, New York 10014.
JOVE and the "J" design
are trademarks belonging to Penguin Putnam Inc.

PRINTED IN THE UNITED STATES OF AMERICA

10 9 8 7 6 5 4 3 2 1

Acknowledgments

Special thanks to freelance writer and naval aviation analyst Brad Elward for his assistance with the air combat scenes. Brad writes regularly for *Combat Aircraft* magazine and *World Air Power Journal* and his book, *The McDonnell Douglas A-4 Skyhawk*, published by Crowood Press, was released in July 2000.

ONE

Heat blistered up through the soles of his worn boots, seeped through two layers of socks, and drenched his feet in salty sweat. Ali ben Wadi could feel his feet baking in their own juices under the desert sun. The rest of his body was parched and broiled. The fine sand crept into every opening, sifting through clothes, clogging his nose, mouth, and eyes with gritty pain.

For all the discomfort, he reveled in the feelings, letting the pain and physical challenge wash over him like a cooling bath. Hell on earth it might be to some, but it was his hell, his home. As hostile as the desert climate was, it was a familiar inferno, one that he had grown up knowing and come to respect.

In contrast, the climate of the northeastern part of the United States would never be familiar, no matter how many years he spent in it. Four years at Harvard for his undergraduate degree, another two for a master's degree, and then the final six months starting his doctorate degree, and every second of the time he'd longed for the harsh reality of his desert home.

Yes, it had been a sacrifice, but one he'd undertaken willingly. His government asked him to go, asked him to apply himself as best he could to knowing the ways of the United States, soaking up the knowledge, making contacts and learning to pass as a native—and then to return home, bringing with him his knowledge like a motherlode more precious than the oil beneath his feet. Over the last several decades of conflict and a return to traditional ways, there was one lesson that Iran had learned the hard way—to take advantage of what was offered by the incredibly naïve United States.

Wadi was considered a rarity in some circles. This experiment had been tried too many times with weaker men—never women, always men. Few women of any character or ability would have shamed themselves by choosing to live in such a decadent, sinful society, as evidenced by the fact that so few chose to return to their homeland after a taste of the American lifestyle. Even the men, his brothers and cousins born to this hard land had succumbed, whining from a distance about being allowed to remain in the West, advancing flaccid arguments about how they could better serve their people by remaining on station inside the Western world and insinuating themselves into the fabric of the culture as spies and subversive elements. Wadi had listened to their whining and vowed never to be the same.

A memory cropped up, seductive and enticing. The smell of Boston streets after a rain, the first scents of spring curling through the still-chilly air. He pushed it away, determined to divest himself of those weaknesses. To have enjoyed it while there was simply a matter of acculturation, of better coming to understand the weak and foolish people that made up that land. To reflect on it now, with hot sand under his boots and hard sun beating down on his shoulders was simply indulgence.

No, not indulgence, because that implied that there was anything at all pleasant about the experience. No, it was weakness, a sin of pride, and one that must be routed out at all costs. There was too much to do in the weeks and months ahead, too much at risk. He would not allow the petty temptations of physical comfort to distract him from his destiny.

His cousin, Jemal Hassan, turned to him. "Here, do you think?"

Wadi surveyed the area. To a Westerner, one patch of desert looked like the next. Flat, hot, sand—what more was there to understand about the country?

But to Wadi and Hassan, there was a richness to the subtlety of this land. There were prevailing winds to consider, the patterns of sand accumulation, the probability of a sandstorm whipping through and transforming this landscape overnight from hard-baked clay and sand into an ever-shifting dunescape.

"Yes." Wadi made an impatient gesture. "The council has already approved it. This is merely a formality and a final chance to detect any problems."

"Even so. I would wonder that we are so far from the ocean." Hassan shifted a bit, as though a trickle of sweat was coursing down inside his traditional garb. Wadi allowed himself a moment of self-satisfaction. So long away from this land, and yet he tolerated it better than his weaker cousin.

"Irrelevant. We could be practically on the eastern border and still have the plan work." The reaction times were so short on the scale that the Americans understood that a few minutes here or there made no difference.

"Yes, but—"

"Have you any valid points to offer?"

Hassan fell silent, but Wadi could feel his seething frustration. Not everyone had welcomed him back to Iran with open arms. His return had rearranged power structures and alliances that had grown in his absence, the way water flows in to fill a void, and the process of reestablishing his position within the family was still going on.

"I thought not." Wadi hammered the point home, allowing a few moments for his cousin to feel his disdain. "Then we are done here."

They walked back to the military vehicle in silence, each preoccupied with his own thoughts. For Wadi's part, he was pleased with the encounter.

A few days to allow their report—his report, since he would ensure that his cousin's name appeared nowhere on it—to circulate, and then the construction would begin. The foreign crews were already standing by, along with their equipment. It was a pain working with them, but few Iranians were willing to soil their hands with physical labor. If the riches that flowed from the black oil underfoot had one drawback, it was that easy wealth seemed to have eroded the willingness to work to survive that had characterized his people before.

Or was that a faulty perception, one that he'd picked up in the West? Yes, that was it. The wealth now allowed his people to take their natural place in Allah's great plan, leading this part of the world into a return to traditional values, to following his sacred commands. It was not that his people were lazy or unwilling, it was simply that greater matters occupied them now. A man could not be expected to spend his days in hard physical labor when he had his leadership responsibilities to the rest of the world to consider. Let the lesser races take their appropriate place, working to redeem themselves from their sinful ways, sweating out their evil for the good of Iran. Yes, they died. Died from heatstroke, from snakebite, from what they complained of as poor nutrition and sanitation. Yet were these not the very conditions that had tempered the Iranian spirit, fired them into the proud and indomitable people that they were now? The days of toadying to American interests were gone, the interest of the oil companies nationalized, and Iran was moving steadily toward her proper role in the world.

Within a few weeks, this would no longer be empty desert. Concrete and tarmac would bloom like flowers after a rain. Metal would fill the skies, hard and clean under the sun. And eventually . . .

"Vengeance," he whispered. "Vengeance will be ours."

The slight coolness of early evening, if it could be called such, was welcome.

Just forty miles to the north, the hulks waited on the desert to answer his call. The low humidity was an excellent factor in their preservation, and although the avionics and weaponry were outdated, money could cure that. Money could cure so many ills in the world, when properly applied. It was distasteful to have to deal with the foreign curs who had such expertise, and the prices that they gouged from this holy mission were an evil unto themselves, but all would be repaid eventually. The aircraft would fly again, harder, faster, and into danger's path, piloted by the brave Iranian pilots that had been trained by the very people that they would soon challenge in the skies.

The impunity with which foreigners dared to fly in the airspace, proclaiming their right to keep the peace, even daring to shoot down Arab aircraft over their own soil—well, it would end, and it would end in a way that would show the rest of the world that this part of the world would never again accept such intrusions. Weren't they the civilizations that had given birth to the rest of the world? The cradle of civilization, the very beginnings of mankind? And how far the rest of the world had strayed to turn their weapons on their own fathers and mothers.

Well, no more. Wadi and his people would prove the point, as they had so far. Fashioning together a coalition among the fractious nations of this world had been a difficult, delicate process. There were egos to consider, the different aims of the Shiite and Sunni cultures, the will of the ayatollahs, the guidance provided by Allah. And, like it or not, there were other cultures to consider. India, China—thank Allah that the Soviet Union now lay like a rotting corpse to the north, decades from ever interfering again.

The compromises within his own extended family had been minor compared to the necessity of providing each nation with that which they could not resist. In the end, it had been a matter of focusing them on what they had in common rather than the slight differences—heretical though they were—that divided them. Above all, each had an abiding hatred of the impunity with which foreign nations dominated their skies.

Nine months—long enough for a child to be born but barely enough time for the devout to nurture the seeds of a reborn nation. So long, the waiting, but the centuries of peace that would follow would make it seem but a blink of an eye. And he, Wadi, would be known forever as the father of the new Iran.

TWO

The non-skid coating of the flight deck still held the heat from the day, but for the sailors accustomed to the blazing heat, even the slightest drop in temperature was a welcome relief. The slight breeze even more so—wind chill was a phrase that would never be applied to the searing heat in this part of the world, but air moving was cooler than air standing in thick, cloying masses around them.

It was slightly cooler inside the two F-14D Tomcats pulling alert-five on the bow catapults, but not by much. Yellow huffers were attached to each aircraft by an umbilical, powering the jets to provide air-conditioning, but the hot sun baking down through the shaded canopies still raised the interior temperature to unholy levels.

The Tomcats were fueled to full capacity, and carried two auxiliary tanks as well. The current loadout was two AIM-9M Sidewinders, two AIM-7M Sparrows, two

AIM-54C Phoenix, a flexible, all-ranges antiair loadout. While the Tomcat was also a capable land-attack platform, there were no over-ground attack missions planned for the foreseeable future. Configured as a "Bombcat," the aircraft could carry more ordnance further than its lighter Hornet brethren.

"I'm too senior to pull alert five," Lieutenant Commander Curt "Bird Dog" Robinson said from the forward seat of Tomcat 106. He was complaining over the ICS—interior communications system—to his RIO, Lieutenant Harmon "Music" David.

"Yes, sir," Music answered. "I agree completely. Far too senior."

Bird Dog sighed. They'd had a rash of nuggets arrive in the squadron all at one time, and Music was part of that gaggle. Nice kid, wore glasses—what else could you say about a new RIO? And he seemed to have the proper respect for pilots, which was something you didn't find often enough, in Bird Dog's humble opinion, in the nonflying part of a cockpit crew. Yeah, that was a bit of a relief, especially after about a million years of being paired up with Gator.

Bird Dog's thoughts drifted away from the cockpit and back to the past missions he'd flown with Gator. He knew what the admiral and the squadron thought about the team—there'd been too many times that Gator had threatened to punch out if Bird Dog didn't go along with his decisions. The rest of the Navy seemed to think that this was a good thing, putting a killjoy in the cockpit with an experienced pilot who was more than capable of making tactical decision on his own, thank you very much.

Why, when they'd been up in the Arctic, what would have happened if he'd listened to Gator? The Russians would have fried a whole SEAL squad, and who would have said boo to Gator about that? Bird Dog had punched his way through the landscape to put ordnance on target at precisely the right moment and saved the day. All over Gator's objections. Well, Bird Dog bet he could roust up a couple of SEALs who were more than happy that someone had the balls to—

"Sir?" Music's voice broke in on his reverie.

"What?"

"Nothing, sir. Just wanted to make sure you were okay."

Shit. Like he'd be the first pilot to catch a few winks in a hot cockpit on alert-five. Yeah, he was definitely too senior to be pulling alert-five.

But with nuggets, what were you going to do? You had to pair them with someone that had some experience, that'd managed to prove themselves in more than one combat arena. Bird Dog conveniently ignored the fact that that was exactly why he'd been paired with Gator.

So because BUPERS, the Bureau of Naval Personnel, screwed up and flooded them with newbies, every experienced pilot and RIO in the squadron was flying more hours than normal, trying to whip the youngsters into some sort of shape. Gator was currently sitting in the wardroom on alert-fifteen, pounding back cold sodas and baby-sitting a new pilot. Figured. Gator always did have a way of finagling his way around things.

It wasn't like he was the only one, either. Over on the other catapult, Rat was saddled with Fastball, and he wasn't so sure that he didn't have a better deal than Rat did. Lieutenant Brad "Fastball" Morrow had already earned himself a bit of a reputation within the squadron as a cocky bastard, and Bird Dog felt pretty sure that having a female as his mentor-RIO—even a damned fine RIO—wasn't his idea of a good time. He wouldn't be so stupid as to make an issue of it, but there were a thousand ways a pilot could make a RIO's life miserable without even breaking a sweat.

"You think we'll launch today, sir?" Music asked.

Bird Dog sighed. "Now how the hell should I know

that, Music? And I told you, knock off the sir shit in the cockpit. We're crew, okay?"

"Yes, si—yes, Bird Dog. I was just asking because, I mean, after all—you've been to the War College and all. I thought you might have it all figured out by now."

Bird Dog listened carefully, but could detect no note of sarcasm in the RIO's voice. Well, what the hell—Music did have a point. Even Lab Rat, the carrier's intelligence officer, hadn't been to the War College, and for all that Lab Rat was smart as hell.

"It's just a matter of history," Bird Dog said, and tried to decide whether he was in the mood to lecture for a bit. Not really, but it beat the hell out of getting woken up every few minutes when Music got worried about whether or not he was still breathing. "That's what you always have to understand about the Middle East—all this stuff goes back a long ways."

"But they wouldn't attack an American aircraft carrier, would they? That would be suicide."

"They might," Bird Dog admitted. "That's what you don't get about this, kid. A lot of these people, they figure they go straight to heaven if they kill infidels. That'd be us. Granted, they don't have the training or the advanced weaponry that we do, but that won't keep them from being a pain in the ass if they decide to cause some trouble."

"So maybe we'll launch today."

"Maybe. Maybe not."

"Wow. Thanks. That helps a lot."

Bird Dog tried for a moment to convince himself that he had indeed clarified the whole situation in his nugget's mind, but couldn't manage to buy it himself. For just a moment, he felt an intense nostalgia for hearing the clipped accent of Gator coming out of the backseat. Up until now, he hadn't realized how fast a yes-man suck-up could get on your nerves.

THREE

A young yeoman with curly blond hair rapped lightly on Rear Admiral Matthew "Tombstone" Magruder's door. He pushed it open when he heard Tombstone say, "Come in."

"Admiral? Phone call for you on the secure line in Admiral Wayne's quarters."

Tombstone put down the operational plan he was studying and said, "Thanks. I'll be right there."

What was this all about, he wondered. Anything operational could have been handled on the normal radio circuits or via the encrypted computer lines that link the intelligence agencies around the world. Tombstone followed the young sailor down the passageway to Batman's office.

Batman looked up as Tombstone came in. "It's your uncle, Stony," he said. He stood and came out from around the desk. "I'll give you some privacy."

"Not necessary."

"Your uncle said it was." With a worried look at his old lead, Batman left.

Now what the hell? Tombstone picked up the receiver. "Magruder."

"Good morning, Stony. Or afternoon there, isn't it?" his uncle said.

"Afternoon, sir," Tombstone answered, even more puzzled now. It wasn't like his uncle to waste time on pleasantries, not on a Navy phone. "To what do I owe the honor?"

"There's no way to say this to make it easy, Tombstone," his uncle began after a moment. "It's not about Tomboy or anything like that. But the selection board just met, and while I can't release the results yet, it doesn't look promising. You might give some thought to what you're going to do after you leave the Navy."

Tombstone sat down hard, stunned. Sure, it had always been a possibility. As a pilot, and later as an admiral in command, he had always been a bit more daring than his peers, at times resorting to outrageous and unconventional methods to achieve results.

And results were what counted, right? None of the rest of it mattered as long as you got results.

Or so he had always thought. His uncle had cautioned him several times that the rest of the Navy didn't necessarily see it that way. Sometimes a team player was more valuable than an officer who could get down and dirty with the enemy.

Yeah, there'd been a chance he was stepping in it, but he hadn't expected this, not really. Even though he and Tomboy had talked over their options, he never truly believed that he'd have to face the day when he would be forced to retire. On some level, he had always thought he would die in the Navy and never have to make the transition to civilian life.

"I know this comes as a shock, Stony," his uncle said, as though reading his mind. "And for what it's worth, you're not alone in this."

"When?" Tombstone asked, surprised to find his voice slightly tight. "Not right away, I hope."

"No, not immediately. But soon. We have six months."

It took Tombstone a moment, but then the significance of his uncle's pronouncement "we", hit him like a sledgehammer. "We? Surely you don't mean . . ." He broke off, not entirely sure he could keep his voice steady.

When he answered, his uncle's voice was peculiarly gentle. "Yes, I said we. While the board can't force me to retire, there were certain strong . . . recommendations . . . from other quarters that I give the matter serious thought."

"Who? JCS? The president?" If anything, the revelation that his uncle would also be retiring made the situation even harder to bear. Because, at some level, he thought that his uncle's predicament was probably due in part to allowing his favorite nephew free rein in fighting the Navy's battles. "Oh god, I'm so sorry to hear this."

There was a long silence, and then his uncle finally spoke. "I've had a day or two to get used to the idea. When the subject was first broached with me, I couldn't believe it. But since then, certain . . . opportunities . . . have come to light. And for what it's worth, I think you may be interested in them."

"Opportunities? What do you mean?"

"This is so secret, Stony, I can't even begin to assign a security classification. And there's not much I can tell you, not even on this line. But there are certain operations within the U.S. government that don't suffer the same restraints as we have in the Navy. There are ways of achieving objectives, and some very different departments to take care of them. I've been asked to head up one of them—and if you're interested, I liked you onboard as my chief of staff."

Tombstone leaned forward and put his hands on his forehand, wedging the telephone receiver between his

shoulder and his ear. "I have to think about it. And Tomboy . . . I'll have to talk it over with her."

"You can't. Tomboy isn't cleared for any of this. If
you agree, you'll appear to be working for a defense
contractor. And that's all that Tomboy will ever know."
His uncle's voice took on an urgent note. "I promise
you, Stony, we can make a difference in the world. We
can keep people in the battle group from getting killed,
make missions safer. No dirty tricks, nothing that you
wouldn't approve of—you think I would take the job if
there were? And . . ." His uncle paused, as if to make
sure he had Tombstone's full attention. "It would require
a fair amount of flying on your part. Tomcats, mostly,
but other aircraft as needed. There will be funds to bring
you up to speed on anything that we need to have you
fly. How's that sound?"

Hope leaped in Tombstone's heart. He realized that
his anguish over the prospect of retirement had been
primarily related to the fact that he would never fly
again. Oh, sure, he had his Pitts Special, and he dearly
loved it. But there was nothing that could compare to
the sheer power and grace of a Navy combat fighter. To
contemplate the possibility of never again strapping a
Tomcat onto his ass and soaring wild and free in the air
was almost more than he could bear.

"Flying?" he asked, a new note of hope in his voice.

His uncle chuckled slightly. "I thought that would get
your attention. No uniforms, no regulations, no squadron
CO telling you what you can and can't do. It would all
be up to you. And as the operation expands, you'd have
other pilots under your command. But the choice of who
flies what missions, how much flying you'd do yourself,
would be completely up to you."

"But what sort of missions? How can I possibly make
a decision based on what you've told me?" Tombstone
asked.

"We'll talk more when you get back to D.C. For now,
keep your retirement confidential. The message will be

out in a few days. Then you can start talking about your upcoming retirement, but not a word about this. Keep your plans vague. Say that you'll look for work in the defense industry. Not that you need to—I know that your investments over the years have netted you a tidy nest egg. Between that and Tomboy's active duty pay and your retirement pay, you could live quite comfortably without ever having to work again. But I have a feeling that that won't be enough for you. It never has been."

"It may be a while before I'm back in D.C." Tombstone said.

"Not as long as you think." Again, the peculiarly gentle note in his uncle's voice. "This is Batman's show, Stony. I'm going to recall you, give him free rein. It could be that someday he'll be up for this job, and I need to make absolutely certain that he can handle everything the world can throw at him without you there to keep him honest. He's only standing in your shadow, the way things are now. Now it's time for him to be on his own.

"I've never interfered with how Batman does things," Tombstone said.

He pictured his uncle shaking his head as he often did, the look of grave amusement on his face. "You don't have to. Batman is no dummy. If you're there, he's going to listen to your advice. Whether you intend to or not, you affect his decisions. Primarily for the better, I imagine, but he simply has to be on his own. Like you were."

Tombstone thought about his own early days, the progression in his career into increasingly important positions of responsibility. The time when he had been CAG and had ended up in command of the battle group. The attack on Pearl Harbor, and putting together a pickup team as a battle group staff. All those events, and countless others, had made him who he was.

Had he been holding Batman back without intending

to? Tombstone considered the matter for a moment, then reluctantly admitted it might be true. No matter that he'd never intended it—that would have been the result nonetheless.

"It's a lot to think about, Stony," his uncle said. "And we'll do it on our own time, not on the government's telephone time. I'll see you when you get back to D.C. We'll talk then."

His uncle hung up, and Tombstone listened for a few minutes to the static hissing on the line before he followed suit.

Flying—a new career, and moreover one that involves combat flying. Not the safe, predictable, and boring flights of the commercial airline pilot, or even a pilot hauling freight cross-country. No, although his uncle hadn't given him any details, this sounded like it would be far more serious.

And fun. Definitely fun.

CVIC
USS **Jefferson**
2220 local (GMT +3)

Commander Hillman "Lab Rat" Busby studied the detailed charts lying on the plot table in front of him. The computer-generated historical data tracks were precisely inked on the charts, showing the last four days of air activity around the *Jefferson*. A second chart showed a longer time period and extrapolated the detected tracks into historical patrol boxes.

His leading chief, Intelligence Specialist Chief Petty Officer Armstrong Perry, was tapping a pencil on the top chart. "Nothing out of the ordinary, sir. Not so far as I can see. Computer's not alerting on anything, either."

"I know, Chief." Lab Rat continued to stare down at

the charts. So much data, so little information. While it was true that often historical data could tell you when things were ramping up, it wasn't an exact science. It looked like it was, with these immaculate charts that the laser printer spat out, with the tabulated columns of data and average flight times and load-outs all carefully correlated against external events and the Islamic calendar— just for a second, he felt a flash of yearning for a hand-drawn chart. When you saw erasure marks and wobbly lines, you didn't tend to think of yourself as infallible. You saw the evidence right in front of you that mistakes happened. It was too easy to be lulled into a false sense of infallibility when the charts were so pristine—columns of very accurate numbers calculated down to two decimal points that meant absolutely nothing.

Everything in front of him told him that the situation was normal. Oh, sure, there were the usual diplomatic flare-ups and violations of the Iraqi no-fly zone. Air Force jets still flew bombing missions to the far north in Iraq and the Kurds were still being massacred by both the Turks and the Iraqis. But all that was par for the course for this part of the world. The only real new factor was the continuing American military presence, at least on the time scale that these people used to measure history.

So why this hinky feeling? Where was it coming from, this uneasiness that woke him up in the middle of the night wondering what he'd missed, the uneasy conviction that the storm was building and that it was just a matter of time before all hell broke loose?

Lab Rat saw the chief was staring at him. "You okay, sir?"

"Yeah, Chief. Fine. Charts look great."

"Yes, sir. But it's like . . . I dunno, sir. It's like we're missing something." The chief looked away, as though embarrassed. "I been pulling duty in CVIC on carriers since we had CVICs, and there's something about this . . . aw, never mind."

Chief Armstrong Perry had one of the most keenly analytical minds that Lab Rat had ever met. He saw patterns where others saw chaos, felt the undercurrents of military planning in a way that few others seemed to appreciate. In the two months since the chief had checked on board, Lab Rat found himself relying more and more on the intuition and judgment of his senior enlisted sailor. He hid his brilliance beneath a bluff, weather-battered, and scarred face and a slow Southern drawl. But you underestimated him at your own peril.

Lab Rat patted the chief on the shoulder. "Don't say that. I know exactly what you're talking about. It's that feeling you get just before lightning strikes, like something is happening right in front of you that you just don't see."

"You got it, too?"

"You bet. And if you're feeling it, too, that means we're missing something. Let's go over this morning again—something bothers me about that whole fly-over."

"Yes, sir." Perry pulled out a new printout. "Here's the track."

"Flight composition?"

"What we've seen before."

"Track?"

"Within normal parameters. But sir, I'd bet my bottom dollar that this wasn't a routine surveillance patrol. Something about the flight profile—right here, I guess." The chief stabbed a stubby finger down on the chart. "They're about two thousand feet lower than usual."

"Why would they deviate? Any weather account for it?"

"No, sir. In fact, if anything, they'd want to be higher, in cooler air. It's just a normal scorcher."

"Any unusual activity on the ground around then?"

"Maybe." The chief hauled out a sheaf of photos. "This."

Lab Rat studied the photos. They were a download

from a geo-stationary satellite over the area, and capable of astounding resolution. He'd seen this particular set yesterday when they were fresh off the printer, after the photo intelligence specialists had conducted their analysis, and hadn't been struck by anything in particular. But evidently something had caught the chief's attention.

The picture showed bare dirt and sand, inland about fifty miles from the coast. It was a largely uninhabited stretch of land, except for the wandering tribes that still lived the traditional desert lifestyle. Now, though, it showed evidence of construction activity.

"And this." The chief handed him another photo.

This one showed what might be charitably called a road to the north. A cloud of dust obscured most of the details, but the infrared resolution picked up smears of light easily against the cooler night air.

"A convoy of some sort, right?" Lab Rat asked.

"Yes, sir. That's what we make of it. Originally, we thought it was routine troop maneuvers of some sort, but now I'm not so sure."

"No, wait. No pussyfooting around, Chief. You *are* sure—sure that we were dead wrong on that one." Lab Rat tapped the photo. "Those trucks are headed for the construction site. And you're worried because it's located right next to that aircraft graveyard, aren't you?"

"Yeah. Yeah, I am, sir." A look of frustration passed over the chief's face. "But it doesn't make sense. Those aircraft have been parked there since the first days of Desert Storm and Desert Shield. They haven't flown since Iraq flew them into Iran for safekeeping. Everybody knows that."

Lab Rat felt something jell in his stomach, a deep conviction accompanied by a flood of relief. Exactly how and why he was so certain, he couldn't have said. But Armstrong agreed with him, and between the two of them, they could manage to convince the admiral and his staff.

"Avionics aren't that hard to come by," Lab Rat said quietly. "And the desert's an ideal place to store aircraft."

"Except for the damage the sand has done," the chief supplied. "You know how it is out there. That damned stuff gets in every nook and cranny. The abrasion is something awful."

"Right. But that's not a showstopper. Our own graveyard is located in the desert in the U.S."

"Yes, sir. But those aircraft are usually properly mothballed. Plastic wrapping and nitrogen packing, and there's no way they leave the avionics on them. But these babies—god knows what a decade in the desert has done to them."

The two men were silent for a moment, each caught up in his own thoughts. Every fact they had argued against the former Iraqi aircraft flying again. There was no indication of new trouble brewing in the Middle East. And apart from the two-thousand-foot deviation in the normal flight pattern on this morning's patrol, there were no other indications of trouble.

"They're going to fly again," Lab Rat said softly, utterly aware that it sounded crazy. He glanced over at Armstrong and saw the chief nodding.

"Yes, sir. I don't know how or why, but I'd bet on it. And sooner rather than later, sir. Sooner rather than later."

FOUR

The new ambassador from the United Kingdom caught up with the United States ambassador, Sarah Wexler, just as she was leaving her office complex. Wexler felt herself frown slightly as he approached, and schooled her face into careful neutrality. The man had only been here for three weeks, dammit. The least she could do was give him a chance to settle in before she started making judgments about him.

At least that's what she tried to tell herself. But Wexler knew that she had always had an uncanny ability to form accurate first impressions of people. When she ignored her first judgments, she often found cause to regret it later. Only once had she proved to be wrong, and even in that instance, the jury was still out on whether the long-time ambassador from China was truly trustworthy.

Perhaps it was just the difference in British and American cultures that made her uneasy around Sir Forsyth Wells. Certainly she would never be so shallow as to judge the man merely on his minor annoying personal characteristics. Like the careful attention he paid to his hair, often smoothing it carefully back into place. Like his habit of echoing the last part of her sentences, as though repeating her words for confirmation. Like his too jolly, too eager way of insinuating himself into her personal life.

The United Kingdom and America were long-standing allies, and often stood alone against the rest of the world's opinion in trying to do what was right. And Wells's predecessor had been a true joy to work with. Although some found him condescending, she had found that he possessed a wealth of insight into the workings of nations and international politics, and embodied all that was very good about the British Empire. He had been a wise, older cousin to whom she had turned on occasion for advice, and during her first days at the United Nations, had done his best to make her feel welcome. In subsequent conflicts, she often relied on his suggestions, although she sometimes thought that his long experience with internal European politics had made him cynical rather than wise.

Still, she had counted him as a friend, and hoped that she would be able to do the same with Wells. That relationship had not yet materialized.

"Good afternoon, Ambassador Wells," she said gravely. He was, she noted, flanked as always by an aide and a security man trying to look like an aide. She wasn't sure exactly what was annoying about it—the implication that he didn't feel safe inside the United Nations, or the possibility that he was simply a coward. Certainly she herself did not take elaborate precautions.

It's not his country. Perhaps you'd feel the same way if you were permanently assigned to the Court of St. James for the first time. He doesn't know the city, the people, doesn't see the clues you pick up in people's behaviors.

"I am glad to have caught you before you left," he

said, a broad smile on his face. He looked rather silly, with a permanent curl that always centered itself precisely on his forehead, the too-eager expression on his face. "The arms negotiations package." He splayed his hands open in a gesture pleading. "I'm afraid I don't entirely grasp the significance of the issues. Perhaps if you have a moment . . . ?"

Wexler sighed. And this was precisely the sort of thing she meant. Yet perhaps the prior British ambassador had felt the same degree of impatience with her naivete on such issues as he'd tutored her on the finer points of international statesmanship.

"Of course," she said. "What can I clarify for you?"

"This question of America's new aircraft carrier—the USS *United States*. It comes up repeatedly in discussions, yet I suspect I am not grasping its full importance. Why are Russia and China quite so concerned about it?"

"My office, perhaps?" she suggested, glancing at the throngs of people hurrying up and down the corridors. Certainly she would not be discussing classified information, at least none that wasn't already releasable to the United Kingdom, but it was always wiser to talk about such things in private. There was no telling who might find useful some insight into America's position from overhearing her, or detect some weakness.

"I thought perhaps lunch—that is, if you have not yet eaten," he said eagerly. "Perhaps a quiet corner in the executive dining room."

Wexler suppressed a sigh of annoyance. She had been looking forward to a good, hot pastrami sandwich, but she suspected that would not go down well with the British ambassador. Wells seemed particularly fond of all the accoutrements and trappings that went with his new position, and never failed to take advantage of the UN's facilities. While the food served in the executive dining area was superb, it sure wasn't the hot pastrami with biting mustard she'd had her heart set on.

"That would be fine," she said instead, and led the

way down the corridor to the dining room. Once they were seated in a quiet corner, apparently out of earshot of everyone else, and she had ordered, she turned to him. "You know, to understand this entire discussion, you must understand that it is not only the weapons that are in question. It is the delivery systems as well. Without those, weaponry is useless. And with a move to reduce long-range missiles, there's increasing concern about the use that we can make of shorter-range missiles from closer delivery points."

He nodded. "The same issue that arose during the Germany talks, of course. The U.S. agreed to eliminate shorter-range missiles, but they were replaced with intermediate-range missiles in other parts of Europe. To the Russians, it was all the shell game."

She nodded. "Yes, exactly. And this is what concerns everyone about the new carrier. With our current low levels of aircraft carriers in the inventory, it represents a major addition to our long-range power projection capabilities."

And that, she reflected, was a sad state of affairs. There was a time when the American military was at full strength, when the addition of another aircraft carrier would have been welcome, but hardly a dramatic increase in America's capabilities. Not so these days— especially in an age of increasing commitments, with current forces overworked, underequipped and worn out, the new carrier would be a much-needed addition to the force.

And hence the reason for Russia and China's concern. And, quite frankly, she for one took their objections as evidenced that building the carrier had been exactly the right move.

"Yes, you understand. So where's the confusion?" she asked.

Wells's face shifted subtly, and for just a moment she caught a trace of the capabilities behind the mask of a bumbling fool he presented to the rest of the world. She felt a shock as she realized how much she might have underestimated the man.

"What confuses me—and, I must admit, the prime minister,—is why your country is so insistent on completing the project at all, given the world opposition to it. Surely your country has better uses for its funds, especially during these times of energy crisis? After all, the president has dipped into your strategic reserves simply to hold prices down within your country." He held up one hand to forestall comment. "Not that we would ever presume to question the judgment of our American cousins. Still, having been down that road ourselves, it would seem that America might be wise to concentrate on their internal affairs rather than on building up the military force." He paused, and an ingratiating smile tugged at his lips. "Particular when the world is relatively peaceful."

Wexler almost dropped her fork at the surprise. "This is . . . I wonder that . . . ," she stopped, aware of the danger of speaking even to an ally with her thoughts tumbling over each other in such turmoil. "You raise an interesting point," she said finally, and let her silence speak more than words could ever have done.

And what was this unpleasant turning of affairs, she wondered. That Britain, America's oldest and staunchest ally, would question building additional aircraft carriers? This was an argument one heard from Russia, from China, even from India, that aircraft carriers would destabilize the current balance of power.

Yes, and those countries had reason to worry—although each had made some forays into the field of carrier aviation, not one could match the capabilities of the United States. Britain was even only a distant second.

And Britain had always been a strong supporter of American military building programs, ever since the days of Lend-Lease. They had had reason to be profoundly grateful for America's industrial capabilities then, had they not?

"Aircraft carriers are not built overnight," she pointed out. "This construction has been in the works for almost ten years now. If Britain had concerns, this is certainly the first that we're hearing of them. And I wonder at this late hour—surely it would be completely unreasonable to suggest that we cancel construction now. The keel is laid, the hull completed and most of the systems equipment in place. To fail to complete it would represent more of an economic waste in terms of cancelled contracts, guaranteed performances, and liquidated damages."

He leaned back, a faint gleam of amusement in his eyes. "But there are costs other than monetary," he pointed out. "A peaceful world is economically desirable, is it not?"

"Are you telling me that Britain objects to this project?" she demanded.

He shook his head. "Not in those terms."

"But you're under orders to convey to me the prime minister's displeasure, is that it?"

He smiled again, that enigmatic expression she'd seen for the first time just moments before. "And now I have evidently irritated you. My apologies, madam." The genial buffoon was back, replacing the harder, more manipulative man she'd seen before. "Please, I hope you will attribute my rudeness to inexperience on my part rather than any agenda by my government. After all, this current conversation began with my plea for your assistance. I hope you do not believe I would abuse the privilege of your friendship."

They finished the meal with polite chitchat, Wells actively resisting any attempts to delve into deeper meaning of his comments. Afterwards, Wexler was not entirely certain what they discussed during the rest of the brief meal. She had cut it short just after the main course, pleading a full schedule as well as a full stomach. Wells had graciously been understanding.

Had this simply been naive chitchat between long-standing allies? Or had there been a message in his question, one she was intended to relate to the president himself?

She had, she realized, been foolish to suspect that the British ambassador was any less capable than his predecessor. Certainly, he had a different style of approaching matters, and she suspected they would never developed the warm friendship and personal respect for one another that she had had with his predecessor.

But that was not the main point in international relationships, though diplomacy turned on personal friendships and passions more often than anyone would like to admit. No, if she could establish a good working relationship with the new ambassador and count on him to support her country's policies, that would have to be enough. That he might be personally distasteful did not matter.

Still, she wondered whether this represented a major change in the British government's policy. Certainly, Britain had been long occupied with the Irish problem, and had had to devote more of its resources and attention to their internal problems than before. And, although it looked like there might be a resolution, or at least the semblance of peace, sometime in the near future, she had no doubt that the conflict drained it's resources.

Additionally, she had seen reports that the Socialist party was gaining increasing influence in both the House of Lords and House of Commons, particularly in the latter. Despite the staunch core of royalists inside the United Kingdom, would that signal a major change in Britain's alignment? And if so, how would American cope with the defection of her most trusted ally?

As she made her way back to her office pondering the implications, she resolved to call the president immediately. It might be nothing—but then again, it might already be too late.

The White House
Washington, D.C.
1400 local (GMT −5)

The president had just finished a short meeting with representatives of the American Wheat Society when the ambassador's call was put through to him. His chief of staff had put her on hold for a moment, and the president had been sorry to terminate his meeting with the farmers, although the farmers were quite understanding, and not a little awed at being ringside observers to the highest level of politics.

As the farmers filed out of the office, the President reflected that whoever had selected the delegation had been particularly astute. The men and women he met with were not corporate managers of agribusiness, the ones who never felt sweet dirt between their toes, had no understanding of the rhythms of nature, and depended on salaries rather than the vagaries of nature for their income. No, whoever had selected the delegation had sent him real farmers, and he had enjoyed talking to them and letting himself slip back into his childhood.

The president's roots ran deep in the heartland of the country. Although he was a political creature, one shaped by the expediencies and deals necessary to maneuver in Washington, there were times, more often than he would like, that he realized how alienated he was from real people. These were the people he needed to see more of, the ones that he really represented. The ones who had voted, given him their electoral delegates, and who, in countless small houses around the United States, were depending on him to oversee the good of the nation.

At his most cynical, he sometimes wondered what he had become, why he was here, and whether he really had a chance to make any difference in anything at all. But talking to these men, these farmers who knew the reality of everyday life, who wrested their living from the soil by supplying the rest of the nation with food, he knew why he had been put in this office by whatever higher power oversaw the affairs of nations. It was to remember them, to guard their interests—against people just like himself.

So it was with some reluctance that he picked up the phone, gave up the moment he savored with them, and turned his attention back to the realities of being the leader of the most powerful country in the world.

He listened to the ambassador's observations of her meeting with the British ambassador, and understood immediately why she'd called. It was no secret that commitment to build up American military forces was a bedrock cornerstone of the president's platform. He had kept those promises, he thought, at least as well as he was able to do in the rarefied air of Washington. The carrier *United States* was particularly important to him, and he'd fought hard and long to insure that the project remain funded at optimum levels.

When she finished, the president asked, "Okay, so you told me what happened. Now give me your take on it."

There was a pause, and he could almost see Ambassador Wexler collecting her thoughts. One of the things he appreciated most about her was her ability to cut through the bullshit, her keen insight into the personalities that made up the international community. She didn't shoot from the hip—he had a feeling that Sarah Wexler knew much more than she said about most things—but when she did voice an opinion that was based on intuition rather than objective facts, he listened.

"I need to know more about Wells," she said finally. "He's a funny creature—almost a clown in a way, a caricature of British royalty. But there something about him—he doesn't let it show often—that bothers me. Perhaps it's because he tries so hard to appear harmless. I was," she admitted ruefully, "taken in at first. After dealing with his predecessor for so long, I had certain expectations. Wells comes nowhere near those."

"I think we can both rule out the possibility that Britain has made a mistake in appointing him," the president said. "We know what is public record about him, of course. Let me check with some sources and see if I can get you more background information. Perhaps somebody knows something that can give some context to his words."

"That would certainly be helpful," she acknowledged. The president knew that, while she admitted the necessity of it, Sarah Wexler always thought the connection between the nation's intelligence services and its diplomatic corps to be slightly distasteful. It was something they shared, an almost reflexive belief that men and women of good will could solve national and international problems and issues in an aboveboard, straightforward sort of way. A pipe dream, as they both knew all too well from their time in D.C. and in the U.N., but a basic guiding principle that they clung to nonetheless. For that reason, although Wexler knew exactly where he would get the information, he made it a point not to mention the CIA. He would make sure the information got to her, but the source of it would be disguised to allow them both to maintain the illusion.

"I do feel that there is something to this," Wexler said. "He made such a point of mentioning it to me—and if we operate on the assumption that he's not a fool, then there was a reason for it. In their way, the British are just as devious as the Chinese."

"So what do we do?" the president asked.

"Nothing. We file information away, and look for some later relevance. But I would never recommend slowing down or even canceling the project based on Britain's position, either official or unofficial."

"Of course not," the president said. "Are they after

something else, though? A quid pro quo for not making an issue of the carrier?"

"If they are, we'll hear about it soon enough," Wexler said. "I'll keep you posted, sir."

"Do that." And with that, the ambassador rang off.

The president glanced down at his schedule, and saw that he had an unexpected free fifteen minutes. And just how had that happened?

No matter—he leaned back in his chair and put his feet up on his desk. He shut his eyes for moment, and thought about the wheat farmers.

In her office, Ambassador Wexler was doing much the same, but in her case it involved kicking off her high heels, putting her feet up on a small, embroidered stool, and having a freshly brewed cup of orange oolong tea. Just as she was thinking how nice a cup might be, it had materialized at her elbow, brought in by Brad, her aide, so quietly that she had almost missed his entrance. She murmured her thanks, and cradled the hot cup in her hands, letting the warmth sink into her bones. Outside, it might be a sultry, humid day, but in here the air-conditioning was working overtime.

"Anything I can help with?" Brad asked.

She shook her head. "This is enough," she said, raising the cup in salute. "There are those days . . ." She let her voice trail off.

"There are, indeed." Brad stood in the doorway for moment, and she had the feeling there was something on his mind. It wasn't like him to wait to be asked, though; things that he thought she needed to know, he brought to her attention—even if she didn't know at the moment she would need the information.

"What is it?" she asked, smiling a bit as he had the good grace to look abashed. "You don't hang on my doorjamb like that unless something is on your mind."

"Every day, there are new security notices coming out," he began. He paused, waiting for her protest. They had had this conversation many times before.

Wexler sighed. "What this time?"

"Just a feeling," he said, surprising her. Normally during these discussions of her personal security, Brad would brandish a specific memo warning U.N. personnel to be careful. This time, however, he looked more serious than ever. "I want your permission to put together some contingency plans, Ambassador," he said, a note of formality in his voice. "You've made clear your personal preferences, and I respect that. God knows we could do with more people with your personal courage. But, if you would allow me, I would be remiss in my duties if I didn't ask for this. Nothing that will affect you on a day-to-day basis, you understand. But in case we ever needed certain arrangements, it would be too late to put them in place when we needed them."

Wexler leaned back in her chair and tried to will the tension out of her shoulders. "Seriously, now . . . do you really think the threat has changed any over the last several years?"

"Yes, I do," he answered immediately. "Look at what we're seeing now—terrorist acts inside the United States, including acts of violence by domestic terrorist groups. We can't ignore the fact that this is no longer the Bastion America, that no one would dare to act on our soil for fear of bringing down the full force of our military might on them. I know what you would like to believe," he said, his voice gentler now, "but it simply isn't true. The fact that you refuse all personal security has operated in your favor until now, as your colleagues have taken it as a mark of personal courage. But it's time to start being realistic."

"Oh, bosh. I simply don't like being followed around, that's all." In truth, she had never felt in danger as ambassador. Perhaps it was because she never took herself as seriously as other people seemed to.

"And if word got out that we were increasing my personal security, it could send the wrong signal," she continued. "It's more of the challenge, you know—to prove that you can break through anything. But what glory is there in coming after me while I'm alone? None. Indeed, if anything, they'd look foolish attacking a defenseless woman."

"Just contingencies, Ambassador," Brad continued doggedly. "That's all."

She eyed him for a moment, and then said warily, "And what would it involve in terms of my personal freedom?"

"Nothing. I need a small operating budget, probably from petty cash, to make certain arrangements. I would ask you to memorize a couple of code words and one or two safe locations. That's it—that's all."

"That's all?" She laughed. "Code words and safe houses to memorize . . . nothing like having to learn by heart an entire welcoming address in Arabic." And to this day, she had no idea what she had truly said to the League of Arab Women that had held its international convention there in New York. Whatever it had been, it had been received favorably.

"That's all, I promise you." There was a new look of fervor in his eyes. "I would hold myself personally responsible if anything ever happened to you. You do realize that, don't you?"

Wexler studied him for a moment. "Low blow, Brad. You knew that would get me."

"Nevertheless, it's true. And you know it."

Suddenly weary of the discussion, and tired of going over the issue again and again, she waved him off. "Okay, you've worn me down. Make your arrangements. I'll be a good, obedient ambassador and cooperate." She gave him a sideways look, and said, "As long as it doesn't involve cameras and two-way mirrors in the bathroom, okay? I draw the line at that."

A look of relief crossed Brad' face. "Thank you, Ambassador."

She waved him off. "Oh, posh. All you people fussing about me—I guess the only way to get you to stop is to give in."

FIVE

CVIC was located perhaps a hundred feet astern of TFCC, but the distance between the two was more than merely a matter of hatches and knee-knockers. As Lab Rat walked down the passageway and moved from the highly polished white tile, through the blue plastic curtain and into the blue-tiled flag spaces, he wondered how many times he had made this trip.

And every time he walked through that blue plastic curtain, he shifted hats from his role as part of ship's company to his role in the battle group. On the ship's side of the blue curtain, the primary considerations were internal: the care and feeding of the air wing on board, the machinery that kept the carrier cruising safely through the water, self defense against sea-skimming missiles, and station-keeping with the other ships in the battle group.

But once you crossed over into the blue-tiled passageway, you were in a different ballgame. No longer

were the concerns merely about the carrier. No, Admiral
Wayne commanded the entire battle group from this passageway, and that staff dealt with far-reaching strategic
objectives: the safety and well-being of every ship, aircraft, submarine, and support service in the theater. Their
concerns were global, not limited to the area around the
aircraft carrier. They maintained a broader perspective,
a higher level of focus.

But knowing the different orientation of the battle
group staff didn't mean that Lab Rat's role in CVIC was
any less important. Without a coordinated intelligence
picture, the battle group staff could not function effectively. Yet it was interesting that the primary intelligence
coordination organization within the battle group was
housed in ships spaces rather then along the blue-tiled
corridor.

Perhaps, Lab Rat thought, as he pushed aside the blue
plastic curtain, it was more a matter of how easy it was
to move around the ship. Personnel were supposed to
avoid the blue passageway, the flag passageway, unless
they had business with a battle group staff. To have extended the blue tile down to CVIC would have meant
placing another of the short passageways that ran across
the ship off limits.

Lab Rat walked through the admiral's conference
room into the small foyer that led to both TFCC and
SCIF, the Specially Compartment Intelligence Center.
The hatch to TFCC was standing open, as it often was
during underway operations. He stepped over the knee-
knocker and searched in the darkness for the admiral.

As he had suspected, Batman was pacing in the small
space, stopping from time to time to talk to a sailor or
an officer, signing messages and papers that were thrust
at him, occasionally conferring with his chief of staff.
Most of these matters could have been handled more
easily in his cabin, but Lab Rat had noted over several
cruises that Batman was almost incapable of remaining
in one place for very long. How he had survived in the

Pentagon was beyond the intelligence officer's understanding, given Batman's fondness for pacing.

And why was he spending so much time in TFCC? Did he feel that same uneasiness that Lab Rat and the chief felt, the lingering sensation that things were not as they seem to be? Perhaps—Batman was an extraordinarily intuitive individual, Lab Rat had found, and seemed to have a sixth sense for trouble.

"Lab Rat," Admiral Everette "Batman" Wayne's voice boomed. "What you got?"

"I'm not certain, Admiral," Lab Rat said. With other officers, he might have to try to appear more confident than he actually was, but his experience with Batman told him that the admiral preferred the straight scoop. "There are some alterations in patrol fly-by altitudes, some unusual activity along the border between Iraq and Iran. I'm not sure what they're up to, but it all seems focus on a desert area next to those abandoned aircraft hulks."

Batman eyebrows shot up. "You think they're going to try to fly them? Is that even possible?"

"I don't know. All I know is there's a change in the activity patterns, and that worries me. That, coupled with the latest political reports—well, take a look yourself. You'll see what I mean." Lab Rat passed the admiral the pictures of the construction taking place in the desert.

Batman immediately saw the significance to it. "It's going to be an airfield," he said, his voice quiet. "I don't like the looks of this at all."

"I recommend we increase our CAP," Lab Rat said. "Just as a precaution, Admiral. Not that I really think anything is about to happen, but—"

"—but if it does, there's no time to get ready. Yes, let's do that. I don't like the way this is shaping up at all."

The rest of the TFCC watch team had been surreptitiously eavesdropping, and Lab Rat saw the flag TAO already picking up the white phone to speak with the ship's TAO further forward along the 0-3 passageway.

"Launch the alert-five Tomcats," Batman said to his TAO. "And bring everybody else up a notch." He cocked his eyebrows at Lab Rat. "Anything else?"

"Are all of our close-in weapons systems already in full auto?"

"Yes, Admiral," the TAO answered immediately. "I'm not sure about the cruiser, though."

"Tell them," Batman said. "Captain Henry is a sharp guy—he'll understand."

Captain Frank Henry, the commanding officer of the Aegis cruiser USS *Lake Champlain*, was indeed no dummy. A graduate of the Naval Academy, with postgraduate work in nuclear engineering at Stanford, along with a host of military higher education including the Naval War College. Lab Rat had found him to be an extremely down-to-earth officer, one equally capable of handling himself in the Pentagon or on the deck plates with his sailors. He would get the message immediately—something was up, even if no one knew what it was.

From overhead, they heard the low, hard rumble of Tomcat engines spooling up to full military power. On the plat camera, they could see the flight deck crew scurrying about, preparing for launch. The alert-five Tomcats had already been sitting on the catapult, fully manned up and preflighted. They could be launched within a matter of minutes. The jet blast deflectors, or JBD's, were already rising up from their flat position on the flight deck to shield the rest of the flight deck from the tornado-force winds blasting out of the jets' engines.

"Two flights—four Tomcats," Batman said reflectively. "I hope that will be enough. But since we don't know what is starting, and what we have to be ready for, we have no idea of what constitutes enough."

Flight Deck

"Now, this is more like it," Bird Dog said enthusiastically. "Sure beats sitting in the ready room, doesn't it?"

Yep, the worst day of flying is better than the best day on the ground. Now, let's see what Music is made of—damn, I hope he's not as much a pain in the butt in the air as he is in the on the ground.

Bird Dog pressed himself back against the seat and braced himself for launch. He watched the catapult officer's hand signals, circled his stick through its full range of motion for a final check on all his control surfaces. The plane captain made one last check of the pin holding his nose wheel steering gear to the steam catapult shuttle, and finally they were ready.

The catapult officer snapped off a salute, then dropped down to touch the deck. With his hand in the air, he pressed the pickle switch on the catapult actuator.

The Tomcat built speed slowly at first, but within a matter of moments accelerated to full takeoff speed. It shot down the catapult, held in place by the shuttle, and was unceremoniously tossed off the pointy end of the ship.

The Tomcat dropped below the level of the flight deck, and, as always, Bird Dog had a moment of shrieking panic that they weren't going to make it. That was when you knew for certain whether you had gotten a soft cat from inadequate steam pressure behind a catapult, and whether or not you had enough airspeed to overcome both drag and gravity.

But his trustworthy Tomcat bit into the air, enormous engines straining against gravity, and the thrust gradually lifted them up and away from the hungry ocean. Over the ICS, he heard Music start breathing again.

Bird Dog concentrated on gaining altitude, making sure not to go nose-up too fast and stall. As soon as they were clearly flying, he cut hard to the right, breaking off and heading for his CAP station.

"It must be serious, sir—Bird Dog, I mean," Music said. "They just pulled the alert-fifteen crews out to alert-five."

"Serious—hell, that's great!" Bird Dog crowed. "Gator will have his butt parked in the backseat out there just like we were—it doesn't get any better than that."

Once they were clear of the ship, his wingman joined him, taking position on his right side and slightly back. Bird Dog didn't know that much about Fastball Morrow—the gossip in the ready room was that he was a good stick, but anybody could look good in the training pipeline. He hadn't finished his first cruise yet, so as far as Bird Dog was concerned, he was still a nugget. And nuggets were dangerous, at least until you learned what they were made off.

USS **Lake Champlain**
2340 local (GMT +3)

Inside the combat direction center, or CDC, Captain Henry was just getting a quick overview of the situation from his TAO when the admiral's call came in. He recognized the admiral's voice in the call-up and took the mike from his TAO. He listened to the admiral's suggestion that his CIWS be placed in full auto, and nodded.

"Roger that, Admiral. We're already in full auto, but I appreciate the heads up. Anything specific we ought to be watching for?"

"Nothing I can pinpoint for you, Captain," Batman's voice boomed down over the speaker. "You know how it is sometimes—you get that hinky feeling it's all about to go to shit. And I've got an intelligence officer here who agrees with me."

"Lab Rat?" Henry asked.

"Yep, he's the one. You should have Tomcats overhead shortly, Captain. Just keep an eye on them, make sure they don't get out of line."

Captain Henry chuckled slightly. Like the cruiser would really have any control over the pilots manning the Tomcats. Still, it was nice of the admiral to ask. "Will do, Admiral." After he replaced the mike, Captain Henry made a visual check on the CIWS system status.

As he had told the admiral, the key arming it in full auto was already inserted, and all stations were reporting ready for action. But if anything was going down, CIWS would be their last resort.

The Aegis fire control system itself was still in manual, requiring human intervention to launch missiles. They could, if in high tempo operations, configure the Aegis computer for fully automatic operations. But in the constrained waters of the Gulf, with the airspace overhead cluttered with commercial flights, transports, as well as the occasional Air Force tanker who forgot the check-in with Red Crown, full auto was not the preferred mode of operation.

"You heard that?" the captain asked his TAO.

The TAO nodded. "Yes, sir. We're ready—count on it."

"I know we are. But the question is, ready for what?" He studied his tactical action officer for a moment.

Lieutenant Commander Abe Norfolk was his weapons officer. Norfolk was a veteran of the cruiser community, experienced and capable, well on his way to a command of his own someday. Captain Henry had liked him immediately from the moment he checked on board. Not that that was a requirement, of course—all he really demanded from his officers was that they demonstrate superb tactical competence. But in the close quarters of a cruiser, it helped that everyone got along.

Abe stood six-foot four inches tall, and weighed in at around 230 pounds. He was a massively boned black man, and one who clearly took working out seriously. Like everyone on the cruiser, he had a difficult time finding both the time and the facilities to maintain his conditioning program. Captain Henry was not entirely certain how he managed it, but he suspected Norfolk had not lost one inch of mass in the three months they'd been at sea.

In addition to his imposing physical condition, Norfolk was also a Rhodes scholar. He had attended undergraduate school at the University of San Diego in California, majoring in physics. He had quickly put that knowledge to use in conducting departmental training, and now most of his enlisted technicians sounded as though they had completed the graduate course in weapons engineering. Captain Henry often found himself chuckling over the phrases that he heard coming out of his enlisted men's mouths and he felt an intense flush of pride when he saw the occasional equation scribbled on the hard plastic surface of the enlisted mass dining facility tables. Writing on the tables, particularly in pen, was strictly forbidden.

But there was no way he was going to do anything about it—hell, he was tempted to cut those scribbled-on pieces out and mount them on the bulkhead, point to them with pride as he showed others around the ship and shout, "This is what these men and women are capable of, given the chance. Don't ever underestimate them—not ever." For some of his toughest cases, kids who had barely graduated from high school, Lieutenant Commander Abe Norfolk was a god.

"Captain, you want to set general quarters or air defense conditions?" Norfolk asked.

"What would you do?" Henry responded. It was his policy to use every second for training that he could, to test his officers as well as his enlisted people on their readiness to advance to the next level of responsibility. Not that he had any doubts about Norfolk—no, not at all.

"I would pass the word quietly around ship, sir," Norfolk said. "Key personnel, but then decide who needs to know. Knowing these folks, they'll soon start drifting into Combat just to keep an eye on things. General quarters—no, not yet. It will only wear them out, use them up before we really need them. Besides, that Commander Busby—he's one smart spook." Norfolk used the Navy slang word for intelligence or cryptological officer. "If it were serious enough to be setting general quarters, he would have let us know."

"Exactly so," the captain answered. And it wasn't a polite comment—Norfolk had reacted exactly as Henry had.

During the pre-sail conferences and staff conferences since they'd been underway, Captain Henry had taken Norfolk with him several times to the carrier. There, they both got to know the rest the staff, and when messages like this came in over the wires, they knew who they were dealing with. And Norfolk was right about Lab Rat—the intelligence officer had an instinct for trouble that was simply uncanny. If it had been more urgent, Lab Rat would have let them know.

"Tomcats are on station, sir," the air track supervisor said. Two blue symbols were arrowing out from the carrier to the cruiser, the target numbers displayed next to them and the shape of the symbol showing that the computer had identified them as friendly contacts. One of the modes of the IFF was especially encrypted, and would have identified the contacts to the computer as a friendly military platform. Even in full automatic, the Aegis cruiser missile system would not have attacked them.

"Any more word on that submarine?" Henry asked Norfolk.

Norfolk shook his head. "Not a word, sir. But Chief Clark and Petty Officer Apple are champing at the bit to get hold of it."

Norfolk didn't have to tell him that. He'd seen Chief and Apple in the sonar shack already, and each one gave the appearance of having been there for several hours.

It was clearly not their watch, but they were there anyway, just watching. "Don't let them wear themselves out," he warned Norfolk. "They will if you let them."

Norfolk nodded. "I threw them out about four hours ago, with orders to hit their racks. You think they look rough now, you should have seen them then. It's a definite improvement."

"Good thinking." He grinned down at his TAO, absurdly pleased with him. For just a second, he considered placing his hand on the man's shoulder, giving it a hard shake. But then he drew back. As satisfied as he was with Norfolk's performance thus far, it never worked to let an officer think he'd achieved every goal set before him. It could lead to laziness—he was certain it wouldn't in Norfolk's case, but that's not the way he trained his junior officers.

"I'll be in my quarters," Henry said. "Call me if you need me."

Iranian Shore Station
Tuesday; May 4
2350 local (GMT +3)

Wadi walked in on an argument raging inside his operations center. He stood just inside the door, watching the chaos for a few moments. The men, most dressed in traditional garb with only a few in uniform, flowed and eddied around the wide open space, shouting, gesturing, each one louder than the next. His cousin Jemal stood in the center, striving to be heard over the noise as he shouted at another man instead of attempting to regain control of his people. It was, Wadi knew, his cousin's greatest failing, this inability to see the big picture, to step into a position of leadership. If he could not control even his own staff, how could he be expected to deal with powerful heads of neighboring Arab states?

No, Wadi was the one to seize the reins of leadership, to take the Middle East into the next era. It was so clear now as he stood there and watched his relatives, his subordinates, his entire staff disintegrate into a squabbling mob in the absence of strong leadership.

And the way to settle this was not to be the loudest, to participate in this game. No, there were other ways.

He stepped into the center of the room, a powerful presence. The men around him who were arguing faltered, tried to carry on their arguments but could not do so under his calm, impassive stare. He let them feel this presence, not speaking, reaching out to each one of them to exert his influence over them.

Quiet spread out in ripples around him, within a few minutes reaching to the farthest corners of the room. Only Jemal refused to yield, continuing—or at least trying to continue—an argument with another officer, deliberately ignoring Wadi's presence in the room. Finally, when his disobedience became ludicrous even to himself, he capitulated. He turned, and a bright smile of friendship spread across his face.

"Cousin," he boomed, making a welcoming gesture. "Welcome."

Wadi stared at him, his face still impassive. He let the full meaning of his displeasure sink in with his subordinates. It was as though he could actually see the power draining away from his cousin, coming to him. Finally, when his cousin's smile began to falter, Wadi unbent slightly. "Is there some problem?" he inquired, as though sincerely concerned. "I wish be able to make a full report to my father."

His cousin recognized the threat for what it was. "Of course not," he said, perilously close to losing his own temper again. "We were simply discussing the next step."

"Which needs no discussion," Wadi said smoothly. "The sequence of events is well-established. And all is ready?"

"Yes."

"Are you certain?"

"I said yes." Wadi could see his cousin struggle to keep his voice down.

"In one hour," Wadi said calmly, "I will return. The first phase should begin two hours after that, unless I am mistaken." He glanced around the room, as though inviting comment. "I am not mistaken, am I?"

"No, of course not. All will go as scheduled," Jemal replied.

Wadi crossed the room in a few strides to reach his cousin's side. He clapped him on the shoulder and said, "Excellent. And just to make sure, I will assign you to the missile station itself to look after the details. After all, who can I trust more with the sensitive assignment than my own blood?"

His cousin turned pale. "I am of more use here."

Wadi leaned forward, and dropped his voice to a whisper. "You are of *no* use here. Go—go now while you still have the chance. If my father hears of your performance here, you'll be executed before dawn. You understand that?"

His cousin trembled visibly, although no trace of discomfort showed on his face. Wadi silently gave him credit for that. "But the Americans—they will retaliate immediately," he stuttered. "If I'm there . . ."

"If you are there, you'll take the same chances as your men. You'll be by their side, and Allah willing, you will be spared. Then again, if you were to perish today, you would take your rightful place in paradise. I can only envy you the opportunity."

Wadi turned to his chief of staff. "My cousin is leaving." His voice was pleasant. "Arrange the transportation immediately. I am depending on you to make sure my orders are carried out." With that, Wadi turned and left the room. It remained silent behind him.

He walked out of the compound, past the armed guards standing duty at the fence, and headed for the desert. He was aware that he was not yet fully acclimated, yet he found himself with an overwhelming desire to test himself against the desert, to feel it suck the water from him.

He walked out into the desert until the station was just a blurred smudge on the horizon. He felt every care in the world sloughing off him as it receded, felt his soul peel down to its essence until he stood naked before Allah. He fell to the ground, prostrated himself on the hard-packed sand and dirt, and prayed.

It is time. Lead us now, my God. Show me the way. I am so unworthy, yet I am all that there is. Guide me, that I might unite your nations into one powerful force, capable of showing the world the glory of our faith. Guide me, and show your face to us that all might come to your will.

Wadi lay facedown on the desert until he felt the still, cool peace descend over him. Then he rose, renewed, and headed back to the compound. He had work to do.

SIX

Lieutenant Brad "Fastball" Morrow slid the dual throttles of his F-14D back into idle, allowing his bird to slow as he turned into the northeastern leg of his combat air patrol (CAP). Morrow and his lead, Bird Dog, were flying a counter-rotating CAP along the northeastern threat axis toward Iran. Four such CAPs were stationed around *Jefferson*'s Battle Group; two consisted of F/A-18s and two of F-14Ds. CAG would have used all Tomcats but for the fact that there were only ten available, and he needed the Tomcats for their LANTIRN and TARPS capabilities.

Fastball had joined the squadron just a few weeks prior to cruise and was still a "nugget." The first thing anyone had learned about him was that he was a San Diego Padres fan—in fact, fan was too mild a word. If ever the beleagured team from southern California had had the perfect fan, it was in him. Fastball had a baseball shirt with Tony Gwinn's number on it, and he could cite statistics and details of every game for the last ten years. He had compared flying the Tomcat to throwing the perfect fastball and the name had stuck. It was only with great difficulty that his squadron mates convinced him that playing baseball on the flight deck would not only result in a dinged aircraft and dangerous conditions, but that they would lose more balls over the side than could easily be replaced.

Fastball had been crushed. Somehow, he had gotten it in his head that it would be possible to form a battle group league and have teams from each ship ferried over to the carrier for games. No one had been able to convince him that as impossible as it was to play baseball on the flight deck, the smaller ships faced even more serious limitations.

Morrow checked the radar picture on his Tactical Situation Display (TSD), then clicked his mike. "What do you make of this, Rat?" he asked his RIO over the ICS.

Lieutenant Johnnie Davis had been watching several groups of aircraft forming up just about ten miles off the coast of Iran. The E-2C had told her of three separate groups: one group of four MiG-29 Fulcrums from Bandar Lengeh, and eight Su-24 Fencer-Ds from Chah Bahar. Four F-5E Tiger IIs were also airborne near Kish Island and circling. Two Iranian F-14As were circling far to the east, over Iran, probably providing AEW for the pending strike with their AWG-9 radar, she thought. The Iranian F-14s were already registering a feint return on her Radar Warning Receiver (RWR).

"I don't know, Fastball. They did the same thing this morning, too, but then broke off at the last minute. It may be a feint to draw us in closer to their SAM range. They've got SA-2s all along the coast." Rat focused on her Tactical Information Display, also called TIDs. She had selected the Link-16 data link, which fed radar information directly to her display from the E-2C via the JTIDS. The link tracks appeared as a small upside-down "Us" for friendlies and a upside-down "Vs" for hostile.

She then noticed the group had joined and had turned toward the picket destroyer, *Algonquin*. *Jefferson* had a smaller air wing (CVW-14) than normal, due to down-sizing—about seventy aircraft. Also with the CVBG were two Middle East Task Force destroyers, HMS *Liverpool* (Sheffield-class) and the Canadian destroyer *Algonquin*.

Tomcat 106
CAP station two miles west of Tomcat 109

"Hammer, King, picture. Two groups, southeast Chicago, twenty miles," came a monotone voice over the tactical comm. "Suspect second group are strikers. Both groups hostile, repeat, both groups hostile. Recommend commit." The call was from the E-2C Hawkeye II airborne early warning aircraft circling near *Jefferson*. The Hawkeye II's sophisticated APS-145 radar allowed it to see out some 300 miles over the horizon, spotting both air and surface threats. "Chicago" was the brevity code word for the Iranian airbase at Kish Island and served as a fixed reference point for all friendlies. The distance and direction was from that reference point.

"Hammer One, contact, your call," Music responded. "Hammers committing." Music checked his scope. "That's it, Bird Dog. Let's get 'em."

"Hammers, committing bandits, southeast Chicago thirty miles. I've got four MiGs in-bound leading the strikers." Music quickly sorted through the contacts with his powerful APG-71 radar confirming their formation, then called out a short target modification to the pre-flight brief. "Hammer Two, target trail group."

Tomcat 109

"Two," Rat acknowledged. She began to set up her shot, slewing the cursor over the lead Fencer-D of her group. Her Tomcat's radar scanned ahead of her in Track-While-Scan mode, watching all of the in-bounds. "Just like we briefed, Fastball. Just like we briefed."

"Don't worry, Rat. I've got it under control." Fastball jammed his throttles into full burner. The kick of the mighty F110s bumped her in the butt. She looked up from her TIDs for a moment considering Fastball's comment. This new pilot's arrogance was getting old fast. And Johnnie, as a rather diminutive female in what was still a man's career, knew all too well what it was like to be on the receiving end of an attitude. But her demeanor usually kept her from acting on it. She didn't expect to be treated special, but she was his senior, and she had two cruises under her belt. Plus, she was fresh from TOPGUN, which meant she knew a hell of a lot more of tactics than some "fresh-from-the-RAG" nugget. "Just watch the gas. Rats don't swim well," she finally replied.

Tomcat 106

Bird Dog swung his Tomcat southeasterly, separating from his wing. As he leveled, he glanced left, noticing that Fastball was well ahead of where he should be and speeding toward the Fulcrums.

"What's that kid doing, Music?" Bird Dog hollered over the ICS. While he had only flown with the new kids on three occasions, he could already see himself a few years earlier—young, cocky, fully of over-confidence. And perhaps about to learn a few lessons. *There's one thing about rising in the ranks,* Bird Dog thought. *You see life come full circle.*

Tomcat 109

Rat finished her Phoenix firing solution on the two Fencers. "Fastball, your dot," she said, meaning that the shot was set up and ready to launch.

"Why aren't we getting the MiGs, Rat? This doesn't make any sense. We kill them and we can play with the Fencers all day."

"Leave the strategy to Bird Dog. Just fire the damned missile."

"But . . ."

"*Fire* the missile."

"Fox Three on lead MiG, 20,000 feet, south group," he finally called the shot, then watched as it soared ahead and climbed to its attack altitude. Although a Mach 5 missile, much of the Phoenix's punch came from its death dive toward its target, rather than its engine thrust. The missile was "fire and forget," which meant that, unlike the Sparrow, several Phoenix could be simultaneously targeted and launched without waiting for each missile to hit its target.

"Second shot ready, your dot."

Tomcat 106

"Two is Fox Three. And . . ." Music called in a calm voice, "it's your dot."

"Take it, Music."

"Roger," Music smiled as he reached for the button. "Fox Three on the lead Fencer, angels 15, main group." His eyes followed the two Phoenix missiles for a second, then rechecked the overall situation.

"Bird Dog," Music said. "We should join on Fastball. Those northern MiGs are closing on him fast. The southern guys are still with the Fencers. Let's get the Hawkeye to watch them."

"Roger, make it happen." Bird Dog considered his new RIO. As much as he enjoyed flying with Gator, he had to admit that this new guy was good, and, to Bird Dog's satisfaction, he knew when to talk and when to shut up.

"King, Hammer One. Monitor southern group, Chicago south at three-five. We're heading north." With that, Bird Dog rolled his bird on its side and headed toward his wingman.

Tomcat 109

Rat watched her TID, waiting for the Phoenix to find their prey. She gave a quick glance outside, then returned her stare to her screen. It had been ten seconds since the launch and the two missiles had just gone active. She could see the small blips making their way toward the . . .

"Splash one Fencer!" she shouted, followed quickly by a "Splash two." Seconds later, Music called the same. Four Fencer-Ds were now heading into the Persian Gulf, burning and in pieces. That left only four for the *Algonquin*'s air defenses.

"Hot damn!" Fastball yelled, feeling the rush of adrenaline over come him. "That'll teach them to play with Uncle Sam."

Rat now turned her full attention to the remaining contacts—the Iranian MiG-29As. The four had separated into pairs and the northern two were speeding toward her Tomcat. At ten miles, she gave her required HUD call, "Out of blower, switching VTR from TSD to HUD," signaling Fastball to activate his HUD recorder. Powering out of afterburner also reduced his heat signature now that he was within range of the MiG's infrared missiles. "Ten right, ten miles, twenty degrees high", she called, using the standard "bearing, range, elevation" format. "Wing should be left and low."

"Now let's get some MiGs. Select Sparrow."

"Locked, and ready," Rat said, hooking the next target, then hesitated for a second. "Fastball, can I take this one?"

"No, this is *my* plane, Rat. Fox One," he called without waiting for her response.

Johnnie shook her head in disgust, but held her anger only for a moment. "We're spiked!" she said, indicating that the enemy had a missile lock on their aircraft. "Launch at our one o'clock, high." Rat set up her ECM gear, then reached for her dispensibles. "Jammers on, popping chaff."

Fastball pulled into a tight banking turn just long enough to break the lock, then nosed back toward the MiG. He was determined to get his first MiG kill and join the small cadre of fellow pilots, whose beginnings dated back to the skies of Korea.

"They're splitting," Rat called out, watching the two northern MiGs trying to set up a position. She had seen enough sorties at the Fighter Weapons School to know that this wasn't developing into a good situation. "I don't like this, Fastball."

"I'm going north. Let's bag the one running. Switching to heat." He clicked his weapons switch.

"Fastball, turn into him. Go nose to nose. We can't have him on our—"

"*No*, this guy's giving me his pipes. Just watch your MiG!"

"Tally on the southern mover." Rat grunted, but kept her eyes peeled on the trailing Fulcrum. The thought quickly struck her that this kid wasn't about to give her experience any deference. She'd have to fix that when . . . if they made it back to the *Jefferson*. "Trailer's slowing to come around. He's setting you up, *Fastball!* It's a drag! *Reverse right! Reverse right!*"

"I've got him, Rat!"

"Fastball, reverse now! We're spiked, trailer!"

Tomcat 106

"Music, we better get over there. Fastball's getting himself in deep. He's locked up by that second MiG."

"Bird Dog!" Music answered. "We've got our own problem. Spiked, three o'clock. Break left!"

Tomcat 109

"Missile in-bound," Rat hollered. "Four o'clock high."

"I see it." Fastball jerked his stick hard right, placing the missile on his starboard beam. The MiG's radar, the Slot Back, guided the missile and giving it a flat return surface temporarily broke the radar's lock. "Chaff, now!" Fastball called. Rat responded with three small clouds.

"Missed. That was close!"

Fastball pulled his nose back around. "You're mine," he called, then cranked his Tomcat into firing position.

"Smoke!" Rat saw another missile loosed from the bottom of the MiG and quickly released a stream of flares. "Brad, this MiG's on us bad! He's at our four . . . coming around . . . climbing . . . he's going over the top." Her breathing was getting heavy. "Smoke! Smoke!" she cried out. "Six o'clock! He took a shot." She quickly pumped another trio of hot flares into their jet stream. "Dive! Break . . . right!"

The missile exploded just aft of the Tomcat's right engine, sending a shower of perforated rods into the Tomcat's tail structure. The jolt shook the Tomcat, forcing Morrow to fight to recover his bird. The rudder was now bent and one of the stabilizers torn. Both of them felt the sudden deceleration.

"Fastball, we're hit!"

"Son-of-a . . . Our burners are out!"

Rat quickly relocated the MiG. "He's coming around! There's another MiG. Crossing our nose going north. He's climbing to turn."

Tomcat 106

Bird Dog focused on the MiG chasing Fastball as he listened to Rat's pleas over the tactical.

"Fox Two!" Three seconds passed. "Yes! Splash one MiG."

Music turned his head away from the MiG now leaving the scene. "Second MiG's bugging out." He quickly checked his JTIDS display. "He's heading back toward Iran."

"Find Fastball!" Bird Dog's eyes scanned the horizon ahead of him, using the smoke and missile trails to locate his wing. "There," he said. "At two o'clock. Going to burner."

"Got 'em, boss."

"He's in trouble. Music, get a lock on that Fulcrum *now*! Use a Sparrow."

"Working on it!" Music fiddled with his gear then a tone rang out over their headsets. "Got em. Dot's yours, Bird Dog."

"Waiting . . ." he watched the MiG weaving for position on Fastball's Tomcat.

Tomcat 109

"He got him! Bird Dog got him!" Fastball shouted.

Rat swiveled her head from side to side trying to padlock. Things were happening at such a frantic pace. Even with her training, she was fighting to keep her situational awareness. "Jesus, where'd he go . . . wait, got 'em. Hammer One, Two's blower out with a MiG at our three."

"Rat! MiG twelve o'clock low, climbing!"

"I'm on the northern MiG. He's at our three . . . turning . . . he's in guns range . . . *firing!*" Rat's eyes opened wide as she watched the stream of 30mm rounds from the Fulcrum cascade toward her F-14 in a downward arch. "He missed!"

Fastball fought his sluggish stick, jerking his Tomcat from side to side in a jinking maneuver. "Spanking the pony," he used to jokingly refer to that in the RAG. Suddenly, with his life on the line, he didn't feel much like joking. He was using every trick in his book and quickly discovered that maybe he wasn't quite as "hot" a pilot as he had thought. Maybe he should have listened to his RIO. This MiG had him and his only hope was his lead, who was still too far away. It was a setup and she had seen it coming.

Tomcat 106

"Come on!" Bird Dog cried out. "Get a lock, Music!"

"Lock!" The tone rose sharply.

"Hammer Two, break left on mark three . . . two . . . one. *Break!*"

"Fox One!" He fired, not waiting for a reply.

Tomcat 109

Fastball heard an *umphf* from his backseat as he yanked his Tomcat hard to the left and up, sending his bird into a steep, climbing turn. "You're . . . killing . . . our . . . speed." Rat grunted. *"Fastball!"* She felt her vision narrow against the heavy gs.

"He'll blow right by!"

"He'll shoot us!"

"He's firing!" *Thud thud thud!* Three rounds ripped across the Tomcat's frame, just missing the aft cockpit. Rat knew the MiGs giant 30mm rounds would tear her to shreds even if only one managed to strike her. "Fuel leak. We're leaking fuel."

"Rat, were done, get ready to eject!"

"No, not yet!"

"Get ready to . . ."

Boom! The MiG at their three o'clock suddenly broke into two and burst into a fiery ball of red-orange. The pieces fell toward the water. There was no chute.

Tomcat 106

"Splash one Fulcrum, southbound at angels fourteen," Bird Dog called. "Music, where's the bandits?"

"Heading east. They're leaving."

"Thank God." Bird Dog sighed.

Tomcat 109

Johnnie waited a moment for Fastball to respond, but he said nothing. He hadn't said a thing since the dogfight ended. Finally, she checked her gauge. "Oh my God. Hammer One, state is three point nine. We are *way* low. And our blowers are out. Leaking fuel. Need a Texaco fast."

"Roger, making it happen."

She switched to the ICS. "Fastball, I told you to watch

your state. You stayed in burners way too long. We'll be lucky to make it back to the tanker."

He didn't respond.

"*Fastball!* I'm talking to you."

"Not now, Rat. Save it for the boat."

SEVEN

Admiral Wayne paced in the small compartment, too annoyed to stay in his elevated leatherette chair. The attack on his two CAP made no sense, no sense at all. Why would the Iranians start something now?

"Answers, people. I need answers," he said into the silence broken only by the calls from the tanker as the fuel-low Tomcats chivvied in line. "What just happened up there? And more importantly—why?"

Lab Rat watched the admiral pace. "Sir, I think . . . that is, Chief Armstrong agrees with me . . . well . . . it may have something to do with the construction taking place in Iran."

Batman paused. "The photos you showed me before?"

"We initially classified it as something else, but the look this morning caught a convoy of trucks with heavy equipment headed into the area."

"Where? Show me again," the admiral ordered.

Lab Rat held out a sheaf of photos.

"In the conference room," the admiral said. "Red light's too hard."

Lab Rat followed the admiral into the conference room located just off TFCC. Batman spread the photos out on the table, and the intelligence officer walked the admiral through their analysis. When he finished, the admiral said, "Okay, so they're building an airstrip. But why jump us now? What sense does that make?"

"No answers, sir. But the two are related somehow—I can feel it."

"Find out," the admiral ordered. "And make it fast, Lab Rat. I got a feeling that we don't have much time."

Tomcat 109
local (GMT +3)

"Rabies" Grill held the KS-3 tanker at a steady course and speed as the fuel-starved Tomcat made its approach. The rigid basket streamed out behind the aircraft, a small but critical target for the approaching fighter.

"Come on, Fastball," Rabies said. "You done this a thousand times before, buddy. Just snuggle on up here right now, come on, you got it . . ." Rabies kept up a calm, confident chatter as he coached the younger pilot in on the basket.

And just how the hell had Fastball gotten so low on fuel? Never mind that—Rabies thought he could probably guess what had happened. The bigger question was why Rat had let it get to this state. She was the one who knew enough to keep an eye on the gas gauge even when her idiot pilot figured that playing afterburner was a free ride.

But now wasn't the time to talk about it. There'd be plenty of time to assign blame later, after they got this stupid nugget and his starved Tomcat back on the deck.

"You're looking good, good, real good," Rabies said

as he watched the approach. "Just a hair lower, mate, that's it."

A hair, hell. That damned idiot was bouncing around the sky like a yo-yo. They'd be lucky if he plugged it on the first pass.

But he had to, didn't he? Fuel state almost at the flameout point—just two snorts less of fuel, and that Tomcat was about to be just another hunk of metal on the ocean floor. Hell, if he were a RIO, he would have punched out by now and left it to the pilot to explain to the CAG why he'd returned without his canopy or his RIO.

"Bingo," Rabies said, as against all odds the green light on his panel lit up, indicating a good seal with the Tomcat. "Hold on, buddy. You gonna be feeling a lot better here in a second." Rabies's copilot flipped the pump switch, and aviation fuel started pumping into the nearly-empty Tomcat tanks.

"Now if he can just hold on a few minutes, get that stuff shifted into his online tank," the copilot muttered. They both knew what the problem was—the fuel was going into the fuel tank not in use, and had to be pumped from that one to the one in use before they could be sure that the Tomcat wouldn't flame out.

As they watched the fuel transfer figures click over, Rabies started to breath easier. Finally, when their gauge indicated that they'd transferred two thousand pounds to the Tomcat, Rabies felt at ease.

"Okay, Fastball. That's enough to get you home with some left over for sightseeing," Rabies announced. "Pull on out of there, buddy. We got other customers lined up."

"Roger," Fastball said, all business and no hint of the disaster that had almost happened in his voice. And no thanks, either, for the job they'd done coaching him in and not ragging on him about his fuel state. The young-ster's attitude pissed Rabies off.

"You know the way home?" he asked. "Because if

you don't listen to Rat for a change, you're not going to have enough fuel to get back onboard."

"Roger, holding TACAN," Rat's voice said, and Rabies winced at the coolness in her voice. He'd just screwed up—not as bad as Fastball almost had, but enough so Rat would make sure he heard about it later. It was one thing for a RIO to rip her pilot a new asshole—another thing entirely for the tanker toad to rag on him, no matter how egregious the sins.

"Thanks, Rabies," Rat said finally, as the Tomcat unplugged and dropped quickly below and away from the tanker. "I owe you one."

Hey, okay. Rabies allowed himself a slight smile. There was something about Rat that had always attracted him, and maybe he hadn't blown his chances entirely with her. Not if she was willing to talk to him like that.

"Save some auto-dog for me," Rabies answered, referring to the soft-serve ice cream dispensed in the dirty shirt mess, the product of which looked uncannily like dog turds. And not very healthy dogs at that.

A single click from Rat's mike acknowledged his transmission. Rabies had a feeling that that was the most he'd ever get from Rat.

EIGHT

Captain James Bellisanus had not slept much in the last three days, and he'd long since lost track of whether it was day or night outside. His crew maintained their normal three-shift rotation, but aside from his XO, there was no one that Bellisanus could really delegate his duties to. Not that he didn't have a number of competent officers in his crew—he did, and he was justifiably proud of the fact that each one was far more qualified in submarine operations that any he'd ever worked with before.

But that didn't change the fact that *Seawolf* was steaming in exceptionally dangerous waters. The water outside the Straits was damnably shallow, for the most part, although there was one deep rift that ran outward from the confined waters to dump into the Indian Ocean. Still, for the most part, it averaged far too shallow for Bellisanus's liking.

Adding to the problem was the fact that, after the

Mediterranean, this was one of the most heavily traveled passages in the world. The constant stream of deep draft commercial vessels, smaller fishing boats, and general shipping kept the crew in a constant state of edginess. They had to stay deep, in order to avoid problems.

Additionally, sonar propagation was exceptionally poor. The water was too shallow, too warm, and cluttered with noise. The final fly in the soup was the presence of the massive oil-drilling rigs. They, too, added a tremendous barrage of noise to the sea. They also were poorly charted, particularly the undersea pipelines that ran across the ocean floor.

No, it was not a good environment for a submarine. And Bellisanus had his suspicions that the *Seawolf*'s operating circumstances were going to get a lot worse before they improved.

His XO, Lieutenant Commander Francis "Frankie" Powder, was equally pessimistic, although he tried not to show it. But the message that had come in late last night had given them both reason to worry.

"They're not serious, are they?" Powder asked for the second time. He held out the offending message.

"I'm afraid so. And it's not like it's unexpected news, is it? Submarines have been operating in the Gulf since Desert Storm, and there's no reason for us not to go on it," Bellisanus said.

And if truth be known, submarines had been in the Gulf for a lot longer than that, although Bellisanus wasn't sure that Powder knew just how long. It was a closely held secret—in the earliest days, it had been common wisdom that no submarine would ever deploy in the Gulf. The water was too shallow for concealment, the sea floor too littered with uncharted dangers.

And just because it was common wisdom, the Navy had decided to prove that it could be done. Submarines, some operated by the Navy, others under the control of agencies identified only by initials, were quietly slipped into the warm bathtub. It went on for years before Desert

Storm, and now accepted wisdom was just counter to what it had been then. A submarine could operate in the Gulf. Maybe not as comfortably as in open water, maybe not as safely, but it could be done.

And every submariner Bellisanus had ever met hated the whole idea with a passion. It ran counter to the guiding precepts of submarine operations and risked the submarine's primary advantage—the ability to remain hidden, undetected, until it was time to strike.

"Yes, sir. Jeez I just hate it there, though," Powder said.

"That makes two of us. The crew's ready for it, though."

"Yes, sir. I'm certain they are." Powder was responsible to the CO for crew training, and Bellisanus had been impressed with his innovative training techniques and his absolute patience as he walked through the problems. The junior officers knew that Powder's scenarios would challenge them, but they also knew that he'd be right there beside them, guiding them to the proper solutions and keeping things safe. As a result, they'd gained confidence and expertise far greater than most crews.

"I think so, too. And we've got some experienced people on board," Bellisanus said.

"Not enough. That's okay—we're growing our own. Trained *our* way."

Your way, you mean. Bellisanus did not begrudge giving his XO the credit he deserved. "Tomorrow, I think. After sunset, of course. Any comments on that?"

"No, sir," Powder answered. "When's the carrier going in?"

"Day after. We'll go in ahead of them and sanitize the area for the carrier." Bellisanus paused for a moment. *Just what the hell had Iran been thinking when they'd launched a deliberate attack on the* Jefferson's *CAP? Didn't they know that would immediately provoke the U.S. into a strong and pointed response? And much as they slavered about having American forces in the Gulf, you'd think they'd do what they could to keep us out, and taking a shot at our CAP sure isn't the way to do that. They've seen that principle demonstrated often enough since Desert Storm.*

"Anything more on that suspected diesel?" Bellisanus asked.

"Not in the last traffic, but we'll get an update before we leave. According to intell, all hulls are accounted for. Two tied up at the pier, one in rework, and one . . . well, we know about her."

"Yes, sir." The last hull, the *El Said*, was a hulk on the bottom of the Gulf. She'd rammed a pipeline—and what did that say about the Iranian military, that even their own subs didn't know about pipelines?—and had been lost with all hands. Rumor had it that part of the crew had survived in an after compartment, but that Iran had not been willing to allow foreigners to attempt a rescue. They'd left their own men there on the sea floor to die of asphyxiation, drowning, or injury.

What must it have been like, assuming the rumors were true? To live out your last few hours, knowing that your military had abandoned you, left you to die? Had they cursed their leaders in the end, finally seen things for what they were? Or had they kept to their faith, knowing that they were dying as martyrs assured of a place in heaven? Every time Bellisanus checked the chart and noted the penciled-in correction adding the hull of the El Said as a hazard to navigation, he wondered about the men left down there to die.

"We'll have eight hours to conduct the sanitization," Bellisanus said. "Then the carrier will move into the safe haven, and her assets will take over keeping the subs at a distance. We'll move slightly north, not too far from our launch basket."

And pray to god we don't have to launch. If there is a submarine out there, and if we do launch Tomahawks, then our survival odds go down a great deal. Because then there's no more guessing—they know exactly where we are.

"Steak and lobster tonight?" Powder suggested.

"Sure." While submariners ate far better than their surface counterparts, the steak and lobster was always a favorite. "At least you might have a shot at filling Pencehaven for once. I swear, the supply officer has to recalculate all our provisions since he came onboard."

"Worth it, though," Powder said.

"Yep."

Sonarman First Class Otter Pencehaven had arrived onboard just five months before the cruise began. If Bellisanus had been pressed to describe him in one word, he would have called him the original blithe spirit. Nothing in the world seemed to bother him; if the submarine ever, God forbid, sprang a critical leak, the captain suspected that Otter would be seated at his console, having a little snack—snacks were important to Pencehaven—that ineffable smile on his face as he stared off into space and invented the one device that would save the submarine from certain disaster.

Pencehaven was a tall, lanky man, without a spare inch of flesh on his sparse frame. His tall form was topped by a smiling, cherubic face at odds with the rest of his body. He was skilled in all areas of sonar operations, but passive acoustics proved to be his true strength. The other men swore that he could find black holes in the ocean.

Shortly after Pencehaven arrived, he was followed by Sonarman Second Class Renny Jacobs. Jacobs was a good eight inches shorter than his friend, and sported a stocky frame. If Pencehaven was a brilliant theorist, Jacobs was the engineer that made his friend's ideas work. Together, they made a formidable team in sonar. They had served together onboard the *Centurion*, quickly formed an inseparable friendship, and they had requested orders to the *Seawolf* together. They were already legendary within the sonar community, and their detailer quickly made arrangements to honor the request.

The one thing the detailer had not told Bellisanus about however, was Pencehaven's formidable appetite. He easily ate as much as three men would, and the captain even worried with the doctor that he might have a tapeworm. But the doctor laughed, assured him it was just the blessing of the strong metabolism, and suggested that the supply officer stock up.

"They've got a bet on, you know," the XO said. While gambling was not allowed on Navy ships, wagers that challenged the professionalism of crew members were quietly allowed.

"On who detects the submarine first?" the captain asked.

The XO shook his head, a smile crossing his face. "Not exactly. They're betting on who misses it first."

And that, the captain reflected, was his exactly how the two operated. Each one was superbly and unshakably confident that he would make the first detection. There was no point in betting on a sure thing. Allowing for the possibility that they might simultaneously detect the submarine, they elected to wager on who would screw up first.

"Some of the other sonarman are making side bets as well," the XO said. "The chief is keeping an eye on them to make sure it doesn't get out of hand."

"Who did you bet on?" the captain asked.

Now the XO did grin. "Sworn to secrecy, Captain." He leaned forward, his voice quieter. "But if you're a betting man, the only safe option is to bet on both of them. That way you at least won't lose money."

NINE

The cruiser loitered just outside the Straits of Hormuz, on antiair picket patrol. Using her SPY radar and the AWACS aircraft circling further to the southwest, she had a complete and comprehensive picture of the entire Gulf area.

Threat conditions were normal, if anything could be said to be normal in this part of the world. After decades of Mideast patrols, the real lesson learned was to be ready for anything.

Captain Henry strolled into Combat, his ever-present cup of coffee in his hand. He walked over to his TAO and tapped him on the shoulder. "How's it going?"

LCDR Norfolk jumped. He had been concentrating on the voices in his headset, monitoring the progress of the undersea game being played out inside the Gulf. While it was not the cruiser's primary mission, she did have ASROC torpedoes available that she could use to assist if necessary.

"They got her pinned down, sir," he said, using his trackball to circle around the enemy submarine symbol on his screen. "With two helos, there's no way she's getting away, not in these waters."

The captain nodded. "I don't believe they'll need our help, but we'll stand by. I see you already got that under control."

The TAO was mildly gratified to have the captain notice his preparedness. "Yes, Captain. We're ready."

The captain studied the tactical plot again, thinking over the TAO's words. Yes, they were ready, but for what? Over the last several days, there had been several indications and warnings of increased preparedness on the Iranian's part. Nothing hard, other than the new shore station springing up in the desert. Nothing you could really point to and say *this is the first sign that the world is about to go to shit.*

Yet, even though he couldn't articulate his reasons, the captain was certain that was exactly what was about to happen. He had done too many patrols in the Gulf area himself not to have a deep-rooted suspicion of anything out of the ordinary.

The Middle Eastern nations were given to grandiose tactical schemes, on par with the time they tried to set the Gulf on fire by breaching oil pipelines. Although they had not stated that was their intention, the captain was quite certain that's what they had meant to do.

The captain pointed with his free hand toward the symbol indicating the new shore base. "You have them keep a real close watch on that area. There's something about it—"

"TAO, Track Supe! Launch indications from Intell— launch indications."

Just then, the new symbols popped up on the screen. The captain swore violently and sloshed hot coffee over his hand. "General quarters—now!"

The distances and times inside the Gulf are so truncated as to allow virtually no reaction time. Even as the missile symbols rose up from the new shore station located near the Straits, the TAO flipped the Aegis cruiser into full auto. While reaction times of the humans who inhabited her might be too slow to deal with every threat, the computer was not. "If it flies, it dies," the Captain said. "No questions—weapons free—now!"

Within the depths of the computers system, tactical decisions were already being made. The computer weighted each bit of radar information and matched that detection with the previous ones over previous seconds, generating track data and linking detections into contacts. Then it evaluated altitude, speed, and course to decide whether or not it posed a threat to the ship or to the battle group. This took just microseconds.

If the threat parameters were met, the computer automatically designated weapons to each track. The ship could ripple off its antiair weapons at speeds far in excess of those that any mere mortal could have achieved.

The tactical plot resolved into four missile symbols, all of them inbound on the cruiser. As they inched their way across the display toward the ship, the cruiser shuddered violently. In sequence, four hatches in the vertical launch system popped open, and antiair missiles rose majesticly out of it, wavered for a moment, then turned to point unerringly at the incoming threats.

But a head-on encounter was a bit like throwing telephone poles at each other. At a high rate of closure, there was no room for error, no room for the slightest course deviation. And if the standard missiles didn't take out the threat, it would be up to the close-in weapons system, or CWIS.

Iranian Shore Station
0312 local (GMT +3)

The telephone sitting on the station commander's desk rang, making him jump. It was linked to a very special headquarters, and rarely rang. He hesitated for an instant, then, aware that his hesitation could send the wrong message, he picked it up and said his name.

He listened for moment, and replied, "Yes. It shall be." He replaced receiver, and turned to look at the rest of the crew. It was a small group, one that lived and worked together in close, isolated circumstances. Here on the tip of the Strait, their small installation was isolated from everything else by three fences and numerous guards. The compound itself housed living quarters as well as the actual purpose for the site. It was completely self-contained.

He stood, and took a deep breath. "It is the time we have been waiting for—the time we've trained for." He turned to his second in command. "We are ready, are we not?"

"Of course."

"Then execute Plan Vengeance." Immediately, the room broke into a flurry of activity. Technicians darted to consoles, and others ran down the stairs to the underground compartment below. The commander scribbled a set of coordinates on a piece of paper and gave it to his second. "Now. It must be now."

"You realize what this means?" the second said, his face composed and a look of religious fervor in his eyes. The commander nodded. "Yes. It means that within the next thirty minutes, we will look into the face of Allah himself."

In the underground bunker below them, technicians ran to the missile launch room. There, the long-range antisurface missiles lay staged in their quad canister. It was a knockoff of the American design for Harpoon missiles. The Harpoon design had been reverse-engineered by the Chinese, and these substitutes made available to a select certain few on a very limited basis.

Outside, dozens of laborers rushed to shovel the thin layer of sand covering the outer hatch off. That accomplished, they manually retracted the massive steel plate. The covering of sand was necessary to disguise the launch hatch, both visually and thermally. The sand proved to be an excellent insulator, and even infrared satellite photography showed no change in the surface temperature around the installation. It was one of Iran's most heavily guarded secrets.

Within three minutes of the order, an amazing time for men who dared not practice their skills, the launch hatch was clear. Below, the technicians manned consoles, and on the commander's order, launched four antisurface missiles at the USS *Lake Champlain*.

The first missile suffered from the inattention of a Chinese technician who had been hungover on the day he had assembled the delicate microcircuitry in its guidance system. While it launched satisfactorily, it quickly veered off course, heading south for a while, then turning back inland. It eventually detonated in the desert when it ran out of fuel.

The second missile fared slightly better. It launched as it should, rose to altitude, and immediately homed in on the *Lake Champlain*. But a bit of sand that had worked its way into the housing clogged the fuel line, and, although it had more than sufficient fuel onboard, the clogged line starved the rocket motor propelling it. While still ten miles from the carrier, the engine shuddered, coughed, then went dead. The missile fell into the ocean to join the growing collection of debris there.

The third and fourth missiles, however, performed just as advertised. They bore straight in on the *Lake Champlain*, everything functioning smoothly.

The third missile was six miles away from the cruiser when an antiair missile caught it. Although the standard missile only grazed it, the impact was enough to shatter the casing and send the Harpoon tumbling into the ocean.

The fourth missile, however, was still on course. The standard missile targeting it bore in with uncanny precision. But the head-on encounter at the higher rate of closure proved to be the problem. A gust of wind caught the Harpoon, veering it ever so slightly off course just at the moment of impact. The standard missile whizzed by, its wake rocking the Harpoon, deflecting it slightly, but it soon regained its course. It bore in steadily on the cruiser.

USS Lake Champlain
0314 local (GMT +3)

"Three down, one to go," Norfolk said. The cruiser launched two more missiles at the Harpoon, but even as he watched the geometry unfold, the TAO knew that they were too late. It would be up to the close-in weapons system to save them now.

And even if CWIS worked perfectly, tracking the missile with its independent radar system and firing its 2000 rounds per minute of depleted uranium pellets, there was still a substantial danger to the ship. Even if the missile were destroyed, it would not be completely obliterated. The air around them would be filled with shrapnel and those that hit could be almost as damaging to the cruiser as a direct hit.

The close-in weapons system picked up the target immediately, and its R2D2-like form swivelled as it followed the missile inbound. When it judged that it had an optimum range and angle, the CWIS started firing. It sounded more like an angry *whirr* than a gun going off.

Everything functioned perfectly. The missile was peppered with super-dense projectiles, and immediately disintegrated. But the mass of metal that composed its body, along with its warhead, continued on their same path, and rained down on the cruiser.

Inside Combat, the impact sounded like hail on a tin roof. One bit of shrapnel shattered a window on the bridge, adding sharp shards of Plexiglas to the barrage pelting the bridge team. Two larger chunks penetrated the skin at Combat, and ricocheted through the compartment, causing considerable damage. Six more found their targets just above the water line, piercing the skin and generating leaks.

But the worst damage came from those bits of the missile that found the antennas and radars on *Lake Champlain*. There was no way to harden them from the possibility of damage.

The first one ripped across the -49 radar, immediately rendering it useless. The second slammed into the SPY-1 system, destroying two-thirds of the small radar elements housed there.

Inside Combat, the screens went blank.

USS Jefferson
0315 local (GMT +3)

One by one, the four missile symbols disappeared from the tactical screen. There was utter silence in TFCC as they watched the drama unfold.

"Launch the alert-five Tomcats," Batman snapped. "Then get everything else we have on the deck turning. If this is the start of a full-scale attack, we've got to be ready."

The flight deck exploded into a melee of confusion. To an outsider, it would look like utter chaos, but to Batman's experienced eyes, everything was running quite smoothly. Pilots were pouring out of the hatch from the handler's office, having hastily signed out their aircraft. They ran around each jet, doing an abbreviated preflight, and then were up the boarding ladders and into cockpits within minutes.

Yellow shirts coordinated the entire evolution, snapping out commands to the green-shirted technicians and brown-shirted plane captains who were dealing with small maintenance problems, critical maintenance problems and moving the aircraft around. The Tomcat that was down for a hydraulic gripe was quickly towed aside as more fighters jockeyed behind him, each pilot eager for his shot at the catapult.

Batman felt his gut churn as he watched the fighters launch. Every second that passed by seemed more and more perilous. When would the wave of missile attacks start? And the enemy fighters? Could they get enough air power up quickly enough to cover for the crippled cruiser?

At the moment the final missile fragments hit *Lake Champlain*, the tactical screen wavered for moment, and then *Lake Champlain* disappeared from the screen. She was still floating, and evidently suffered no serious structural damage other than the destruction of her radars in one antenna. Then she reappeared, being reported in the LINK by the other ships, as well as the AWACS, but had no independent transmit and receive capability herself.

The battle group circuit crackled and then *Lake Champlain*'s skipper came on. He summarized the damage to the two radars, then concluded, "We're in no danger of sinking, but it's going to take a while to get our radar and data link capabilities back up—if we even can. I'll need priority on a couple of parts, I think. As it stands now, I have to rely on CWIS."

Had the data link at least been up, *Lake Champlain* could have targeted her missiles using radar data from another ship. That was standard procedure, and no problem for *Lake Champlain* or crew.

"Can you shift to a different antenna for LINK?" Batman asked.

"It's not the antenna, sir, it's something in the processor. I don't know if it was an electrical short, vibration damage, or what, but the entire console tripped offline during that last hit. I have technicians on it now, but we'll have to change out just about every part in her. It's going to take a little time." Batman could hear the frustration in the captain's voice. Without a radar, the cruiser was virtually useless. Without her data link, the cruiser's missiles were no of use.

"I keep waiting for the next set of missiles to target the carrier," Batman said. He glanced at the status board, and was relieved to see he now had fourteen Tomcats and Hornets airborne. There was also tanker support, as well as E-3 electronic support and SAR helos. "But it looks like it's not going to happen. I guess their objective was to knock out our advanced radar capabilities."

"We're down for a bit, but we're not knocked out completely," the captain said, his voice determined. "But as I said, Admiral, it's going to take time."

Batman made his decision instantly. "I want you to close the carrier, then. Take station on our starboard beam, five thousand yards. You'll be well within our antiair envelope, and at that range your CWIS won't pose a danger to us. I'd much rather defend you close in—that way, I don't have to break off an extra set of fighters for you."

"Aye-aye, Admiral," the captain responded. "I don't like it, but—"

"But you'll do it. Not only is it an order, but you know as well as I do that you're a sitting duck while everything is down. I know it's tough, but get your ass in close for now. The fighters will carry the load for now.

As he watched Batman saw the symbol representing *Lake Champlain* execute a turn and head back for the carrier.

Batman picked up the phone linking TFCC with SCIF, the special intelligence unit located immediately next to TFCC. "Where did it come from?"

Lab Rat answered, his voice calm and certain. "The Straits. We have the launch indications from national sensors, and AWACS confirms it. Right there." A new symbol popped into being on Batman's tactical screen.

It was located on the eastern side of the Straits of Hormuz. "We're certain of it, Admiral."

Batman turn to the TAO. "How many of those Tomcats are loaded with bombs?"

"Four. The rest are strictly antiair."

"Break off all four Bombcats, as well as two fighters for escort. Ten minutes from now, I want to be looking at a sheet of fused glass where that installation is right now. You got that?"

The TAO nodded, but he looked uncertain. "Admiral . . . no clearance from higher authority? I mean, it is an attack on the land mass."

Batman wheeled on him. "You think I don't know that? When I need some snotty-nosed junior officers to question my decisions, I'll pin the stars on your collar instead of mine. For now, you follow orders. You got that, mister?"

"Yes, of course, Admiral." The TAO was visibly shaken by the intensity of Batman's anger. His fingers trembled slightly as he picked up the radio to make the call.

Batman watched him for a moment, then turned back to the screen. Okay, maybe he had blown his top. But there wasn't time for questions, was there? Not when there could be another wave of missiles raining down at any second. And had he made a mistake committing two of his fighters as escort for the land attack? He wondered if he should clear it with Fifth Fleet . . . okay, maybe he should, but dammit, it was his cruiser that was crippled. They attacked him, not vice versa. An entirely different set of circumstances than if he launched the attack without provocation.

Still, he had to give the TAO credit for having the balls to speak up. Not every junior officer would have done that, and there might be a time someday when just such a question would keep him from making a serious mistake.

He walked over to the TAO and put one hand on the

man's shoulder. "It was a good question, Tom. Don't you ever stop thinking, okay? Someday, when you got the stars on your collar, and you're sitting in the same position I am, you remember this, okay? Remember it, and know that even admirals lose their temper sometimes." He turn back to the screen, ignoring the startled expression on a TAO's face that slowly transformed itself into a grim smile.

USS Seawolf
0317 local (GMT +3)

It was Sonarman Renny Jacobs who had the first warning that all was not well. The submarine was running in quiet ship, all of her active sensors secured. Input from the passive sonar array was their only means of examining the water around them.

At first, it was nothing that Jacobs could put his finger on. The background noise changed slightly, shifting upward in frequency, slightly quieter on certain bearings. The change was so faint as to be almost undetectable, and it took him a few seconds for his tired ears to process exactly what was happening. It wasn't something that you ran across every day.

In the first microsecond, all he knew was something had changed, and change was dangerous in the world of undersea operations. He turned to the chief, intending to ask him, then cold, clear certainty washed over him. His hand darted out to toggle the switch to the bitch box. "Conn, Sonar! Obstacle in the water, slightly off our starboard now!"

"What sort of—?" the conning officer started to ask, then the XO cut in.

"Hard left rudder!"

The submarine immediately began to turn, but it was difficult to change the direction of that much sheer mass and inertia moving through the water. Renny felt the deck shift slightly, and held his breath, hoping that he had been fast enough. He damned himself for the seconds of delay, even as he knew it would not have made a difference.

At first, it was a humming metallic sort of sound, as though a tuning fork had been struck. It quickly crescendoed into an all-encompassing squeal, a hideous howl of metal against metal. The ship jolted violently to the left, the deck slamming up at a ten-degree angle and throwing every piece of loose gear across the compartment. Strapped into his seat, Renny felt the harness cut into his abdomen.

Seconds later, screams were added to the cacophony as the ship's motion caught the rest of the sailors off guard—the dull sound of bodies hitting steel bulkheads, the clatter of pots and pans and plates in the galley crashing to the deck.

Within seconds of the initial impact, the captain was by the XO's side. As far as the XO could tell, he had not even shut his eyes, yet the clock indicated that he left the control room over an hour ago. It was not possible that he could've remained awake the entire time.

It seemed to go on for hours, each second louder and more horrifying than the previous one. Finally, the sound tapered off, and except for the moans of the wounded, there was silence on the submarine.

"All stations report!" The XO's voice snapped.

In control room, the XO was not aware of any panic. Fear, yes, coupled with anger that this had happened to the ship. But the need for immediate action to prevent flooding and further damage to the submarine took priority over all their human emotions.

He knew within the first seconds what had happened. This entire body of water was a maze of uncharted pipelines and obstructions. Wrecks from the Gulf War still littered the ocean floor, although most of those were charted. No, it was the truly incomprehensible predilection for these nations to build undersea pipelines and conduits without bothering to inform any international charting agency of their existence. That was undoubtedly what had happened to *Seawolf*—she had rammed a pipeline.

As the report began coming in, the XO was relieved to hear that they had apparently suffered a glancing blow to the pipeline. The sonar dome had taken the hardest hit, along with part of the conformal array that ran the length of the hall. But structural integrity had not been breached, and the only real problems were a few broken pipes.

Indeed, the crew suffered more than the submarine. Their bodies were not built to withstand the pressures and impacts that the ship was.

The final casualty count was four seriously injured, and ten minor injuries. Of the serious injuries, the worst was a sailor who had been next to a steam line that had snapped. Fortunately, it was an auxiliary steam line, not the main steam line, although even the lower temperature steam had inflicted third-degree burns over twenty percent of his body. Two broken legs, and a burn from the galley rounded out the collection of serious injuries. The rest were walking wounded—bruises, one greenstick fracture to an arm, and other assorted injuries that could be dealt with onboard.

But the burn patient, Fireman David Harding, was the most critical. According to the doctor, he needed to be in intensive care, in a specialized burn unit. But there was no way to evacuate him short of surfacing and attempting a risky helo transport from the submarine to the carrier outside the Gulf.

The XO glanced over the captain, who was evaluating a damage control report. Had the captain been awake? And if so, did that mean he did not trust his XO? That he left the control room merely to placate the XO, but had remained wide awake and worried in his cabin.

Under the circumstances, it appeared that his concern was justified.

In that moment, the XO was very, very glad he was not in command of the *Seawolf*. The captain would have to decide whether to give up the submarine's cloak of invisibility, her primary defense, and expose the warship to the enemy—or to make the even more agonizing choice of staying hidden and hoping that Harding would pull through.

TEN

It wasn't until after they were airborne that Rat seriously contemplated whether or not the best course of action would be to shoot Fastball in the back of the head and then punch out. While they were waiting their turn for launch, Fastball started his bitching. He complained about everything from the condition of the cockpit—grease on the instrument panel from a technician's work—to the slowness of the other pilots in getting on the catapult, to the tight fit of his flight suit, and progressed down the list to a series of comments on the inedibility of lunch served that day. At first, Rat had tried to answer him, but then realized that he was bitching just for the sake of bitching.

Things hadn't improved any since the launch. According to Fastball, there was no one else in the Navy who knew how to maintain proper station as a wingman except him. Sure, she had to admit he was good—they'd been welded onto Bird Dog's wing ever since they gained altitude after launch. But it wasn't like the rest of the squadron pilots were slouches, either.

Finally, she realized what his problem was. After they'd landed and refueled, their Tomcat had been loaded with a ground attack payload instead of antiair weapons. And, from Fastball's perspective, that signified a lack of confidence on the part of CAG, especially since they'd just proved their worth in ACM. The real fighters were just that—fighters. With fighter weapons. Sidewinders, AMRAAM, and Phoenix and Sparrows. Not bombs, laser guided or otherwise. Additionally, he complained that the weight and shape of the bomb payload made a marked difference in the Tomcat's aerodynamic handling. Although Rat couldn't see much of the difference, she wasn't a pilot.

Did Gator have to put up with this from Bird Dog? The exploits of the two during their earlier days were legendary, and she often heard Gator moaning about his life as Bird Dog's backseater. And while Fastball was no Bird Dog—not yet, anyway—he sounded an awful lot like the stories Gator told.

Finally, when she could take it no more, she said, "What's the matter, can't you fly this thing without moving your lips?"

"And I suppose you're happy about this," Fastball retorted. "Yes, that's it probably there's a whole lot less chance of the seeing action with this load-out, isn't there? You chicken, Rat? Is that it?"

For moment, Rat was too purely stunned to speak. Then the anger started, curling around her gut, building up through her chest until she could feel the veins in her forehead popping out. She clamped her hands down on the side of her seat, willing herself not to unbuckle her ejection harness and crawl through the space between the front seat and the canopy to choke the living shit out of him.

"I have my hand on the ejection handle," she announced, aware that her voice sounded cold even with all the rage boiling inside of her. "You have five seconds to take that remark back. After that, you can practice your speech to CAG explaining why you returned to the carrier without your backseater. Because I'll be damned if I'll fly with a pilot who thinks I'm a coward."

Fastball started to speak, but she interrupted him. "And as for you, you little shithead, if you can't suck it up and understand that the mission is more important than your testosterone-loaded dreams about aerial combat, then I'm requesting a new pilot as soon as we get back onboard. I don't fly with people who aren't team players, asshole. And if it ever there was someone who didn't understand what the hell he's doing, it's you."

She waited a moment, and said, "Four . . . Three . . . Two . . ."

"Okay, okay," Fastball said, evidently realizing she was deadly serious. "I'm sorry. You happy now?"

"You're sorry for what?"

"You're not a coward, okay? I didn't mean it like that."

Suddenly, the radio interrupted their spat. "Tomcats flight, Bird Dog—execute ground attack mission alpha against the following coordinates." The operations specialist read off a latitude and longitude, concluding with, "Chain-link fences, three small buildings. That's where the attack came from. The admiral wants—hold on, I'll quote him exactly—a sheet of fused glass. Any questions?"

"*Jefferson*, Tomcat flight, no questions. Tell the admiral he's going to be able to shave in the sand after we get done with the place," Bird Dog answered crisply. "Okay, Tomcat flight, get hot. There's no time for a dry run, no time for a practice shot. We're operating on very little intelligence on short notice. Just follow my lead, we'll go in at two thousand yard intervals, with each RIO calculating each individual release point. Accuracy counts, ladies and gents—let's give the admiral what he wants."

"Hammer flight, this is the admiral," Batman broke in. "Bird Dog, I'm counting on you."

"Roger, sir. You want fused glass, you got fused glass. Although I can't promise that there won't be a couple of gaping holes in the middle of it."

"All right," Fastball said. "Now this is more like it. Just watch this, Rat. Now you're going to see a real expert at work."

Rat had her head buried inside her radar screen mass, working on the exact ingress course, release point, and rollout parameters. The RIOs in the four aircraft traded information, then settled on a plan of action. The pilots might like to believe that they were the important part of this, but each RIO knew that putting metal on target was entirely their problem. As long as the pilots did what they were told, there was a pretty good chance of success—Rat herself was the second runner-up in the squadron bombing accuracy contest.

"Ten minutes," she said. "Here's the profile." She snapped her data picture over to his HUD.

"No problem," Fastball said. "No problem at all."

USS Jefferson
TFCC
0322 local (GMT +3)

"Ten minutes," the TAO announced. "Bird Dog says he'll roll out to the south, and he'll need a tanker when he's done. He's also asking for the latest update on any SAM sites."

"What does Lab Rat say?"

"Lab Rat says," a voice said behind him, and Batman turned to see his intelligence officer standing there, "that there's a good chance they've fielded some portable units in the immediate vicinity. A high probability, at least." Lab Rat shoved some satellite surveillance photos at Batman. "This is how they did it, sir. And I'm betting there're some SAM sites that are concealed the same way."

Batman studied the sequence of photos, showing the remarkably clear figures of men frantically scraping and shoveling an otherwise unremarkable stretch of sand. The next photo caught the glint of sun on metal, as the steel missile door was partial exposed. The final shot showed the cover fully retracted, and a blur of motion as the first missile launched. "Damn them," Batman said softly. "You're right—how the hell did they set this up without our knowing about it?"

"We did know about it, sir." Lab Rat saw the look on Batman's face, and added, "We, as in the Navy, sir. Not me personally. Evidently the powers that be decided that the information was too sensitive to release to the fleet. It's only after the fact that they're passing it on."

Batman swore quietly. That's the problem they always had with intelligence. The really good stuff was so sensitive that you didn't get it when you needed it. He could understand reasoning—it was the same problem that the British faced with Coventry. Do you evacuate the city, and tip your hand to the Germans that you've broken the Enigma code, or do you sit by and watch your own people killed in order to protect the greater secret? It was a decision that Batman had never had to make—and he wasn't so sure how he would've reacted if he had been in charge of deciding Coventry's fate.

"So if they've got this concealed underground, they've probably got others as well." Lab Rat shuffled the photos back together, and handed them off to an assistant. "I'm pinging on them as hard as I can to make them release the information, sir. But nobody is saying for certain—or maybe they just don't know. At any rate, my best guess would be that if they can do this with one facility, they can do it with others."

Batman turned to the TAO. "How many of those Tomcats are carrying HARMs?"

"Only one, sir."

Batman nodded. "That will have to be enough."

The HARM missile, an antiradiation homer, was designed to execute a kill against enemy radar facilities. The later versions of the missile locked on to the emissions and even if the enemy shut down the facility, it would remember the location and take it out anyway. It was a fire and forget weapon, and a high priority weapon for the battle group.

"Tell Bird Dog he may have a problem getting it," Batman said. He listened to the TAO relay the details to the Tomcat flight.

Then another circuit snarled to life. "*Jefferson* this is *Seawolf*," a voice said, thin and tinny. "We've got a problem."

The Seawolf. *What's she doing on the roof?*

"I've got a few problems of my own right now, *Seawolf*," Batman said. The worry on his face was immediately evident. But what was the submarine doing breaking her cloak of visibility, exposing herself to detection and prosecution? Especially under the circumstances.

But *Seawolf* couldn't have known that when she came to communications depth. It was only now, as the high-speed link brought her database up to speed, that she would see that she'd surface in the middle of a complete clusterfuck. Not that she was completely surfaced—only a small satellite antenna would be above the surface of the water, but that was enough of the visual to give away her location if anyone happen to be looking there.

"I can see that now, sir. Bad timing, is it?"

"Understatement. *Seawolf*, can it wait? Because things are about to get pretty nasty here. I want you safely submerged. Get down, and make best speed to clear the area just in case someone saw your antenna. Get to a

safe location, then come back up. But for now, I'm just
a little busy."

"Roger that, sir. *Seawolf* out."

"Wonder what she wanted?" Lab Rat asked, a worried
expression on his face. "I didn't like the sounds of that
at all."

Batman turned back to the tactical screen. "Whatever
it was, it will have to wait."

USS **Seawolf**
0340 local (GMT +3)

Bellisanus replaced the microphone in its holder and
turned to his XO. "Get us out of here. You see what's
going on."

And indeed, the XO did. The details that were unfolding on their now updated tactical screen were truly
horrifying. The missile attack on the cruiser, the air thick
with fighters—no wonder the admiral hadn't wanted to
talk to the submarine, absent a report that they were
sinking.

"Right full rudder, flank speed," the XO said to the
officer of the deck. The order was repeated to the conning officer, and then again to the helmsman, who ech-
oed the orders and reported his compliance with them.
The submarine started to pick up speed.

"Conn, Sonar. We're making a lot of noise, sir." The
concern in Jacobs's voice was evident. "If there's a sub
in the area, there's no way she won't hear us. We're
generating flow tones over the damaged sonar dome like
crazy."

The XO swore quietly. The hull might be intact, but
the damaged sonar dome resonated to the flow of water
over it. As the water passed over the jagged edges, it
generated sounds a bit like blowing on a Coke bottle.

No competent antisubmarine warfare person could possibly mistake the sound for anything else.

"Sonar, Conn, aye. There's nothing we can do about it right now, Jacobs. We're noisy as hell, but be grateful we're not sinking. Just keep your eyes peeled for any unfriendlies in the area.

"Will do, sir, but we're putting so much noise in the water that it's hard to see much of anything. We're not only noisy, but our own detection capabilities are degraded."

"Roger. I want to do a high-speed sprint and then we'll slow down. You let us know when we quit generating the flow tones, okay?" the captain said. He then turned to the XO. "Five miles, that ought to give us a head start. I'm open to suggestions."

He was open to suggestions. After the one time he left the control room and the XO had run the sub into a pipeline. A feeling of unworthiness swept over the XO. If he could just come up with the right answer now, just find some way to . . . wait. That was it.

He thought it through a second time, then turned back to the captain. "Sir, I recommend we return to the area where we struck the pipeline. If they're not paying attention, they may mistake our flow tones for current rushing over the broken pipe. Additionally, it's going to take a while to shut down the oil flow. I bet it's still pumping. That will foul up the water enough that there won't be any chance of a visual, and will also reduce the acoustic propagation characteristics of the area. It's the best place to hide right now."

The captain's face was unreadable. "Downside?"

"Fresh water," the XO said. "There's a real danger it will foul our sea chest, and that could mean serious trouble. But not as bad as being detected right now, I suspect. We can deal with the fresh water problem later."

The captain's face relaxed slightly. "I agree completely. Make it so. And pass the word to the crew—we're on strict water hours until I say otherwise. No showers, no flushing. I know, I know, it's going to get pretty foul. We can't waste a drop until we're certain we can clear the area safely."

The XO nodded, gratified that the captain had approved his suggestion. "Come right, steady on course zero three zero."

Bellisanus watched his orders translated into action. Yes, they'd clear the area all right—of that he was confident. But at what price? How long could Seaman Harding hold on without advanced medical facilities? He felt the pain deep in his gut as he forced himself to acknowledge what he was doing. Yes, Harding desperately needed to be medically evacuated to the carrier, and if he'd asked anyone in Harding's family—or most civilians, for that matter—he suspected the reaction would be the same. Surface, insist that the carrier send a helo immediately for the young man.

Yet this was why the burden of command was such a grueling, demanding pressure. You spent years honing the judgement and skill of your officers, inculcating in them the ability to make decisions such as this. You hoped and prayed that when the time came, they'd make the right ones, but you knew that it would twist them into knots just like it did him. Because as much as he wanted to get Harding off the ship, take care of him the way a captain is entrusted to care for his or her sailors, he couldn't. His priority had to be the safety of the ship, the mission, and other hard priorities that were so distant from the concerns of one family over one sailor.

And you hated doing it, but you did it anyway. And the day that it quit hurting, that you stopped caring about your sailors and still forced yourself to make these decision, why, that was the day that you ought to retire.

He'd visit Harding later today, after things settled

down. He'd tell the lad that they'd get him off as soon as they could, urge him to hold on. And the real bitch of it was, the thing that would keep him awake at night would be the look of understanding in Harding's eyes, the forgiveness he'd see there.

ELEVEN

Tomcat 103
0319 local (GMT +3)

"Two minutes," Rat announced. "Then descend to two thousand feet and come left to course 340."

"Got it," Fastball said. He let the aircraft slide back slightly until he was behind Bird Dog rather than on his wing, and then descended. He stayed slightly to Bird Dog's right, avoiding the turbulence directly behind the Tomcat in front of him.

Below him the land was clearly visible now, flat, hard baked desert sand, filthy blue water lapping at the shore. The compound itself was no great shakes either. The three sets of fences strung around it looked ominous but tattered. Guard towers and searchlight emplacements were set in each corner. Inside were three concrete buildings, none of them with any windows. They were crammed together in the middle of the compound, with wide open spaces between the buildings and fences. For increased security? he wondered.

Men were running around a compound, obviously alerted to the incoming aircraft. Rat peered around over Fastball's shoulder, then blinked. It looked as if . . . as if . . .

"Fastball," she said urgently. "The sand—it's moving. I think I'm seeing—"

A blast of smoke blew up from the shifting sand, and then, impossibly, an antiair missile was barreling straight for them.

Immediately in front of them, Bird Dog broke hard to the right. Fastball broke to the left, and started climbing, kicking into full afterburner as he did so. Rat was jammed back against the seat, and she tensed her muscles and grunted, forcing oxygen into her brain. It wouldn't do to gray out now—not when everything depended on what she did in the next few moments.

Then Bird Dog completed his circle, descended to one thousand feet, and continued on in. "Hammer flight, on me," he said. "It should be a piece of cake—these guys are bad shots."

Fire flared briefly under Bird Dog's wing, then a HARM missile shot out. In seconds, it nailed the entire radar, thus effectively eliminating the SAM threat.

"On me," Bird Dog repeated. "We're on our own for about forty-five seconds, people. Then its back up to altitude with our fighters. And there'll be one less dirty little SAM sight in the world. Fused glass—that's what the admiral asked for and that's what he's going to get."

Rat shut her eyes for a moment, and offered up a prayer. *Please let Fastball be good enough. Please let Fastball do what I know he can do. Thank you.*

Fastball was gyrating the Tomcat through the atmosphere like a rock and roll dance partner. The tail end of the Tomcat slew around violently, throwing her first against one side of her ejection harness, then the other. She fought the blackness that nibbled at the edge of her vision, forcing her breath out in hard grunts as she tried to remain conscious.

"Stay with me, Rat," Fastball grunted, his own voice tight. "Fifteen seconds—get ready."

They continued to descend, the compound and the men so close she thought she could make out their individual features. She watched the target marker inch along their flight path, and then, at precisely the moment indicated, she toggled off the payload.

The Tomcat jolted upward violently, suddenly two thousand pounds lighter. At the same instant, Fastball broke hard to the left again, kicking in the afterburners and pitching the Tomcat into an almost vertical climb.

This time, Rat lost the battle. She saw the gray creeping in, saw the color leach out of her vision. She tried to fight it, but the blackness eventually met in middle of her field of vision as she passed out.

"Rat! You okay?"

No answer.

"Dammit, Rat, stay with me!" Fastball tried to lean forward, as though that would somehow magically increased the speed of the Tomcat and get them safely out of antiair range. While the SAMS might be destroyed with their radar, they could not ignore the possibility that there was another site somewhere nearby.

Finally, at altitude, he cut back on the afterburners and converted into level flight. "Rat?"

"Oh. I'm here," she said, her voice groggy yet determined as she fought her way back to consciousness.

"I got it," she said, as she regained her tactical awareness. She had only been out for about five seconds, but it was the longest five seconds Fastball could remember in a long time.

As he formed up on Bird Dog, staying within the circle of their accompanying fighters, it occurred to him that that was the essential difference between a Tomcat fighting team and single-seat fighters. In a Tomcat, you were part of a team. You depended on your RIO to feed you information, became accustomed to the steady patter of instructions, advice, and second opinions echoing in your ears. During combat, it was as though you were one person, one person with two brains. In a good team, your thinking eventually synchronized almost completely with your RIO, and sentences became shorthand, clipped phrases that were incomprehensible to anyone else.

Not so in an aircraft like the Hornet. There, you were completely alone, with no one to second-guess your judgment or give you a sanity check. There would be a certain freedom about that, he supposed, somewhat like the trainers he learned in. But in combat, two brains and two sets of eyes were always better than one. And in those few moments when he thought—even rationally knowing exactly what happened—that he has lost her, he had known real panic.

"Tomcat flight, good job," a new voice said on tactical. "It looks like a direct hit for everyone."

"Yes!" Fastball said. "Good going, Rat. Good going."

"Thanks."

For a few minutes, Fastball concentrated on maintaining his position in formation as he vectored toward the tanker waiting for them. Then he said hesitantly, "Rat? About what I said . . . I really *am* sorry. I was wrong." And he was—this time he meant it. It wasn't just words to keep her from punching out—and really he had no doubt she would have done it—but an honest admission of his error.

"Some good flying back there, Fastball. Not everybody could've gotten us out of that alive."

"So . . . we still a team?" he asked.

There was a long pause, and he felt a flash of dread at what her answer would be. But finally she said, "Yeah, sure. Just as long as you remember I've got an ejection handle back here, too."

"Put it in command eject. From now on, if you go, I go."

"Touching," Rat said dryly. "I'm very moved. But you know, I think right now I would be even more touched if you just concentrated on getting this bitch tanked and back on deck."

"Yeah, sure." Fastball let it drop, but inwardly he was fuming. Hey, he made this big reconciliation thing, and

what did she do? Take the cheap shot, remind him of
the last time he lost his nerve on a tanker approach.
Well, she might be a good RIO, but she was still a bitch
as far as he was concerned.

In terms of pucker factor, tanking was right up there
with landing on the carrier. At least they were fortunate
that the weather was good. And from looking at the
flight schedule, Fastball had seen that Rabies Grill was
in the cockpit of the tanker. Now that was good news,
as much as Rabies bitched about tanker duty. No one
flew a steadier pattern than Rabies.

"How about it, 103? You ready for a drink?" Fastball
recognized the voice of Rabies's copilot.

"I sure could use a tall cold one about now," he answered. "How about you just funnel one on back here?
I hear the S-3 has a cooler full of beer onboard just to
keep you guys occupied."

"Yeah, right," Rabies broke in. "Listen, junior, you
just take care of business, okay?"

*Now what was that all about? What had he done to
incur Rabies's wrath?*

Fastball concentrated on lining up on Rabies, approaching from below and slightly behind. He eased the
Tomcat into position, concentrating on the basket, trying
not to overcontrol. On his first pass, the probe slid
smoothly home. The green light lit up on his console,
indicating a solid plug. "I have a green board," he announced.

"Green board," the copilot agreed. "Three thousand
pounds, Fastball. Don't say I never gave you nothing."

Fastball watched as the fuel indicator showed aviation
fuel flowing into his tanks. He probably wouldn't need
that much, although his two runs on afterburner had
eaten at fair amount of fuel. Still, he could feel this was
a good day for the deck. Three wire, first pass. There
was no doubt in his military mind that this was going
to be one hell of a landing. No doubt.

Within just a few minutes, the refueling was completed. "Disengaging," Fastball said, watching the indicator. As soon as the light turned red, he slowed ever so slightly, and dropped down below the tanker. Once he was well clear, he broke right, descending in a clean, sweeping turn as he headed back to the carrier.

"That went well, I thought," he said cautiously, trying to find some noncontroversial subject to approach with Rat.

"Not bad," she replied offhandedly. "I've seen better."

Damn the bitch! Couldn't she find anything nice to say? Fastball concentrated on putting it out of his mind, compartmentalizing and maintaining his focus. He slid smoothly into the starboard pattern, taking his place in the queue of aircraft waiting to get back on deck. He watched the aircraft ahead of him, descending and spiraling down as one by one, the lowest Tomcat in the stack broke off to make an approach. Finally, it was his turn.

"Tomcat 103, inbound," he announced.

"Roger, 103, maintain course and speed and call the ball," the operation specialist said.

The ball was a Fresnel landing light located on the port side of the carrier. The combination of green and red lights told a pilot whether he was too high or to low on approach. The last two miles behind the carrier were a critical time during which Fastball lined up with the carrier, shot his approach, and eased 60,000 pounds of Tomcat down gently onto the deck in a controlled crash.

In addition to the Fresnel lens, he would rely on the judgment of the landing signals officer, or LSO. The LSO was an experienced Tomcat aviator who would make visual observations on Fastball's approach, verifying the correctness of his needles, or his glide path indicator, and pitch into a perfect landing attitude.

When he spotted the ball, Fastball said, "Ball, 103."

"103, ball," the LSO agreed. "Say needles."

"Needles high and right," Fastball said.

"103, disregard needles. I have you on path, at altitude. Continue on."

Damn. A slight annoyance, but no major problem. For a wide variety of reasons, the needles were often off.

The carrier deck which looked so small at altitude now loomed before him. It looked like a cliff rising out of the water, a dangerous cliff at that, as though the ship was an iceberg just waiting to smash his Tomcat to bits. He concentrated on looking at the lens rather than the shape of the ship. As long as the light was white, he was on the correct glide path and would not smash into the ass end of the ship, called a ramp strike.

"Looking good, 103. Keep coming," the LSO said. His voice was calm, confident, pitched so as to reassure any pilot strung out on adrenaline or shaky on his approach. It was like having a RIO, Fastball thought. A RIO standing on the stern of the ship.

Three wire, three wire . . . it would be a perfect landing, he decided. People would talk about it in the ready room later, as they always did. Each squadron LSO maintained a list of each pilot's landings, rating them according to whether there were any problems or whether they were satisfactory. The ratings were posted daily on the bulletin board for everyone to see.

Still, there were good landings, and there were *good* landings. The really good landings and traps were those that might draw a quiet comment from the captain, maybe a slap on the back in the dirty shirt mess. Yes, this was going to be a good one.

Suddenly, the Tomcat coughed, an abrupt sound that made his balls draw up close against his body. Microseconds later, the Tomcat rolled hard to the left, trying to do a barrel roll on its own. Red lights lit up all around the cockpit.

"Fire in the port engine," the LSO shouted, his voice more agitated now. "One zero three, you've lost your left engine—punch out. Eject, eject."

But it was already too late. Fastball looked up to the

canopy and saw black, hungry water. If he ejected now, the rocket engines mounted beneath their seats would simply drive both he and Rat far below the surface of the ocean. But they had to get out—the Tomcat was clearly out of control and there was no way to survive hitting the water in her. Incandescent jet engines plus cold seawater equal explosion. Even if the impact didn't kill them, fragments of metal and turbine blades from the jet engines would shred the cockpit, destroying everything in the path. No, they had to eject, but—.

"No!" he shouted, knowing that Rat was already reaching for the ejection handle. "No, hold on two seconds while I . . ." the Tomcat completed its wing-over and rolled back into level flight for just a few moments. Just at the right instant, Fastball yanked down hard on the ejection handle.

The explosive bolts on the canopy fired, blowing the canopy away from the fuselage. Microseconds later, the ejection seats themselves fired, the RIO's four-tenths of a second ahead of the pilot's. They arced out at different angles, so as not to collide, both clearing the fuselage.

The next few seconds were a dizzying kaleidoscope of flashes of sky, water, and gut-wrenching, all-encompassing nausea. He spun violently through the air, the seat falling away and his parachute deploying. His hand went instinctively to the handle of the secondary chute, even as he knew that there would be no time. They had one shot, maybe not even that. So close to the water, too close—no ejection should take place at this altitude. It simply wasn't survivalable. He felt a hard jerk upwards on his groin and shoulders, and saw the canopy billowing overhead. It tried to fill with air, but there simply wasn't time. It was enough to break his fall, but no more.

Too fast, black water closed over his head. He lost consciousness on impact, for only a split second, then the warm water lapping over his face, filling his nose and stinging his eyes shocked him back into consciousness. He tried to scream, and was rewarded with water trying to flood his lungs.

Actions practiced so often in flight school came back to him as though they were instinct. It was reflex, ingrained so deeply on purpose into every pilot that they might have a chance of doing the right thing even under the most grueling circumstances. He slapped the release latch, freeing himself from the now-deadly parachute cords. He was still descending into the water, the pressure on his ears growing more painful. It was dark, as though the sun had been doused as well. Something snaked around his right arm, and he jerked, disoriented, trying to figure out which way was up. A sea snake, small, yet deadly? But it was only a line from his parachute trying to trap him.

Training again took over. He watched the bubbles, blocking out all other thoughts, and saw which way they were moving. Up—follow the bubbles. With his lungs screaming for air, he kicked hard and felt a flash of deep, deadly pain in his right leg. Broken? No time for that now—if he didn't make it to the surface soon, he was certain his lungs would explode.

It seemed to go on forever as he struggled to reach the surface. Minutes, maybe hours, passed. The water around him grew lighter and lighter, and then, just when he thought he could bear no more, that he must suck down a lungful of anything, even seawater, to douse the pain building there, he broke free at the surface.

His life jacket had deployed automatically, but the buoyancy alone but not have been enough to get into the surface in time, he thought.

He sucked down great lungfuls of air, coughing up seawater as he did, desperate to get oxygen into his brain.

As the pain in his lungs eased, the agony in his right leg took over. Noise flooded in—the slap of waves, slapping him in the face, the loud noise of a helicopter overhead beating the water down around him. He concentrated on staying afloat.

Seconds later, there was a splash in the water near him. A rescue diver swam over, approached him from behind and put him in a carry position.

"It's okay, I got you. I got you," the swimmer said, his voice almost as calm as the LSO's had been. "Are you hurt?"

"Leg," he gasped, still unable to spare the oxygen to say more.

"It's all right—don't talk, just breathe. I'm going to slide you into a stretcher, sir. Just take it easy. You're okay."

"Rat?" he gasped, aware that the question would make no sense to the rescue swimmer. "RIO?"

"They're going after her," the swimmer said. "Let's just get you onboard, sir, and you can see for yourself." There was a splash as the stretcher was lowered from the helo overhead. The rescue swimmer slid him into it, manhandling him but trying to be gentle with his injured leg. Once he was strapped in, the helo ascended, then ferried him over to the carrier and lowered him gently to the deck. Corpsmen surrounded him, efficiently stripping off his ejection harness. Four sets of experienced hands ran over his body, checking for injuries.

Fastball tried again. "My RIO?"

The corpsmen ignored him. After a few seconds, satisfied that he was conscious and not bleeding, they picked up the stretcher and hustled for the island.

Yeah, clear the area for Rat's helo, if she didn't already beat me here. She'd like that, wouldn't she? Get picked up first from helo. She'd say it was because RIO's were smarter or something.

He tried to think of where he had been in relation to the carrier, tried to calculate whether the angle at which her ejection seat shot out would put her safely in the water or—*no, don't even think about it. She didn't come down on the deck. She didn't slam into the side of the ship. She couldn't have—it didn't work like that. No, she had to be all right.*

USS Jefferson
0320 local (GMT +3)

Everyone in TFCC wanted desperately to give an order. Any order, it didn't matter what. The compulsion to take action even when there was nothing they could do was almost overwhelming. And Batman, more than all the others, wanted desperately to do something.

He'd watched the Tomcats approach, quietly confident that each one would get back onboard safe and sound. They had lost no aircraft to antiair missiles, and there were no enemy fighters. Absent the operation of Murphy's Law, there was no reason to suppose that all the aircraft wouldn't be recovered safely.

But then, as always, the unexpected happened. Batman had watched in horror as Tomcat 103 departed from a perfectly normal approach into uncontrolled flight. He had watched the Tomcat wing over, out of control, driven only by one engine. It was possible to recover from such a casualty, but it took experience, more experience than he thought Fastball possessed. He had been certain they were both dead.

And in those moments of horror, he saw the pilot demonstrate true nerves of steel. How many of them would have had the presence of mind to hold off of the ejection, to coldly calculate the moment when the aircraft would be oriented properly to the sea, that split second in which the flight crew could safely eject into empty air instead of being rocketed down into the sea? It had been such a chance, almost unbelievable, because it was every chance that the Tomcat would not have returned to the proper orientation at all.

Yet Fastball had pulled it off. Batman vowed silently

that if he pulled through, he would be wearing an air medal before the day was over.

"What about the RIO?" Batman asked for the tenth time. "Any word?"

"No, Admiral," the TAO said for the tenth time. As though he could add anything more, since he and Batman were both listening to exactly the same communications from the SAR helo.

Damnit, it couldn't end like this. That boy had pulled off too amazing a stunt to have the story end with a dead RIO. No, she had to be out there—she had to be. "Keep them out there. Keep them out there until they find her." Or her body, he added silently.

Suddenly, the SAR helo broke into an excited yell. "We got her! We got her!"

A cheer broke out in TFCC. "About time," Batman said coolly, hoping that none of them could tell how truly touched he was. "Typical RIO—off on their own."

The seconds ticked by with agonizing slowness as he watched the recovery unfold on the monitor mounted high in one corner of the compartment. Why was the helo approaching so slowly? Couldn't they do it any faster than that? Batman raged inwardly, resolved to have a stern conversation with the SAR helo pilot when he landed, knowing all the time that if anyone was more worried about the recovery than he was, it was the helo crew. They took it even more personally than the admiral did.

"Swimmer in the water," the speaker announced. "He's on her, he's on her—yes! We have a thumbs up!" Again the cheer, and this time Batman joined in.

So she was alive, but how badly was she hurt? She was unconscious, but she was breathing. The carrier housed an advanced medical suite capable of performing almost any medical miracle in the world. If anyone could pull her through, short of a major trauma facility, it would be the doctors and medical staff onboard the *Jefferson*.

The same procedure that they'd followed with Fastball was repeated, a stretcher lowered into the water, and
transported to the flight deck. Batman watched the
corpsmen crowd around her, then hustle her into the ship
before they'd even completed their initial assessment. It
was bad, it had to be.

Keep her alive, boys. Just keep her alive, Batman
prayed silently. *I'm counting on you.*

Just as the helo touched down, the TAO let out a yelp
of surprise. "Admiral—look!" At the same moment, Lab
Rat dashed into the compartment, a look of consternation on his face.

"What the hell?" Batman asked as he turned to stare
at the screen. It showed four missiles in flight from
Northern Iran headed for the coast. "Get those fighters
back up," Batman shouted. There were still ten Tomcats
in the pattern, but most of them were at the low-fuel
state—sufficient to get onboard, but not nearly enough
for aerial combat.

But even as he watched, the situation became even
more puzzling. Because the missiles were not aimed at
the *Jefferson* or the battle group at all. Instead, they were
arcing out from a facility further to the east and headed
directly for the station the Tomcats had just destroyed.

Batman turned to Lab Rat. "What the hell?"

Lab Rat shook his head. "No data. But, if I had to
guess, I'd say Iran's in the process of putting together
their version of the truth." As they both watched, the
missiles disappeared from the screen just as they reached
the bombed-out facility.

TWELVE

The submarine moved silently toward the entrance to the Gulf. The Straits of Hormuz were a particular dangerous area for her. The water was shallow, barely deep enough to cover her conning tower. The traffic was also much denser, and by the time they completed the transit, everyone would be worn to a frazzle.

Powder had just finished setting the maneuvering detail when the captain finally reached his decision. He motioned to the XO, drawing him off away from the rest of the crew.

Bellisanus studied Powder for a moment, taking his measure. A good man, with a bright career ahead of him. The captain knew if things went terribly wrong, it would affect not only his career, but that of his XO as well.

That was the reason for his decision to make this an order. He would insist that the XO log his protest in the deck log, as much to protect him as anything else. Had there been any other way, he would have taken it.

Funny that the thought of sacrificing their life in the service of their country was something that every man had already dealt with, at least on some level. Particularly on a submarine, where they were isolated from the rest of the world and knew at some deep, instinctive level the dangers of sailing beneath the surface of the water. Not a single man on the ship would hesitate, if it were necessary—not that they would die eagerly, but they would if they had to. So why was he worried about his XO's career?

"You understand the tactical situation, XO," the captain said, his voice unusually formal.

"Yes, Captain. I do." A determined look crossed Powder's face. "We've got to get into the Gulp to protect the carrier, but the situation has gone to shit. We can't stay holed up here hiding next to the pipeline."

He knows. He's already figured out what he would do, and it's exactly what I intend. That doesn't mean he has to like it—and that doesn't mean he should take the fall for it.

"You know what international rules require when we transit the Straits—we have to surface, show flashing light. It makes a lot of sense. The traffic here . . . they'll be able to see us. And we have the right-of-way over everyone else, under the same rules." He paused and saw the XO's expression grow more determined.

"Of course, Captain. I understand." The XO waited.

"XO, I'm making this a direct order. It is my intention to log your disagreement in the deck log—no, you have no say over that. This is ultimately my decision, and no one else's. If subsequent events . . ." the captain stopped, not entirely sure the phrase covered the consequences that they would face if something went wrong.

When he spoke, the XO's voice held a note of quiet confidence. "You want to go in submerged, don't you, Captain?" He nodded, as though the captain had already answered. "I concur completely. And the men are ready for it—we can handle this, Captain."

A wave of profound humility swept over the captain again. To serve with such a man—how had he indeed been so blessed?

"I do not accept your concurrence, XO," he said quietly. "Listen to me, understand this . . . you will face the same decision at some point in your career, and I intend for you to have a career left when this is over. We need people like you commanding these ships. Don't be a fool, Powder. Do it my way."

"Not a chance, sir. I concur completely in your decision, as does everyone else on the ship. If you falsify the deck log and indicate that I disagree, I will immediately log a retraction. It's absolutely necessary to go in submerged, as dangerous as it might be. If we are detected going in, then it makes our task all the more difficult. That's the whole point of having a submarine here, isn't it, sir,? To be an undetected force?"

"Dammit, Frankie!" The captain's voice was full of exasperation. Not that he hadn't expected this—indeed he would've been surprised had his XO reacted in any other way. "This is no time for you to attempt to usurp command prerogatives. When I give an order, I expect it to be obeyed."

"Yes, Captain. But the good of the ship comes first. And that includes everything from the material condition to the crew's morale. Just how do you think it will affect them if we make believe there's a disagreement between us? Because there's not, you know. There's not at all. So, sir, in my estimation, ordering me to log a disagreement with your decision would do more harm to the ship than good. Therefore, I must respectfully decline."

The captain swore quietly. He had counted on some resistance from Frankie, but not to this degree. How the hell was he supposed to cover for his XO if his XO refused to cooperate?

He wasn't. Commander Powder was ready for command himself. And one of the qualities that had gotten him to that point was a sense of honor. He would not be party to this—and if he had, the captain knew that it would have struck more deeply at the man's soul than any later reprimand for what they were about to do. The captain smiled slightly. While it was true that command was among the most lonely positions in the world, there were moments such as this that made it all worthwhile. Yet it was still his decision alone, and he would bear the ultimate responsibility for it.

"Then let's do it," the captain said quietly. "XO, take the deck. Take us in."

Captain Bellisanus watched the numbers on the fathometer roll over silently. The fathometer was a low power, highly directional seminar, virtually undetectable. As the numbers inched their way down, the floor of the Straits crept up to meet them. With each foot of depth they lost, they increased the risk to the ship.

Additionally, the captain had elected to transit at the very edge of the marked channel. With the proper timing, he hoped to be able to fall in with a line of merchant ships, and carefully keep distance between them. They had waited for an hour, watching for just the right spot.

"Conn, Sonar. I think we might have a shot, sir," Otter said in his quiet, normally sunny tone. "In about five minutes, Captain. Want to take a look?"

The captain stepped back into sonar and looked at the plot Jacobs and Pencehaven were maintaining. Sure enough, it looked like there was a sequence of merchant ships coming up and maintaining station well. There was just enough space to slip in between them, riding the outside of the channel, if they could be counted on to maintain their stations.

Otter pointed at the lead contact. "That one there, she's riding shallow. So is the one right after her, but the third one in the line looks loaded down. I figure our best bet is to slide in between the two shallow draft ones. That gives us a little bit more clearance in case—" Otter stopped abruptly. He looked over at his captain for encouragement.

"Always good to have a margin of safety," the captain said mildly. "Any clue as to what they are?"

"Tankers," Otter said promptly. "The third one is a container ship, probably a RO-RO."

"Give me a time hack," the captain said.

"Three minutes at . . ." Otter stopped and watched the second hand on the chronometer. ". . . now!" Although their desired target was still five minutes off, Otter had to allow for the time it would take the submarine to build up speed. That much metal in the water doesn't instantaneously attain the desired forward speed.

Three minutes—a lifetime when you are trying to stay submerged and play a delicate game of follow the leader, sliding your massive submarine into the line of ships moving ponderously. The seconds ticked by, and no one spoke other than Otter to give the deck officer—the XO—time hacks at two minutes, one minute, thirty seconds, and then a countdown from ten seconds on. As Otter reached zero, the captain felt the slightest vibration change under his feet. The XO brought them up to eight knots at standard accelerations to match the speed of the ships. Simultaneously, he moved them slightly to the west, maintaining position just on the edge of the channel.

The captain watched the green lozenges on the sonar plot march closer and closer, advancing incrementally toward their own position. Then, after the XO had started his approach, he held his breath. Once they were in position, it might be easier going, but for the next few minutes, everything depended on Otter's ability to position the other contacts by passive acoustics alone, and the XO's skill at steaming in formation.

For a brief moment, the captain considered lighting off the active sonar system. Just one ping, no more. Hard evidence to verify that the geometries unfolding in front of him were correct.

But no, even one ping would be enough to blow exactly what they were trying to accomplish with this dangerous, most certainly illegal maneuver.

It was always easier to ask forgiveness than permission.

The speakers picked up the low rumble of the merchant ship just in front of them. Massive thrashing merchant propellers, probably powered by diesel engines or low-pressure steam turbines, churned up a violent mass of bubbles in front of them. The cavitation was particularly severe because the vessel was so lightly loaded, and her propellers were shallow.

In addition to posing some danger if they did not detect any maneuvers on her part, the noise generated by two large ships close aboard effectively blanked out their detection capabilities any further out. Their world was defined for and aft by screamingly noisy merchant ships who gave no thought to quieting techniques.

"How long?" the captain asked the navigator.

The navigator was hunched over his plotting table, carefully supervising the maintenance of a paper plot to supplement the computerized one. He measured off the distance of the Straits transit with his dividers, and did the quick calculations mentally. "Four hours, ten minutes," he answered almost immediately.

The captain studied the chart again, although there was no real need to. He had this particular stretch of water memorized. There were no obstructions that he could see ahead, though one could never be certain in these waters.

Otter stared at the scope, his eyes focused, his hands clamped over his headset. To the captain watching him, he seemed to shimmer, to merge with the advanced electronics and computers that made up the heart of his sonar gear.

Jacobs seemed to anticipate Pencehaven's every thought, and was always one step ahead of him, adjusting volumes, refining track frequencies, handling all the details from his side of the console while leaving Otter free to perform his black magic. The chief, wisely, simply stepped back and let them work.

Suddenly, Otter stiffened. He stopped breathing, and glanced over at Jacobs. Jacobs turned pale. "Captain, the aft ship is picking up speed. Look." A few microseconds after Jacobs spoke, the lines displayed on Otter's console shifted slightly.

"How much?" the captain demanded.

"Two, maybe three knots. I don't know what she's thinking—if she keeps this up without a course change, she's going to hazard the vessel in front of us."

"It may be temporary," Otter said, speaking for the first time since falling in between the two behemoths. "Closing the distance, maybe traffic coming up behind her. Wait," he finished, and shut his eyes, held his breath for about twenty seconds. Then he opened his eyes and said, "Yes, that's it exactly. There's another ship behind them coming into fast, and they're giving her some room. But it sounds like it will pass well to the west of us."

"Orders, captain?" the XO asked.

"Take us slightly to the east, just slightly. I don't want to bottom down, nor do I want to be crushed. And bring us up to match speeds with the stern contact," the captain ordered. Almost immediately, he could feel the vibrations under his feet change as the submarine added two knots to her speed.

The captain glanced over at Otter. He looked relaxed, but then Otter usually did. "That do it?"

Otter nodded. "Should, Captain. I don't hear anything new ahead of us, and I think it will . . . yes. She's slowing back down, Captain. We can slow back down and maintain station."

The captain breathed a sigh of relief.

For the next four hours and ten minutes—and it actually turned out to be fifteen minutes, but the captain did not hold that against the navigator—the captain paced between Sonar, the control room, and the navigator's chart table, keeping a careful eye on everything. Powder retained the officer of the deck position the entire time as well, and his smooth, competent voice giving rudder and conning orders did much to steady the nerves of the crew. By the time they cleared the Straits, it had become absurdly routine, this ponderous underwater dance between the submarine and the two surface ships.

Finally, when they were able to open distance on the merchant ships and head for slightly deeper water, everyone on the crew breathed a sigh of relief. That they would ever consider three hundred feet of water a safe haven would have been absurd under any other circumstances. But after what they had been through for the last four hours, it was exactly the case.

"Engineering, this is the Captain. Any change in hull integrity on damage control status?" Bellisanus held his breath. After their daring submerged transit, his major concern was the damaged sonar dome and the noise it generated.

"No change, Captain," the engineer replied. "We're still watertight."

"And now," the captain said, "Let's get down to business." He turned back to navigator. "You have the search pattern laid in?"

The navigator nodded. "First leg, come left to course 270, speed five knots," he advised. "Leg length thirty minutes."

For the next twenty-four hours, the submarine would execute a silent search of this part of the water. And when the carrier was ready to inchop, *Seawolf* would be certain of one thing—that she was the only submarine in these waters.

THIRTEEN

Iranian Shore base
Wednesday, May 5
0800 local (GMT +3)

The large Aeroflot jet traveled down the runway, awkward and ungainly now that it was on the ground. A few streaks of rust showed on its side, and there was a trickle of hydraulic fluid from one engine.

Wadi contemplated it gravely. Perhaps not the best aircraft, but then again, there were no Iranians riding in it. It would do for the cargo it transported, in some ways more precious than gold or oil.

The aircraft finally came to a halt near the hastily erected terminal building. A boarding ladder was pushed up to it as the hatch opened. Two security guards came down the ladder and stood guard as the aircraft disgorged a flood of civilian technicians.

The heat hit them like a physical blow. While many parts of Russia were not hospitable, there was not much in the world that could match the baking sun in the Middle East.

Wadi's assistant stepped forward. He spread his arms wide in a gesture of welcome. "We are very glad to see you, my friends. Very glad indeed."

Ilya Gromko, the leader of the group stepped forward. "Thank you. If we could perhaps get out of the heat, we can discuss the progress schedule. My men are eager to get to work."

And to get out of the Middle East, I suspect, Wadi thought. He let no trace of his thought show on his face. "Of course, of course."

He led the way into the terminal building, where they were rewarded with an icy blast of air-conditioning, then they crowded into the room. "All work will be done, of course, in air-conditioned bunkers," Wadi said.

"For investments, if you like. Especially hardened." He paused to let this reminder to the man that they were in dangerous territory. "Do you anticipate any additional problems?"

"No. Not as long as we can get the parts," Gromko said.

"Oh, that will not be a problem," Wadi assured him. "My government has the most cordial of relationships with yours." *As well as hard cash. Very convenient, that the nation who has the technology we need is sorely strapped for that. Hard-up enough, certainly, to send a full crew here on the mere possibility of a contract.*

"I have reviewed the production schedules. Most impressive."

The Russian leader grunted. "It's not anything we are not used to. The stories I could tell . . . well, I shall not bore you. We will conduct our preliminary assessment this evening. After that, I will assign six men per aircraft. An assembly line, three days per aircraft. I would estimate no more than two weeks to have all the aircraft operationally ready. Do you have sufficient pilots to fly them?"

Wadi drew himself up straight. The man was offensive, intolerably so. Yet for the time being, he needed his help.

Of course he had the necessary pilots, all of them eager to join battle. They had the benefit of the most advanced training, tutors, and the instructors who attended the U.S. Navy's best school decades ago. And as for the skills they did not possess now, well, there was no shortage of combat instructors for a nation as wealthy as Iran. And if that didn't work, there was always the threat of their biological weapons.

But for now, he must allow the insult to pass. He yearned for the day when he no longer needed these man nor their talented hands and spare parts. And most assuredly the Soviet Union—Russia—would be offended if he executed them for offenses that would have warranted execution had they been citizens.

Oh, but someday soon, they would pay. And pay dearly. After Iran took its place in the civilized world as a superpower once again.

FOURTEEN

Flag Bridge
USS Jefferson
Wednesday, May 5
1200 local (GMT +3)

Batman paced the length of the flag bridge that was located immediately above the ship's bridge. His watch team, consisting of a flag watch officer, a quartermaster, boatswain's mate, and an assortment of pilot fish, watched him uneasily. They were all familiar with his restless temper and moods, his need for physical action when under stress. They had seen it often in TFCC, when Batman eschewed sitting in his elevated leather chair and tried to pace in the much smaller compartment. Here, at least there was room for him to move without stepping on everyone's headset cords.

At most times during the transit into the Gulf, Batman had been content to remain on the 03 level, checking their progress in TFCC and watching the plat camera monitor. But this time, some deep instinct seemed to have gotten him all wound up. And while none of them could pinpoint the cause—indeed, Batman himself could not put it into words—his staff immediately picked up his attitude. There was something wrong, something out of the ordinary, something waiting for them.

Lab Rat was also concerned, but his worries had a specific cause, one that Batman knew as well. The shore station in the desert in Iran was continuing to expand. Intelligence reported that an Aeroflot jet had touched down there yesterday, and although a sandstorm had masked most of the details, it couldn't be good. Additionally, there was some HUMINT, or human intelligence, coming out of the region that indicated Iran was on the move and in a big way, serving as a focal point for the constant pernicious aspirations for Arab unity. With last night's walkout at the United Nations by all the Middle Eastern delegates, the situation was not looking good.

Most of the commentators, including ACN correspondent Pamela Drake, viewed the walkout as purely symbolic. They seemed to find it incomprehensible, despite the continued fighting in the Middle East, that the Arab nations could actually intend evil or that they could constitute a threat to the American forces there. Lab Rat viewed their analysis as shortsighted and self-serving. There was no more volatile area in the world, as far as he was concerned, and Iran did nothing without a purpose. As the Shiite Moslem groups claimed more and more power within the United States's former ally, the situation became more precarious. He doubted that all of the Middle Eastern nations could ever put aside ancient rivalries long enough to form a united front, not for long anyway, but last night's actions certainly increased volatility in the region.

Batman's pacing had an almost hypnotic effect on Lab Rat. He found himself shifting his weight to follow the admiral's pacing, felt a compulsion to join him. Finally, simply to break the hypnotic effect, Lab Rat moved out from behind the chart table and stood in the middle of the bridge.

At five feet two inches, Lab Rat was dwarfed by the

admiral's mass. In recent years, Batman had had a tendency to put on some weight around the middle, adding bulk to his already large frame. Although he was a few inches shorter than Tombstone, Batman easily topped six feet. His shoulders were broad, his face deceptively placid except for the brilliant blue eyes.

At first, Lab Rat thought that Batman did not see him and would simply stride right over him as he paced. But Batman stopped and stared down at the diminutive intelligence officer. "You got something for me?"

"No, Admiral. And you?"

Batman shook his head. He touched Lab Rat on the shoulder, and said, "Come with me." He led the way out to the starboard bridge wing. As soon as they stepped out, the heat and humidity hit Lab Rat like a blow. It was well over 100 degrees, with the humidity at least 90 percent. The air itself sucked the energy out of your bones, reducing you to a mass of flesh that barely wanted to move.

Batman seemed not to notice. He stared at the coast to the right, an almost hungry look his eyes. "You see that? You know what the problem is here, Lab Rat? Everything is too damned close together. There's no reaction time, no margin of safety—you can't afford to be wrong even once. And the bitch of it is, by stationing a carrier here all the time, we're accomplishing just what the Arabs want us to." He glanced over at the intelligence officer.

"How's that, sir?"

Batman straightened up and made an all-encompassing gesture. "The thing we forget is that this area is ancient. So ancient we can't even begin to understand it. Any solutions to the problems here will have to come from inside the Middle East. The peace we impose is an illusion." He slumped down and put his elbows on the highly polished wood railing. "And yet we come here anyway. And every time we do, we help them achieve the one thing they can't do on their own—build Arab unity. Because the enemy of my enemy is my friend, you know? We give them something they can all hate together, a reason to put their differences aside for a little while. And when we do that, maybe we get them to start working on solving their own regional problems. We can't play police here forever—it's just not feasible."

Lab Rat nodded. Batman's position was not an unreasonable one, although he doubted that most politicians thought that way. Everything he'd seen on the media following the walkout at the United Nations seemed to indicate that no one was taking it seriously. It was a gesture, the commentators said, a demonstration of unity. Nothing more.

But like Batman, Lab Rat thought it was very much something more. Everything had a purpose, and it wasn't necessarily the meaning that an American mind would assign to it.

And in a way, could you blame them? How would the United States feel if a coalition of outsiders started imposing their will on American society?

To the right, Iran. To the left, Iraq. Both nations had so much in common, a history they shared that spanned centuries, and every reason in the world that they ought to be left to settle their own affairs.

He glanced further astern and saw the crippled cruiser limping along, mainly keeping station. Her search radar was turning, and Lab Rat knew that inside her hull, technicians were working feverishly to bring the other systems up as well.

Batman followed his gaze. "Yeah . . . and there's that. We can't let them get away with that, not at all." He slammed his fist down on the railing in frustration. "Rock, hard place—for once I wish there were some easy answers."

FIFTEEN

USS **Seawolf**
Wednesday, 5 May
202 local (GMT +3)

"Conn, Sonar. Possible machinery noises to the north."
Jacobs spoke with quiet confidence. Pencehaven had left
the sonar shack for a few minutes, probably for a snack
and a head break, but Bellisanus had no doubt that Jacobs was completely competent on his own. Still, since
this was a passive detection, he'd wait for Pencehaven's
concurrence. Now how not to offend Jacobs while still
buying some time?

"Lot of traffic out there, Renny," Bellisanus said carefully.

"Yes, sir. But this is subsurface. Come see, sir."

"Take her, XO," Bellisanus said. He walked the short
distance to the sonar shack and stuck his head in. "So
let's see it."

"There." Renny pointed out a thin set of lines tracing
their way down the green waterfall display. "Main
power, SSTGs."

The ship's service turbogenerators, or SSTGs, provide
main electrical power for a submarine. They run off
main steam produced by the reactor, stepped down to an

appropriate temperature and pressure. On most submarine, SSTGs were among the most heavily shock mounted and noise isolated of equipment.

"You're sure about that?" Bellisanus said, wanting more confirmation even as his guts told him that Renny Jacobs was right.

"Yes, sir. That's an SSTG, not a motor alternator."

And that made it worse. Because an SSTG was only found on a nuclear submarine, and the Iranian diesel they'd been warned about wouldn't have it.

"Whose?" Bellisanus asked.

"Russian," Jacobs answered. "I'm pretty sure, but not absolutely."

"Any other possibilities?"

"A Russian knockoff. Or . . . and this is going to sound pretty crazy sir, but it's possible . . . a submarine that's towing an acoustic augmenter to make us think she's a Russian submarine."

"And it couldn't be a surface ship with an augmenter?" Bellisanus asked.

Pencehaven came back into Sonar at that moment, and leaned over Jacobs's shoulder to study the display. Bellisanus caught the faint odor of peanut butter on Pencehaven's breath.

"Yep," Pencehaven said, and settled into his seat. "SSTG. Could be an augmenter, though. Awful stable."

"I guess it's possible," Jacobs admitted, and suddenly Bellisanus felt a whole lot better. You couldn't beat the ears on Jacobs, but once in a while you could come up with an alternative explanation that he'd buy. "Yes, sir, now that I think about it, that's certainly possible."

"All right, then. We don't have any intell on any Russian submarine in these waters, so for now I'm going with that possibility. We'll make a slow transit up there to keep our own flow noise down and have a look. And keep an eye on that signature in case it turns out to be a motor alternator instead."

"Yes, sir," Jacobs said, but Bellisanus could hear the

denial in his voice. It might be something towed by a surface ship, but there was no way he was going to convince Jacobs that it might be a motor alternator.

Bellisanus went back into the control room and filled his XO in, concluding with, "Have Ops draft up a message. Let's rattle their cages a bit, see if somebody knows something that they haven't bothered to tell us."

"Aye-aye, Captain," Powder said. He turned the deck of the submarine back over to his skipper and went aft to find the operations officer.

As Bellisanus settled back into his normal scan of people, gauges and machinery, one thought kept nagging him. If it was an augmentor—and the more he thought about it, the more convinced he was of that—then why did someone want to make him believe that there was a Russian submarine in these waters? And more importantly, who was behind it?

After a brief consultation with his navigator and another moment checking the location of the *El Said*'s hulk, the *Seawolf* headed north in search of her prey.

"The Russians wouldn't risk it," the captain said bluntly. "They've been supportive of U.N. efforts in the Gulf ever since the earliest days. Remember how odd that was, during Desert Storm? Seeing the Russians listed as a friendly force?"

The XO nodded. "But they haven't actively contributed military forces to peacekeeping in the last five years," he pointed out. "Wonder what that means?"

"It means just what you think it might. We can't be entirely certain that they haven't deployed an asset down here." He held up one hand to forestall comment. "I know, I know—there's no intelligence on the Russian unit being in the area. But intelligence has been wrong before."

"Or it could be classified above our level," the XO pointed out.

And that was a hoot, wasn't it? Of all the areas of

classified data within the military—indeed, the entire national security system—few were more closely guarded than those secrets associated with the operation of a nuclear submarine. Why would intelligence not trust them with the information, particularly when it directly affected their area of operations? The captain shook his head, as always slightly bemused by the issue.

"Well, it does change the way we're operating in the Gulf, doesn't it?" he said bluntly. "It changes everything."

And that would be reason enough for someone to want us to think that. To slow us down for a bit, to make us think there's more going on than there should be. Because it's one thing to take on a Middle East military unit—hell, they don't have the hardware or the training to use what little they do have. That's why they've been depending on nuclear, biological, and chemical weapons—maximum bang for the buck. But if I were running Iran's show, I wouldn't mind having the U.S. think that there were other parties involved. That maybe our own alliances were shifting in ways we didn't really expect. Because it does change things, doesn't it?

"Let's bump this up the chain of command," the captain said. "Let the carrier know, and sideline it back to Fifth Fleet as well. Maybe if we start asking questions, we'll jar loose some data. It's worth a try, at least." *And we'll let those who are supposed to sort out this sort of stuff figure out what's going on.*

I'll pass the word to the sonarmen, though. Let them keep their eyes and ears open for it. Because the odds are, if the Russians are involved here, we're going to have to deal with them before we get guidance. And particularly if they head for the carrier. Because I'll be damned if I'll let one within weapons-release range of the carrier.

If Bellisanus had slept in the last three days, the XO didn't know when it could have been. He had been in the control room almost continuously, his eyes roving constantly over the instruments, alert to every minute change in the submarine's operating condition. Yet even after days of sleeplessness—hell, they were all running short of sleep, weren't they?—the man showed no trace of the fatigue that must be building up in his body.

How did he manage it? the XO wondered. And would he himself ever be able to sustain that level of effort if he were in command of a ship such as this?

It wasn't often that the XO doubted his own capabilities. He glanced around the control room again, listened to the faint sounds of reports being relayed over the sound powered phones. Bellisanus had left training primarily up to him, and if he did say so himself, he thought he'd done a pretty good job of it. The crew was relaxed, confident, but not too relaxed. There was an undercurrent of cold professionalism running throughout the ship that told him that if and when—and it would be most assuredly when—the time came that the submarine had to fulfill its mission, she would not be found wanting. The sense of being part of something larger, of having contributed to the molding of this collection of people into a tight-knit, potent team made him feel humble.

Humble? He realized with a start that that was exactly the right word. Not proud, not gratified, not anything else that was personal. Just humble that the Navy should have chosen him to lead this group of men.

And maybe, just maybe he had one more responsibility. He glanced over at the captain, until he felt a surge of certainty that it was true. He moved quietly to the captain's side, then with a slight shift of his head, indicated that he would like to speak privately. It was this way with men that spent so much time in close quarters as a team. The merest glance, the slightest gesture, could convey the depth of meaning that didn't need words.

The captain walked over to a corner of the control

room and leaned forward. He was perhaps three inches taller than the XO, and it was not something the XO noticed unless they were in close quarters. Right now, it felt entirely right to be looking up slightly to this man who bore such a burden.

"You could use some rest, Captain," the XO said quietly. He motioned to the control room, taking in all the crew members. "They're doing well. It's quiet right now. But it won't always be like that. I can handle this for now, sir, but there's going to be a time when the only thing that keeps this ship safe is you. And, with all due respect, sir, I need you in top-notch condition *then*. Not now." The XO waited.

The captain drew back slightly, and for just a moment the XO thought he'd overstepped his bounds. Bellisanus started to speak, then shut his mouth with an audible click. He looked at his XO with new respect.

"I insist that the men get food and sleep," the captain said slowly. "But I've always thought myself exempt from those requirements. It's something, you know . . . well, maybe you don't, not completely yet. But you will someday when you have your own ship." He paused for a moment, and XO thought that the captain was going to gently suggest that the XO mind his own damned business.

Then the captain continued, "And when you command your own ship, I hope that you are blessed, as I have been, with an XO like you. There aren't many people who can tell the captain to go get some rest. That you consider that part of your responsibilities tells me you're ready for command."

Then, without further word, not even a caution to call him immediately should it be necessary, the captain turned and left the control room.

The XO stared after him, even more humble now. He turned back to the crew. There was not a flinch, not a quiver, not a trace of uneasiness with the captain out of the control room. That gave him more confidence than any words of reassurance from the captain could have. Because the captain's judgment was that of one man, albeit a man with several decades of experience in submarines. This quiet, this confidence from the crew, though, was the judgment of a collection of men with over 200 combined years of time onboard a submarine. He challenged himself to do his best to live up to the vote of confidence.

The captain slid the door to his stateroom shut, and eyed his rack with longing. He knew the XO was right, and he had known himself for several hours that he was starting to verge on complete and utter exhaustion. But that his XO had spoken out amused him slightly. Had he had that much confidence when he had been an executive officer? Had he?

He couldn't remember, but he hoped so. Without even kicking off his shoes, the captain stretched out on top of his rack. He pulled the blanket over his torso to ward off the constant chill from the air conditioner and shut his eyes. An hour, maybe two, he promised himself. That was all it would take right now to fight of the hard edge of exhaustion that was threatening his judgment. He also knew that on some level he was so attuned to every sound and motion of the submarine that he would be awake immediately if he were needed, even before the XO could call him.

Bellisanus shut his eyes, and was immediately asleep.

SIXTEEN

Viking 701
North of USS **Jefferson**
Wednesday, May 5
1215 local (GMT +3)

Rabies pulled the S-3 into a slow, gentle bank. A gaggle of Tomcats were due to vector in for refueling shortly, and he was on station waiting for them. He'd just tried out his latest composition on his new enlisted antisubmarine warfare specialist, and had been quite gratified at the reception. He wished he could say the same for his own appreciation of the sailor's latest efforts. Indeed, he had made favorable comments, but only because it was polite to do so. In truth, Rabies marveled that the man did not know how tone deaf he really was.

As he worked on the refrain to an idea that had struck him late last night, he kept up his scan of the ocean below. The rest of his crew watched as well, but he knew they were not as committed to the visual search as he was. Well, he would prove them wrong—just wait and see. Maybe he wasn't flying a USW mission, but that didn't mean he couldn't find a find submarine.

Within the parameters of his refueling tasking, he had considerable flexibility.

Just then, his fondest hopes were fulfilled. At an angle, he saw the patch of darker ocean, with a small pole sticking up in the center of it. His heart started beating faster, and he knew the thrill of initial contact on a submarine.

"I got it, I got it," he crowed, jubilant. "No more shit from you guys, OK? Because that down there sure as hell ain't no whale."

Twenty minutes until the Tomcats were due—plenty of time to check it out. "Hold on, boys—we're going in." He put the Viking into a steep dive, and headed for lower altitudes.

Beside him, his copilot stirred uneasily. "They got Codeye you think?" The advent of antiair radar and weapons being installed in the sail of a submarine in the last decade had put a whole new twist to USW. No longer did they stalk a target that could take out their carrier or another ship, leaving the Viking to bingo. No, now submarines had the audacity to be able to attack the ones who were stalking them directly. The helo community in particular, with their slower speeds and operating at a lower altitude, were particularly wary.

Rabies shook his head, intent on flying. "All of the intelligence briefs say no. But," he concluded reluctantly, "Intelligence has been known to be wrong before. I'll play it safe, OK?"

"Let's get them," the copilot agreed.

Behind him, the TACCO was designating the contact as a contact of interest, putting out word of the visual sighting on the data link that transmitted information between all platforms in battle group and to higher authority.

Looking down from two thousand feet, the outline of the submarine was clearly visible. She was coming shallow, a communications mast sticking out over the surface of the water. Rabies gloated over his good luck.

Good luck, hell. Just sheer professionalism, that's what it is. How many other tanker toads would be watching for something like this?

"Give me a flight-to point," he ordered. Almost immediately, the series of symbols appeared on his screen. Rabies vectored over to them, and the TACCO released sonobuoys at each designated point.

"We ought to be able to get something, her coming so shallow like that," the TACCO opined.

"I got prop noises," the enlisted man said excitedly. "Real faint—she's hardly moving at all—but they're there. And," he continued, studying the acoustic display for a moment, "Some electrical sources. Yes, sir, we got us a submarine. And it sure as hell ain't ours."

"Hunter 701, be advised we are vectoring two dippers for hot turnover on this contact." The voice of the USW commander onboard *Jefferson* was gleeful. "Good work, Rabies. If anybody was going to get him, it was going to be you."

Good work? Then why the hell am I still flying tanker duty? Maybe this will convince the CAG that I ought to be off the rotation.

"Return to altitude and continue with assigned mission," the USW commander continued.

"Viking, this is Hound Dog. Interrogative your channelization, sir?"

The TACCO relayed the sonobuoy channel assignments to the helo so that the helo could begin monitoring the correct frequencies. "OK, we got him, sir. I'm holding your data link and your sonobuoys. Don't worry, we'll nail him down."

"But . . ." Rabies started, then fell silent, fuming. It was his submarine, dammit! His submarine! Why the hell did he have to turn it over to the helos?

Because the helos couldn't pass gas to the thirsty Tomcats inbound. Sure, they were nifty to have for localization, with those dipping sonars that they could move around at will. But it seemed so unfair, that they were taking his sonobuoys, using his data, and they would get credit for the kill.

If there was a kill. So far, weapons were still white and tight. But sooner or later, with submarines, it always came down to those moments when the battle group was left with no other choices. The primary rule of warfare was to kill the enemy before he killed you, and submarines were one of the threats that worried the battle group the most.

With a sigh, Rabies took the Viking back up to tanking altitude and began his slow circle again, waiting for the Tomcats as he watched the localization continue on his battle link.

Iranian Shore Station
1220 local (GMT +3)

Wadi swore quietly in his mind, but he was careful not to vocalize his curses. As strong as his position was now, it would not do to give the ayatollahs any reason to doubt the purity of his soul.

But surely if there ever had been a reason for swearing, it was the events that were unfolding on the paper chart in front him. His second in command stood to one side, a look of fear on his face. His master's fits of temper were well-known to all of them, as was Wadi's tendency to execute the bearer of bad news.

"How did they know?" Wadi asked quietly, his voice deadly with menace. He turned to his senior planning officer. "I gave strict orders that the submarine was not to be located. And now I see one of their USW aircraft in the area. Your explanation?"

His subordinate breathed a sigh of relief. Evidently, there would be no messengers executed today. And in the Arab world, that was meant literally rather than figuratively.

The senior planner was just as shaken, although he drew some measure of comfort from his relationship to the ayatollahs. "Our plan was designed to maximize use of the submarine's ability to remain undetected," he said, searching for just the right words. "But one cannot completely eliminate luck from the battlefield, and it appears that that has been what has interfered with our plans now. This must have been so on their part, because the skill of our submarine commander is—"

"Is seriously in question at this point." Wadi shot him a deadly glance. "Unless, of course, it was your planning that resulted in this fiasco."

Someone would die for this mistake today, the ops planner knew. He silently prayed to Allah that it would not be him. "I will institute an investigation immediately," he said with more confidence that he felt.

Why could Wadi not understand that there was little certainty in warfare? You would think that he would know that, with his vaunted years of experience so often held out as a model to the others. Yet when things went wrong, he invariably looked for someone to blame it on, not realizing that uncertainty and chance is the very essence of any battlefiled?

Wadi drew in a deep breath, held it for a moment, then his expression cleared. "Very well. There can be no doubt at this point that they have detected our submarine. There are two helos directly overhead, she reports, and one of their Vikings in the area as well. Should they decide to attack, we have no options."

"Then what would you do, sir?" the planner said, amazed at his own own boldness. In the long run, it would not work, this attempt to shift responsibility back to Wadi. If things went wrong, it would still be his head that would roll. Yet he sought in this his only chance to survive.

Wadi studied the chart for moment longer, and a cruel smile spread across his face. "The best defense is always a good offense, is it not? That is the teaching from every

major battle experience. So, we will take the offensive."
He pointed to the symbol that represented the carrier.
"Starting with that ship."

The planner turned pale. "Our forces—sir, we will be
ready shortly, but right now we are not—"

Wadi turned on him. "More evidence of your incompetence?" he snarled, leaving the words hanging the air
as though they were poisonous gas.

The planner backpeddalcd quickly. "No, no, of course
not. It will be as you say."

"Then make it so without further delay." Wadi turned
back to the paper chart and studied it, scowling as he
did. What he would not give to have the electronics and
data link that the American had, where information was
instantaneously exchange between all units. Instead, he
was forced to rely on this virtually Stone-Age technique
of mapping out ships and aircraft on paper, the information woefully out of date even as it was plotted. Warfare moved too quickly in these constrained waters, with
this modern technology.

Still, if what he hoped to achieve succeeded, Iran
would then be graced with the ultimate in battle technology. There would be no more of this. Instead, they
would have the admiration of the entire world.

SEVENTEEN

Ambassador Sarah Wexler stormed into the suite that housed the Iranian delegation. She ignored the receptionist's angry howls and headed straight for the ambassador's office. She barged in, fire in her eyes, and positioned herself in front of his desk.

At five feet, two inches, Wexler was hardly an imposing figure. She was slim, her age showing in her face and figure, but not in the steely determination with which she approached the grave matters discussed in the international forum. She was known as a tough negotiator, one with a keen understanding of the shifting alliances that govern most of the world, and not above a little skullduggery of her own.

But now, it was clear, Wexler was not in her diplomatic mode. She slammed her fist down on the desk and glared at the large man sitting behind it in traditional garb. "Just what the hell is the meaning of this?" she shouted, leaning forward to stare directly in his eyes.

She knew how uncomfortable a woman in a position of authority made the Iranian ambassador, and most of the time she curried to his cultural idiosyncrasies. But this was no time for being anything other than what she was—the international representative of the most powerful nation on earth. "I demand an answer, sir. And right now."

The ambassador moved back slightly, and rose from his expensive leather chair to tower over her. "Calm yourself, Madam Ambassador," he said softly. "It is so unbecoming to see you like this."

Sarah Wexler's Farsi language skills were minimal at best, but she possessed sufficient command of the language to reply, "Your mother fucks camels." Switching back to English, she continued, "The next words out of your mouth better explain exactly what your position is or I will do my utmost to ensure that the president obliterates your nation from the face of the earth." Her tone of voice left no doubt that she meant it.

"I assume you are referring to a matter of internal dissension," he answered, his voice colder than it had been before. Evidently the remark about his mother had struck home. "If the United States had not interfered, the matter would have been easily settled within our own borders."

"Interfered?" She pointed an accusing finger at him. "Your people just executed an attack on an American cruiser. Fortunately," she lied, "the vessel was not damaged. But there was absolutely no provocation for the attack. Now explain exactly why you thought it necessary to offend us in this matter."

"Even in an Allah-fearing country such as ours, we have dissident elements," he murmured. "One of the hard-line factions, so at odds with our current peaceful government, took control of the self-defense station. It had been all but abandoned, converted purely to research use. Evidently they obtained funding from some enemy of the United States—it is difficult to tell which one, there are so many of them—adequate to supply it with antisurface missiles. As my people were attempting to regain control of the station, the United States provoked them into attack. I cannot, of course, speculate on their motives. But I can assure you their actions in no way reflect upon my government."

"Bullshit," Wexler said flatly. "I don't buy it, and no one else will, either." Just for a moment, her face softened as she focused on what was to come. There would be another Gulf War, and this time she feared the casualties would be much greater. They had been so lucky last time, so well-prepared. But Desert Storm concerned even their allies within the region, and she had been warned more than once privately that such action would not be tolerated again. Any discipline of the rogue Iranian state would come from her neighbors, not from a nation halfway across the world interfering in regional affairs.

No, if war broke out again there, it would be far more costly. Under the guise of assisting the United Nations in enforcing sanctions on Iraq, Iran had secretly countered by building up both her biochemical and nuclear arsenals. Wexler was quite certain that if war came again, countless families across the United States would mourn the loss of sons and daughters.

And for what? Oil? Yes, that, and more. The growth of the fundamentalist religious movement across the region hit her on a personal level as she read about the treatment of women within both Iran and Iraq. Garbed always from head to foot in black garments, sequestered behind walls to their houses, not permitted to own property and forbidden to speak in public, they were truly slaves in every sense of the word.

The Iranian ambassador turned away from her, as though dismissing a subordinate, not his equal. She moved to face him again. He looked down on the her, disgust evident in his face. "If not provoked, we would have settled matters. As it is, our own attack on the station was already under way when your fighters breached our airspace. I understand the guidance of U.N. sanctions, but it also provides that there will be no unprovoked attacks upon any nation without consultation. In this instance, the United States acted unilaterally. He paused for moment, his face impassive. "And if you had information on the attack—and by the way, you might wish to caution your intelligence officers to be more thorough, as I understand the cruiser was heavily damaged—then you will know that the site was obliterated by our own missiles falling shortly after your attack. There was no threat to your battle group—not from Iran." He smiled, and she felt her stomach turn at expression of sheer malice. "Iran is a peace-loving nation."

EIGHTEEN

USS **Jefferson**
1500 local (GMT +3)

In the hours immediately after the Iranian attack on their own installation, no one knew exactly what was going on. Lab Rat's assessment, that the Iranians were readying their cover story, was the only plausible explanation advanced, although at least one staff member insisted that they were intent on eradicating biological warfare weapons stored there.

Admiral Wayne roamed the 03 level of the carrier, unable to settle down in any one spot. It was a growing conviction in his gut that things were about to break loose, and no radar evidence to the contrary could reassure him. Additionally, he was concerned about the odd call they'd received from the *Seawolf*. He was certain they'd followed his orders to clear the area, but he had no way of knowing if they'd found a place of safety. He could have transmitted a message to them by ELF—extremely low frequency—and asked them to come shallow and communicate, but after some debate, he decided that would be interfering with the captain's judgment. He was the one who best knew what situation his ship was in. Batman had told him to get to safety, let things cool down, then try again. He would have to trust the judgment and experience of the captain on *Seawolf.*

But what could have convinced the captain that he needed to come shallow and communicate? A serious engineering casualty of some sort? Intelligence data? Batman wondered if he'd been too abrupt with the man, ordering him out of area, then decided he would have to trust the captain. If it was too urgent to delay, Bellisanus would insisted on briefing him.

That was the problem with being in command rather than on a flight fighting platform by himself. It was one thing to make your own decisions about targets, in-flight safety, that sort of thing. You trained as hard as you could, tried to think everything through, and when it came down to it, you either survived or you didn't. But in command, he had to depend on the men and women below him, trust that they were just as thorough—if not more so—than he would have been in preparing for the same situations.

The radar and intelligence picture for the area was particularly disturbing. There was no indication of any unusual activity; the troop movements, and even the routine patrol flights of the area had stopped. Iran seemed to have suspended most of her normal activities. The smaller states in the Middle East were also quiet, and Batman pictured military staffs in each country trying to figure out what the hell had just happened. So he paced, moving restlessly between the carrier's combat direction center, intelligence center, TFCC, SCIF, and his own stateroom. He felt the compulsion to be everywhere at once, as though something would happen that only he would have the key to. As always, the worst part of any conflict was the waiting.

USS Seawolf
1510 local (GMT +3)

Bellisanus studied the navigational chart, then double-checked their position against the bottom contour map. After twenty minutes at top speed, the *Seawolf* had gone to a slow patrol speed, dropping all of her machinery noises well below the detection threshold of any known sonar. Since they already had hard proof that this area of water was inadequately charted, the captain was particular concerned about another collision with a pipeline or the remnants of the drilling structure. But there was nothing he could do about that, short of turning on his active sonar, and that would be a homing signal to every enemy platform in the area. So he settled for proceeding slowly, making sure he knew exactly where he was, and retracing his path back to the broken pipeline.

According to the chart in front of him, they should be within 1000 yards of where they had run into it. Data processors on the submarine all confirmed that. Engineering was reporting that the water flowing through the sea chest looked unusually nasty, contaminated with oil.

One more issue they would have to contend with—at extremely slow speeds, the *Seawolf* could rely on natural water circulation to provide cooling through scoop injectors, but not so in this water. He would have to use the reactor circulating pumps, and every additional bit of equipment brought online increased the chances of being detected. But the captain thought the risk might be minimal, given the extremely poor sonar conditions in this fouled water.

"We'll give it an hour," Bellisanus said. "Make sure there's no one in the area, and come shallow for a comm break." Once he relayed the details of the man's injury to the admiral, the decision would be the admiral's, not his. He felt a sense of relief, coupled with guilt.

And how long was an hour to a critically injured patients in pain? He turned to his XO. "How is he?"

"Holding his own. Doc says he's still stable, but the odds are that he'll go downhill fast today. We got a little time, but not much."

Not much, indeed. They had to allow time to clear the area and exit the Gulf, then arrange the rendezvous with the carrier. All that assuming that the tactical situation had calmed down enough to allow a medical evacuation. And the odds of that happening, Bellisanus thought, were not too almighty good.

Iranian Shore Station
1530 local (GMT +3)

From his position in the control tower, Wadi stared down at the swarms of technicians around the aircraft. The work was progressing much more quickly than anticipated. There had proved to be far fewer corrosion and structural problems than he had thought, and the primary focus had been on updating avionics and replacing dried-out seals.

Even the Russians were surprised at the condition of the aircraft. Ilya Gromko, their leader, had come to him earlier that day with good news. "Three more days—yes, perhaps four. We will be completely finished." He gestured at the aircraft. "Every one of them will be able to fly. As long as you have the pilots . . ." He didn't finish the sentence.

Wadi felt rage building. Who was this Slavic fool to imply such a thing? Oh, yes, their turn would come. With the aircraft repaired, and when the American presence was eliminated in the Gulf, Iran would buy her own aircraft technology. Anything was available for the right amount of money, and as long as Allah provided the oil in the ground, everything was possible.

But that day of glory had not yet arrived, and for now, he must rely on these sodden oafs to do his work. He forced a smile on his face, and clapped the man on the back in a show of good humor. "Excellent, excellent. I shall have a nice surprise prepared for you when you are finished. A bonus, sorts." He held up one hand to forestall comment. "It is not in the contract, of course. But when a group of men produces such results, it is only proper that it be recognized." He winked, trying to indicate the conspiracy between the two of them. "And for you, perhaps something special. There will be no need to tell the others about it, yes?"

"That is very kind of you," the Russian murmured. Wadi saw his broad, high-cheeked face split into a grin in anticipation of his wealth. "Yes, very generous of you. As much as we admire your lovely land, we will be glad to go home."

Of course you will. To the land of unlimited vodka, to long, dark nights lived in a drunken stupor. And your women, fah—they can be no better.

Yes, I shall have a very special prize waiting for you, my friend. Very special indeed.

"I must get back," the Russian said. "It goes well, but one can never be too careful in looking out for one's people, can one?"

"I appreciate your taking the time to keep me informed. I will not forget it."

Gromko reflected on the conversation as he made his way back down to the air-conditioned revetments. Had his family not been in such desperate circumstances, he never would have agreed to come to this desolate land of infidels. But the lack of hard cash, and government support for the program—which meant more amenities for his family—had proved irresistible. Now, as his heart sank, he knew that the decision had been his final and most fatal mistake.

He knew he was not alone in his concerns. The rumors had circulated among his people since the day they'd set foot on this accursed sand. He tried to reassure them, pointing out that any harm to them would be a direct affront to Mother Russia, but to no avail. And now, he unwillingly came to the conclusion that their collective wisdom had been right.

He gazed around the harsh desert, the sand that blasted them so frequently and crept into every moving part. Even the food tasted of sand. And the vodka, the little of it that there was, had a grainy, unsavory after-taste.

He would die here.

He headed back down to join his men. The Iranians might kill them, but they would leave them a little surprise as well.

NINETEEN

Bird Dog pushed open the swinging double doors to Medical. Immediately inside was a receptionist at a desk. Beyond that was a row of hospital beds with the blue curtains separating them pulled back. Off to the left was another set of swinging doors that led to the surgical suite and intensive care.

"Can I help you, sir?" the corpsman asked.

"The two aviators that were brought in—how are they?"

"Hold on—I'll get the doctor to come out and talk to you, sir." The corpsman picked up the phone and spoke softly for a moment.

A few moments later, Dr. Bernie Green came out of the surgical suite. Bird Dog felt relieved. At least he knew Bernie, and could count on him for the straight scoop.

The rangy Texas native looked like he would be more at home riding a mustang across open fields than in a hospital ward. But Bernie had grown up on the Gulf Coast of Texas, and had a deep and abiding love for the sea. He had attended the Naval Academy, followed by medical school, and *Jefferson* was his second tour of duty. Bird Dog had been trying to find a way to get Bernie up in a Tomcat with him, since Bernie wanted to qualify as a flight surgeon after this tour. The two had become good friends over several lunches in the dirty shirt mess.

"Hey, Bernie. How are Fastball and Rat?"

"Holding their own. Fastball is better off than Rat—he thought he had a broken leg, but it turned out to be a cramp." Bernie chuckled slightly "Pilots. You're all wimps."

"And Rat?"

Bernie's face took on a more serious expression. "The X rays don't show it, but I think she must have hit her head pretty hard when she punched out. I'm guessing a mild concussion, or maybe just shock. She'll be okay in a day or so. You want to see them?"

That was what Bird Dog had been hoping for. "Yeah. That way I can give the admiral a firsthand report."

Bernie led the way back into the intensive care unit. It consisted of six beds, all under the close observation of three corpsman. The array of medical monitoring equipment was slightly daunting. Bird Dog turned to Bernie. "I thought you said they were okay?"

"Just a precaution for the first twenty-four hours. Fastball will probably be cleared to return to flight status tomorrow. Rat probably the day after."

Fastball was in the bed nearest to the door. He struggled up into a sitting position. "Hey. How are you?"

Bird Dog crossed to stand next to him. "The question is, how are you?"

Fastball slumped back down the bed. "Not bad. Considering."

"Yeah. Considering. You know they're going to take the cost of that Tomcat out of your paycheck, right? A hundred bucks a payday for the next million years."

"Yeah, well, make Rat pay for it."

Bird Dog studied him for moment. Fastball looked pale, his face drained. A bruise was starting to bloom on one cheekbone, and Bird Dog figured he'd probably have a black eye as well. A few cuts, scrapes, probably from the impact of the ocean, but nothing serious. "Doc said you'll probably be back in a flight status right away."

"Yeah, I hope so." He cast a worried glanced down at the other end of the room. "What about Rat—they're not telling me much."

"Concussion, they think. She should be fine." Although Bernie hadn't sounded all that sure, Bird Dog figured that reassuring was the way to go. "Good stick, by the way. That's a hard one to recover from."

"Well, I didn't exactly recover." Fastball shifted slightly on the bed. "Man, I feel like I've been beat up."

"All the same—any ejection you live through is a good one."

"You would know, wouldn't you?" Bird Dog held the squadron record for most ejections over a career. He shouldn't have been proud of it, but secretly he was. For some reason, Gator wasn't particularly thrilled about that either.

A good stick—it was the ultimate compliment to any pilot. It meant that the pilot had the overall skills and instincts to recover from virtually any casualty. It wasn't an accolade awarded lightly, and usually bore no elaboration. Good stick—that said it all.

"I'm going to head down and see Rat," Bird Dog said. "You need anything, tell them to give me a call."

"See if she's still speaking to me, will you?"

Bird Dog nodded.

Rat's bed was located just ten steps away, secluded in a corner. A corpsman stood by her side, taking her vital signs. He looked up as Bird Dog approached. "She's still pretty groggy, sir. Keep it short, please." It wasn't exactly a request—more like an order—but Bird Dog let it slide.

Rat's eyes were partially closed, and she looked like hell. But Bernie had said she would be okay. He leaned over the bed and spoke softly. "Rat? How ya doing, kid?"

Rat's eyes focused on him and she looked more alert. "I feel like shit," she said, her voice alert. "What the hell happened?"

"You lost an engine on final. Fastball punched you out." Bernie had said it might take a while to regain her memory, if she ever did.

Rat stirred, then let out a groan. "I hope to hell that asshole feels as bad as I do."

"He does," Bird Dog lied. Maybe not physically, but Bird Dog was quite sure that Fastball wasn't pretending to feel bad about the whole thing. Sure, there was nothing he could do about the flame-out or the engine fire, but that would not prevent him from feeling responsible. Every time a RIO climbed into the backseat with a pilot, he or she placed their life and trust in the pilot. It wasn't often spoken about, but every pilot that Bird Dog knew took it seriously. Even if the RIO were senior, the pilots looked on them as younger brothers or sisters, someone you had to watch out for and keep out of trouble. If a RIO got hurt in flight, it wasn't the RIO's fault—it was the pilot's.

"They said you'll be fine," Bird Dog said, and cast around for something else to say. He wasn't very comfortable being around injured people. No pilot was. It reminded them too much of their own mortality. That something like that could happen to them, too.

Rat murmured something that he couldn't make out. He bent closer. "Say again?"

Rat's eyes opened wide, and for just a moment she was fully alert. "I told him not to do it—I did. But you know how he can be, don't you?"

"Sure, yeah. Told him not to do what?"

"I told him not to try it. The engine was overheating while we were inbound. Intermittent but . . . god, I'm tired."

"So he knew he was having trouble?"

"Yeah. And when we lost it, he thought he could get it back. He was going to roll out, restart—but I punched us out. I put us in command eject and punched us out."

"You weren't in command eject all the time?"

Rat yawned and her jaws creaked. "Naw. He won't let me. He doesn't trust me, Bird Dog. He doesn't."

Bird Dog turned to stare back down the line of beds at Fastball. The pilot appeared to be dozing off. He took Rat's hand, and said, "I'll take care of it." Then he laid her hand gently on her stomach and went back to Fastball's bed. He leaned over, his mouth just inches from the other pilots ear.

"You asshole—why'd you pull something like that?"

"Huh?"

"Rat told me. Jesus, Fastball, you fucking idiot. I'm going to see you fry for this one if it's the last thing I do."

"Hey!" Fastball struggled to a sitting position, and said, "Hey, I was the pilot. It was my call. What I did was—"

Bird Dog cut him off. "What you did was almost get yourself and your RIO killed. You were having problems, and you didn't tell anyone. Climb, call, confess, comply—that ring a bell? What the hell were you thinking, Fastball?"

"I didn't want to punch out."

Bird Dog make a dismissive gesture. "Nobody wants to. You do it when you have to. And when you're a freaking nugget, you leave the switch in command eject. Nobody's going to want to fly with you now, Fastball. You might as well transition to Hornets, because I don't know a RIO in the Tomcat community who would ever get in an aircraft with you again."

A corpsman walked over to them, his stern expression

at odds with his relatively junior rank. He took in the situation instantly, and turned to Bird Dog. "Sir, I'm afraid I'm going to have to ask you to leave." He laid one hand on Bird Dog's arm.

Bird Dog shook him off. "Yeah, yeah, I'm leaving. But you haven't heard the end of this, Fastball. Not by a long shot." Bird Dog stormed out of sick bay and headed for the CAG's office.

TWENTY

The radioman held a message out to Batman. "I thought you would want to see this right away, Admiral." He passed the admiral a single sheet of paper.

Batman glanced over it quickly, noting that it was from the chief of naval operations. He then scanned through the message garbage to the text of the message. And there he paused as a stunned feeling swept over him. He turned to radioman. "Find Admiral Magruder for me, will you? Tell him I'd like to see him as soon as it's convenient." As the radioman left, Batman read the message once again. He had spent enough time in D.C. to see nuances and subtleties in many things that would escape another officer's notice. But he was damned if he could figure this one out entirely.

The message ordered Tombstone Magruder to return to the Pentagon by fastest means available. It was signed by Tombstone's uncle personally.

Tombstone? In D.C.? A fish out of water would be more comfortable.

Although Batman had the greatest respect for his

friend, maneuvering within the political byways of the Pentagon was not one of Tombstone's skills. Oh, sure, he could play diplomacy with the best of them, as he demonstrated in Russia when he was searching for his father. And when it came to combat, there was no one Batman would rather have on his side. But this, this smacked of intrigue and empire building.

And just what did the CNO think that Tombstone would find to do in D.C., anyway? For the last two years, he been a troubleshooter admiral, dispatched by the CNO to problem areas of the world. Was the CNO sending a message that D.C. was a problem area? Or was this something Tombstone should have seen coming? Tombstone's position was unique in the Navy, and Batman had no doubt that the CNO had taken some flak for that.

A feeling of ineffable sadness swept over him. Although he didn't want to admit it, he could see the handwriting on the wall. No, this wasn't about a new mission for Tombstone—it was a sign that the end was approaching, as it did for every officer who didn't quite fit the politically correct profile demanded by today's armed services.

But he'd thought that the CNO could pull it off. That maybe for once the Navy would do the right thing, continue using Tombstone in roles that he had been so valuable in. But if this message was the harbinger of disaster, that wasn't going to be.

Batman laid the message in the center of his desk. *And what do we do as civilians, my friend? Not fly airliners, that's for certain. You'd never be able to resist the impulse to pull a few barrel rolls. Just what will you do?*

There was a knock on the door, and Tombstone came in. Without comment, Batman passed him the message. The impassive face that had earned his friend his call sign was very much in evidence. Even so, Batman had the feeling that Tombstone was not surprised. They'd known each other long enough for Batman to be able to read every subtle change in his friend's expression.

Tombstone passed the message back. "Got any ideas?"

Batman hesitated. His speculation that Tombstone's career was at an end wasn't anything he felt comfortable sharing. "No. Do you?"

To Batman's surprise, Tombstone nodded. "Yeah. That call from my uncle—there's something in the works, Batman. This goes no farther than us, okay? I'm not supposed to tell anyone. But it looks like the board results are out and I'll probably be retiring before long." He held up one hand to forestall comment. "But my uncle's got some ideas. I'll tell you about it when I can . . . if I can. Now, you have any idea about how I'm going to get back there?"

For one of the few times in his life, Batman felt slightly stunned. "The COD. Probably to Bahrain. From there, you shouldn't have any problem—at least, not as long as things stay relatively quiet. Although, given what's been happening, I'm not too confident about that." He shot Tombstone an inquisitive glance. "So there's nothing you can tell me about this?"

Tombstone shook his head. "Maybe never. But the fact that I'm not upset about it ought to give you some clue." Again, that curious grin. "I'll call Ops, get him to save me a seat on the COD. You're on your own from here on out, Batman. You know that, right? Of course, you always have been."

With that, Tombstone left.

Yes, I am on my own—finally! It was with a sense of astonishment that Batman realized just how much Tombstone's presence onboard his carrier had always reassured him. But now, for the first time, he would be alone. For some reason, that both bothered and delighted him.

CAG's Office
1630 Local (GMT +3)

Bird Dog finished telling CAG what had happened with Fastball's ejection, and concluded with, "He's lucky he didn't get both of them killed. You've got to do something, CAG. He can't go around pulling that shit, and from what I've seen of him, he's dangerous in the air."

CAG studied him for a moment. "Some people said the same thing about you."

"Sure, they did. Back when I was a nugget. But as pissed off as I'd get at Gator, I never took us out of command eject. Never. And especially not when we were coming in to the carrier for a trap."

Standard procedure called for the Tomcat seats to be in command eject. The actual controls were located in the RIO's seat area. During an approach, or other times that demanded the utmost from a pilot, it was standard procedure to make sure the switch was set to command eject, which would allow the RIO to punch both the pilot and the RIO out. Otherwise, in its other mode, the RIO could punch out alone. But when a pilot had to keep both hands busy flying the aircraft or might otherwise get distracted, a RIO had to be able to exercise his independent judgement for both of them.

There'd been many times when Gator had threatened to punch himself out alone, swearing that he'd rather take his chances with SAR than spend another minute airborne with Bird Dog. But he'd never followed through on the threat, and Bird Dog wasn't convinced that he ever would. Sure, it'd be a bitch explaining to CAG why he'd come back without his RIO or his canopy, but that would be a piece of cake compared to the problem that Gator would have faced had he followed through on his threats.

"There'll be a Board of Inquiry," CAG said. "You know that."

"Ground him in the meantime," Bird Dog urged.

"Automatic—as you should well remember. But Rat will be grounded as well . . . not that she'd be medically cleared any time soon." CAG hesitated for a moment, then said, "You've been riding his ass some, Bird Dog. I want you to back off for a while. Let things work the way they're supposed to. The Navy's got a pretty good system for deciding who flies and who doesn't."

"If it puts him back in the cockpit, it doesn't work," Bird Dog said bluntly.

"They put *you* back in."

"That was different."

"How? Dammit, Bird Dog, just get the hell out of here!" CAG exploded. "I can manage to run this air wing just fine without your personal assistance, thank you very much."

Bird Dog drew himself up straight. "Yes, sir. I just thought you ought to know what happened."

"Did it ever occur to you that I *did* know what happened? Now get the hell out of here—and don't go spreading rumors around the ship, you hear? I'll take care of things in the manner that I decide most appropriate. And someday if—God forbid—you're ever a CAG, you can sit here and listen to a hothead spout off about what you ought to do."

"I didn't know you'd talked to her, sir."

"You didn't ask, now, did you? And just for your information, it wasn't Rat who told me what happened. It was Fastball."

TWENTY-ONE

Just off of her main office, Ambassador Wexler had a small personal room. In it she kept several changes of clothes, a vanity with a full selection of her cosmetics, and other items, including an emergency evening dress for special occasions. A single bed was in one corner of the room, allowing her to catch a quick nap during times when she simply couldn't leave the United Nations for her house.

Now, standing in front of the vanity, she contemplated her image. Businesslike, yes. But feminine, the light coral fabric lending a glow to her complexion.

She contemplated her jewelry again, then removed a bracelet. Put on everything that's necessary, then remove one piece, her mother had always told her.

Funny how many of her mother's old sayings proved to be a help in the U.N.

She surveyed herself again, then all at once was annoyed with herself. What was the big deal? This was dinner with T'ing, nothing special. Although, she had to admit that the dinners were increasingly becoming part of her regular routine.

T'ing was always a pleasant, cordial dinner partner, a man with a fascinating insight into relationships between nations. She found his insights helpful: On occasion he had even, in his subtle way, made suggestions about how she should approach issues that concerned the United States.

But he was a professional colleague, nothing more. There was no . . . well . . . romantic interest.

Was there? She brushed the thought away. Of course not. They were simply two adults who enjoyed each other's company, no matter that they were almost always on opposite sides of every issue that confronted the United Nations. And given T'ing's subtlety in conducting his nation's affairs, she wouldn't put it past him to cultivate the friendship to satisfy his own agenda.

With a sigh, she took off another piece of her jewelry, then changed the coral suit for a plainer, more business-like suit. She ditched the high heels, and settled for her flats.

And, after all, it wasn't like T'ing was the only one with an agenda. The president had become aware of her growing friendship with the ambassador from China, and had openly encouraged her to pursue it. There were, he said, a number of issues on which they would be confronting China, and it would do no harm to have special insight into one of the great minds to emerge from that nation.

There was a rap on the door, and then Brad, her aide, stuck his head inside. "Your car's here."

"Thanks. I'm ready, I think. How do I look?" She pirouetted, allowing him to assess her from all angles.

"Perfect," he reassure her. "Just the right balance between hegemony and democracy." A sly smile followed.

Wexler laughed out loud. That was one of the things that made Brad so valuable as an aide—his sense of humor. He always seemed to know exactly what to do to lift her spirits, and she never ceased to be amazed at his devotion. When she was worried about something, down in the dumps, or simply boiling over with rage—as seemed to be more often the case than not these days—Brad was always there. With tea just the way she liked it, maybe a snack, or even just an attentive ear to listen while she vented.

At times, she wondered whether Brad was particularly devoted to her or was just exceptionally good at what he did. She'd never asked, and she suspected either explanation could be equally true. Brad was never anything other than the perfect staff officer, and she had no idea of what lay behind his charming demeanor.

Not that it mattered. Brad was also one of the few people who would tell her the truth, point out a loophole she overlooked in pending legislation, or tell her that a color suited her.

"Pacini's?" he asked, mentioning the name of a quiet Italian restaurant nearby.

She nodded. "We're getting to be regulars there."

Brad walked with her down to the main entrance, then handed her off to her chauffeur. "Same thing as usual," she said. "I don't think you'll need me for anything, but if you do, don't hesitate call."

"I will."

Pacini's Restaurant
1810 local (GMT 5)

T'ing was waiting for her in the foyer. His two bodyguards were seated at the bar, each one holding a glass of clear liquid. Soda water, she expected.

If you didn't know anything about them, you would think that they were just businessmen getting off work, enjoying happy hour before going home. That is, if you didn't look at their eyes. That was what gave them away. They were flat and passive, constantly moving over the room, scanning the people coming in, those going out, mentally recording faces and comparing them with their database of threats. There had not been, as far as Wexler knew, any particular threats on T'ing's life. Then again, she suspected he would not have told her if there had been.

T'ing bowed slightly. "They're holding a table for us."

Another advantage of being an ambassador to the United Nations—even the finest restaurants in town always managed to find a table for her, even on short notice. She took the elbow T'ing proffered, and let him lead her to the table. Once they were seated, he opened the wine list and studied it for a moment, then ordered a bottle of Chablis.

She lifted one eyebrow in surprise. It was rare for him to have anything to drink. "Special occasion?"

"It is very difficult to propose a toast without wine," he said gravely. "I try to follow the customs of your country."

"A toast, hmmm? Might I know what we're toasting?"

"In good time. I understand you have been busy today," he continued, deftly changing the subject. It was something he was an expert at. She considered pressing the point, then let it lie. T'ing normally had his own time schedule, and she had learned by now that it was rarely worthwhile to try to rush him.

Briefly, she recounted her conversation with the ambassador from Iran, leaving out her threat to ask the president to deploy nuclear weapons there. It had been mostly bluster, and she suspected that it would turn out to be interpreted as something else entirely if it ever made the rounds.

Finally, she concluded, "They don't like dealing with women. But this is one time they'll have to get used to it."

T'ing listened patiently, and a sly smile tugged at the corner of his mouth. "They would be wise not to underestimate you."

Just then, the wine arrived. T'ing waited while the glasses were filled, then raised his in a toast. "To friendship." He clicked his glass lightly against hers as she repeated toast, and took a delicate sip.

"That's it? Friendship?" she asked.

"Isn't that enough?"

This time she did laughed. "All right, have it your way."

T'ing shook his head. "We know each other too well." He took another sip of his wine and his expression turned grave. "I have heard about your encounter with the Iranians. And what I have heard worries me greatly. I know you travel around the city unaccompanied. I wish for you to reassess that practice. Should you lack for suitable security, I will be glad to loan you a couple of my men."

Wexler sat back, surprised. Was this what this was about? Concerns about her safety? And just exactly what had he heard about her encounter with the Iranian ambassador? She took a deep breath before replying, aware that there were always circles within circles to any offer from T'ing. "Is there a reason for me to be concerned?" She waited.

"Yes. Without a doubt. And if you value our friendship, I would ask that you take this warning seriously." He leaned forward, reaching out and covering her hand with his. "Please, Sarah. The friendship cannot continue in this life if one of the parties to it is dead."

"And you have specific reasons for believing there may be a threat?" she pressed. "Not just vague concerns?"

He nodded. "Very specific. From sources I trust."

Was this another one of T'ing's games? No, the look of concern on his face was real. Although she was quite certain he wouldn't tell her exactly what or how he learned of the threat, she thought she had better take it seriously. She gave his hand a squeeze, then withdrew it. "I shall. Starting right now." She withdrew the cell phone from her pocket and flipped it opened. She speeded dialed Brad's number, and quickly filled him in.

"They will be there in fifteen minutes," Brad promised. "Are you in immediate danger?"

She glanced across at T'ing. "I doubt it. The ambassador's men are here."

"Very well. Do not leave the restaurant until my men have identified themselves to you, understand?" There was a hard note in Brad's voice now, one she had not heard before. Gone was the pleasant, smiling aide she had always known, and her questions about his background surfaced again.

"Agreed." She snapped her phone shut and asked, "Will that do it?"

He nodded. "Your Brad, he is a very competent man, isn't he? In more ways than one."

And just what the hell did that mean? Did he know more about Brad than she did? She wouldn't be surprised. Of course, everyone on her staff had passed a rigorous security investigation, but there was always a chance they'd missed something.

T'ing leaned back in his seat. "And now let us enjoy our dinner. The fish for you?"

For a moment, she thought about the offer she had received from the Red Cross. To take over as its executive director sounded particularly tempting at this moment. Oh, sure, there would be political intrigues, competitions for money, all the sort of stuff you would expect in any large organization. But a threat to her life—she doubted it.

She raised her glass. "To friendship." They clinked, then she said, "And yes, the grouper sounds particularly good."

TWENTY-TWO

The Pentagon
Washington, D.C.
Thursday, May 6
0800 local (GMT −5)

Tombstone pulled up to the parking lot surrounding the Pentagon and felt the familiar sensation of dread and distaste. He understood the need for the Pentagon, and admired men such as Batman who could easily shift between the operational world and the world of politics but it wasn't for him. Never had been, never would be. He had dodged assignments to the Pentagon from his very earliest days.

And look what that's got you. Maybe not the best choice, you think?

But what part of his career would he have given up for a tour in the Pentagon? So many conflicts in so many parts of the world—each one the same, in that deadly force met deadly force, but each one different. And he'd been there in every one of them, right on the front lines. If not flying himself, then commanding those who were.

No, he wouldn't trade a single moment of combat for

a tour in the Pentagon, not even if it would save his career now.

Tombstone parked in the visiting flag officer's spot near the east entrance. It was a typical, sticky August day in the city. The humidity was around 90 percent, the temperature even higher. He broke into a sweat before he reached the entrance. There, he showed his identification card to the guards, and made his way through the world's largest office building to his uncle's office.

The flag corridor was a marked contrast to the rest of the Pentagon, which had taken on a peculiarly tacky institutional look over the decades. Here, thick carpet and paneled walls were the norm.

A Navy captain, his uncle's chief of staff, greeted him. "Go right in, Admiral. He's waiting for you."

His uncle came around from his desk as Tombstone entered. A broad smile split his face, coupled with a look of relief. "I knew I wouldn't believe it until I saw you here," his uncle said, slapping him on the back. "Believe me, I halfway thought you might go UA rather than retire."

Tombstone and his uncle exchange pleasantries for a few moments before they got down to business. Their relationship was closer than that of most uncles and nephews. The CNO's brother, Tombstone's father, had been shot down over Vietnam. Tombstone had been very young at the time, and his uncle had naturally stepped into the role as a father figure. Although he had not been in the home full-time, he had made a concerted effort to stay up on what was going on in the life of his only nephew. Tombstone had been included in his uncle's family outings, along with his uncle's two boys and one girl, and began increasingly to count on his uncle for advice and guidance.

When Tombstone had announced his decision to apply for admission to Annapolis, his uncle, then a relatively junior lieutenant commander in Navy, had been deeply gratified.

Over the years, as they'd each grown older, the nature of the relationship changed. His uncle had accepted Tombstone as a man, as a naval officer, and as a valued colleague. He dispensed invaluable advice when he could, and sometimes said the hard words that no one else would say to Tombstone as he grew more senior.

Events had taken a serious turn on Tombstone's mission into Russia to find his father's final resting place. Tombstone had managed to step on a number of sensitive political toes. That had spelled the end of his aspirations to higher rank. It had been his uncle who had laid the consequences out for him—Tombstone was simply not political enough to survive and be promoted to chief of naval operations. Initially, however, Tombstone was not nearly as disappointed as he had expected to be. He had come to know what was involved in very senior flag positions, and he'd found himself increasingly impatient with the amount of protocol, political, and general ennui associated with higher rank.

Sure, he might be named as one of the fleet commanders, and that of course involved enormous control over fighting forces. But it also brought with it insidious new dangers, in that the slightest politically incorrect statement could immediately torpedo a career. And Tombstone, if he had been anything, had never been politically correct.

So it was with a sense of relief that he heard his uncle toll the death knell on further advancement. Not in a peacetime Navy, he decided. Not for me.

The forced retirement was simply the next logical step after that, although the idea had taken some getting used to. But now, as he felt the years of his naval service start to peel away, Tombstone found that he was eagerly anticipating whatever this new assignment was his uncle couldn't talk about. He felt the thrill of excitement that he rarely experienced outside of flying, and that perhaps had been due to his uncle's emphasis that he would be back in the cockpit.

Tombstone waited for his uncle to bring it up first. And finally, when they had run out of chitchat, he did.

"I know I haven't told you too much," his uncle began. "But there were reasons for that." Tombstone heard a raw edge of excitement in his uncle's voice, something he hadn't heard there in a while. For a moment it bemused him—two men at this age thrilled over the first assignment? How lucky could one man get?

"You know how it is when we need to get something done and can't do it because of political concerns?" his uncle began.

Tombstone nodded. "It's one of the most frustrating things about being in the military."

"Exactly. Well, two weeks, ago the president asked if I'd be interested in heading up a small outfit designed to get around exactly that problem. I said yes, with a couple of conditions. First, that he let me pick my own teams. And second, that he simply tell me what needed to be done, and leave it up to me to figure out how." Tombstone's uncle shot him a glance from under his bushy eyebrows. "I won't be second-guessed by politicians, Tombstone. Not like we were in Vietnam. Mind you, this president is okay, and probably will be re-elected. But in case that changes, I wanted it laid out from the very start what the working relationships were."

"But doesn't the CIA have a number of units doing this for work?" Tombstone asked. "Don Stroh's SEAL team, for instance. I know they get involved in all sorts of high deniability operations."

"You're not supposed know about them, no one is—and no, I'm not going to ask how you do. Suffice it to say that although SEAL Team Six takes care of a lot of the nation's business under very risky circumstances, there are some things they just can't handle. Things that call for more firepower, maybe joint service stuff. That's where we come in."

Tombstone sat forward on the edge of the couch, feeling his excitement build. "You mentioned I'd be flying again."

His uncle nodded. "Yes. In a Tomcat, of course. You can pick your own backseater. Not Tomboy—at least not while she's on active duty. But anyone else you want."

"What sort of flying?" Tombstone asked.

His uncle grinned. "Everything. Some fighter work, some bombing runs. Maybe an occasional covert surveillance mission. I can't tell you specifically, because I don't really know. All I know is that we'll have complete independence, answerable only to the president, and all the operating funds we need. It will be a small group, Stony—none of the bullshit that goes with military service. So, are you in?"

"Did you have any doubts."

His uncle smiled, and Tombstone thought he detected a note of relief. "No, not really. Okay, then." His uncle stood, walked back to his desk, and picked up a folder. "Study this. It's a range of options, all at a very generalized and low classification level. But you get the drift, and you'll have a number more to contribute as well, I suspect. The first thing I will want you to do is start putting together the rest of your staff—decide how many we'll need, and who you want. If they're available, I'll get them for you. They'll have to be dry-cleaned, released from active duty, and hired here as civilians, but each one of them will have the president's personal guarantee that if he or she wants to leave and go back on active duty, they will do so with no prejudice and no loss of career. You have anybody in mind off hand for your number two?"

Tombstone thought back immediately to his last mission in Hawaii, how he'd managed to put together a pickup team to constitute one of the most exciting battle staffs he'd ever worked with. He wondered if any of them were available.

There'd been Major General Bill Haynes, a two-star

Army infantry officer on his way to assume duties as Deputy Commander in Korea. Marine Colonel Darryl Armstrong, deputy commander I Corps, with two tours in special operations, including Rangers, who'd assumed duties as the landing force commander under Tombstone. Armstrong had been a powerfully built man a couple of inches taller than Tombstone himself. Maybe 6'4", 230 pounds, and with an intense, driven air about him that attracted Tombstone's attention immediately. His hair was cut so short as to be almost invisible, and his ice blue eyes seemed to absorb everything without actually looking at anything.

Then Lieutenant Commander Hannah Green, who'd spent most of her time supporting landing operations and special forces teams. She was a tall, willowy blond, with a slim, athletic build. Short blond hair framed a classically beautiful face with blue eyes a couple of shades darker than Armstrong's. She had a photographic memory.

The team had also included other services as well. An Air Force major, Carlton Early, coordinated the tanking and out of theater logistics support. Captain Ed Henry, a Coast Guard ship driver who'd taught them all the Coast Guard way of doing more with less. And finally, Fred Carter, the Air Force master sergeant, who'd supposedly spent a good deal of time managing senior officer matters but who'd also proved to be a handy helo mech as well as a real trooper.

"I have some people in mind," Tombstone said slowly. "I'll have to find out if they're interested."

"Give me the names."

"No, sir. If it's just the same to you, I'll ask them myself. If they're going to be part of my new team, then it's only right that they know what they're getting in to."

His uncle grunted. "Ask my chief of staff for any assistance that you need in locating them. But I'm warning you—I better not hear that any of them just happen to be located on *Jefferson* and you want to go see them in person."

"No, sir. You've made your orders clear. Give me credit for that much, at least."

"I do, Stony. I do." His uncle stood and clapped him on the shoulder. "Now get out of here. Getting fired means I have a lot of loose ends to tie up. And I'm sure you've got some of those as well. Check back in with me tomorrow; let me know how you're getting on with it."

I will, Uncle. I will. The Navy may be shortsighted enough to let both of us go, but I'm going to do my best to make sure I take the best and the brightest with me. We'll fight wars the way they're supposed to be fought— and we'll win. That I'll guarantee. With my own life, if I have to.

TWENTY-THREE

The United Nations
New York
Thursday, May 6
0900 local (GMT-5)

Ambassador Wexler stared across the vast hall of the delegates. As with any other major political body, most of the work was done behind the scenes. By the time a matter came up for a vote, you pretty well knew where you stood. You might make the motion anyway, just to make your point to the international community, but generally if it wasn't cemented down beforehand, and you hadn't corraled shifting alliances in that region, nothing was going to happen. Every ambassador wanted to consult with his home government before making a decision.

But time was short now, events moving at such an accelerated pace that unless something was done soon, there was a good chance that the Middle East would erupt into bloody war while the delegates sat around indifferent. There had not been time, although she had tried. With T'ing's help, there was at least a chance.

Her gaze shifted to the ambassador from Iran. He was

staring at her, a look of sheer malice on his face. And why, she wondered, did he not feel it necessary to mask his feelings in public? It was an axiom of diplomatic art that you never let anyone know exactly what you really thought.

The ambassador made a slight gesture, one that could have been interpreted as downright obscene. She held her temper in check and smile pleasantly. He turned away from her. She could almost feel T'ing's gaze on her from the other side of the room. They had argued long into the night about the merits of trying this now. T'ing's position had been that it was better to wait and succeed than to make the motion now and go down in public defeat.

But what should her real objective be? Putting on a good show show or winning the war?

From her perspective, and that of the president, there was more to this motion than simply making a gesture. They were voicing the nation's outrage over the unprovoked and unwarranted attack on a ship of war. If they let it slide, the UN would interpret it as a sign of weakness. In the end, they had agreed that they had to do something now, because that what was in the American character.

She took a deep breath. The Secretary General looked at her over his reading glasses and said simply, "The ambassador from the United States."

Wexler rose. She paused for a moment, letting her outrage flood conviction into her voice. "As the delegates know, two days ago Iran executed an attack upon an American cruiser. Although the damages were minimal, this is completely unacceptable. Our ship was operating in international waters under the authority of a resolution passed by this very assembly. This attack not only is an attack upon my nation, but on the authority of the United Nations as well. If we are to be able to maintain peace in the world, work out grievances and disputes without the widespread bloodshed of the last century, then we must insist that the delegate nations abide by their agreements and our rulings."

Then she stopped and surveyed the room to see how it was going down. A few nods here and there, other looks of consternation. The ambassador from the United Kingdom murmured a quiet, "Here, here," that carried easily in the silent room.

"Therefore," she continued, "I move that pending further measures, the United Nations immediately issue a condemnation of this unprovoked attack by Iran. Furthermore, we will require reparations."

The Secretary General turned to the ambassador from Iran. "And your response?"

Wexler remain standing as the Iranian ambassador stood, as though she could by the sheer force of her presence force him to admit the truth. He glared across the room at her, and when he spoke, his voice was low and ugly. "We do not consent to any action by the United Nations. The attack was not unprovoked. The United States violated our security in a very real way, as these photos I'm passing out will show." He motioned to an aide, who began distributing photographs along with accompanying text to the rest of the delegates. "When you examine the evidence, Mister Secretary General, you'll see that it is not Iran who should be sanctioned—but the United States." He paused for a moment to let his words sink in.

"However, since that is not a possibility, given that the United States has bought the goodwill of most of you, you will not take action. Therefore, in concert with her brothers in the area, Iran will settle its own scores."

He dropped his microphone to the floor and stormed out. One by one, the delegates from the other Middle East countries followed him.

It was still dark out when the last aircraft was done. The Russian leader watched, feeling the inevitability of the future rushing toward him. There was a peculiarly fatalistic streak in most Russian psyches, and he was no exception. He did not want to die—how he did not want to die!

He contemplated the newly refurbished aircraft. Perhaps it was not much to look at—the finish was still rough, but a few coats of paint would have improved its appearance as well as its aerodynamic characteristics. Still, the engines were sound, the avionics working, and it would do for what the Iranians intended.

But what would happen when they were through ejecting the United States? Would hungry eyes turn northward, to the fertile planes of Ukraine? To Russia herself?

This project was a test of what the Arabs claimed was a new era of peaceful cooperation. Deal fairly with Russia and Russia would deal fairly with you. But betray her, and expect threefold results returned to you.

He summoned the shift leader to him. "Send a messenger. He will want to know we are done, even at this hour." There was no question as to who he was. The shift leader's eyes sought his out, anxious and afraid. "Perhaps you're wrong."

The leader forced a smile. "Perhaps I am."

But I'm not. You know it, and I know it.

Just as the sun reached the horizon, two food service trucks pulled up to the hangar. They discharged huge tubs of iced vodka, vats of Russian caviar along with all the accompaniments. A staff car followed in short order, along with a troop carrier. Wadi emerged, smiling, very awake. He bowed and spread his hands expansively.

"You have done well—well beyond all expectations.

My men are passing out a small token of our appreciation." The soldiers moved among the crowd, handing out packages that contained thin strips of gold. The men gasped, awe on many of their faces. It was more money than they would see in their entire lives.

"Drink, eat." Wadi pointed toward the groaning tables. "Each of you take a bottle and bring it with you. I wish to have a final picture to memorialize the new era existing between your country and mine." The Russians swarmed to the buffet tables, helping themselves. Soon they were talking loudly, boasting, an eager flush of anticipation on each face.

"The photos," Wadi said. He pointed at the horizon. "I would like you in three lines, facing the horizon, facing the new day." Their spirits now buoyed by food and drink, the Russians followed the soldiers. They lined up in roughly three lines. Gromko remained behind to stand with Wadi, who was still smiling.

Wadi turned to him and said, "Several times now, you have asked me whether Iran has the military power and might to make a success of this plan. Have we pilots, have we the technology—your questions become tedious. I will demonstrate to you myself just how determined we are."

With the Russian technicians watching, Wadi withdrew a pistol from his robe and shoved the nose against the Russian's head. "Do you doubt me now?"

The Russian turned smiling and spat in the Arab's face. Wadi pulled the trigger, and the Russian's head disintegrated into a mass of blood, bone, and brains. A second later, the Iranian troops hosed down the technicians, then moved methodically through them, dealing final death shots to those who survived the onslaught.

When they were done, Wadi posed in front of the sprawled bodies for the official photograph. There would indeed be a memento to commemorate the new relationship.

Operations Center

Wadi walked into the operations center, the Russian's blood still spattered on his robe. His aide offered him a damp, clean cloth without comment. Wadi wiped the remnants of brain tissue from his neck and face. He did not bother to try to remove the debris from his clothes.

Let them see it. Let them see it and wonder.

He turned to his operations officer, and asked, "The submarine is in position?"

"Yes, sir. Exactly where she should be." It was clear that the operations officer was shaken by his superior's appearance.

Wadi nodded. "Have her linger near the straits," he ordered. "The American battle group is doomed now." He paused, shut his eyes for a moment and then nodded. "They have a saying . . . something about closing the barn door after the horse is out." He smiled, his teeth stark white against his dark complexion. "Fortunately, it is not one of our proverbs. Instead, we shall let the horse into the barn then shut the gate behind it. You understand?"

"Of course."

"Make sure she is well inside the Straits. Two hours after she passes our last checkpoint, perhaps. Then shut the gate. Permanently."

Iranian submarine
0545 local (GMT +3)

When the message came, the submarine captain felt a surge of relief. The sooner they executed their mission, the quicker he could leave to a safer position. The water was barely one hundred feet deep, almost too shallow to keep the submarine entirely submerged. And around the straits, the heavy traffic posed a constant threat. He had been up all night, supervising the operations of the sonar suite and the officer of the deck as he dodged heavily loaded merchant ships inbound. Their draft exceeded the clearance.

"Two hours?" his second in command asked. He pointed at the tactical chart. "The American aircraft the *Carrier* cannot possibly escape. Even at her top speed, she is three hours from the Strait. I will start the clock now, sir."

"Do that."

USS Seawolf
0600 local (GMT +3)

"I'm satisfied that we have not been detected," Belli-sanus announced. He looked over at Powder and saw a nod of concurrence. "Let's come up to communications depth and tell the carrier what's going on. It wouldn't hurt to have an update on the situation as well. The last I saw, it was going pretty smoothly."

"Aye-aye, sir." The XO turned to the officer of the deck, and listened as the order was relayed and trans-lated into technical terms down to the planesman and helmsman.

This time the submarine rose slowly, careful not to breach the surface of the ocean. They would come shal-low enough to poke their satellite antenna above the wa-ter, spit out the message, and suck down data from the Link. God willing, the whole maneuver would take no longer than five minutes. Every second spent shallow, even with only an antenna exposed, increased the risk exponentially.

"Good data," the data systems specialist announced. The tactical screen began filling with updated positions.

The captain and the XO stared at the screen in horror as the situation unfolded in front of them. The cruiser was devastated, in close to the carrier. *Jefferson* herself just clearing the Straits and now in the Gulf. How had so much gone so wrong so quickly?

"At least it will make the medical evacuation quicker," the XO said. "Doc says the sooner the better."

The captain grunted. "They always say that."

The captain picked up the microphone that fed into the tactical circuit. "*Jefferson*, this is *Seawolf*, over." He listened to the odd warbling over the secure line. A response came back immediately.

"*Seawolf, Jefferson*. Go ahead."

Briefly, the captain sketched in what had occurred, and then said, "We're going to need medical evacuation for one of the men. When can you stage that?"

There was a long silence, then "*Seawolf, Jefferson*. Wait. Out."

The captain hung up the microphone, seething with frustration. He had expected no less, but it was still frustrating.

The flag TAO would have to find the admiral, who would then no doubt need to consult with his staff before he decided whether or not to risk the dangerous evolution. Thirty minutes, at a minimum, he decided. Thirty minutes was lightning speed in terms of planning, but an eternity to a submarine at communications depth.

"Conn, sonar! Holding contact on a subsurface contact, bearing 180, range 8000 yards. I classified this as the Iranian diesel we were holding earlier, sir."

The captain swore quietly. Had they been detected? Had air assets seen their antenna? Or this was the simply bad luck?

No matter. It required immediate action. "Conning officer, take us down." He turned to the XO. "Tell Doc I'll get him answer as fast as I can, but we have a problem to take care of first."

The captain walked back into sonar and took a look at the displays himself. Not that there was much point to it—if Renny Jacobs had made a mistake, the chief would have caught it, and the captain's untutored eyes would have been no help. "Any indication he's doing anything I should know about?" the captain asked.

"No, Captain," the chief said. "He's lying quiet on the bottom, just waiting. Not even moving."

"Are we going to have any difficulty holding him with part of the conformal array damaged?"

"Too soon to tell. Right now we've got him, but I suspect we will have some blind spots on some bearings. I won't know until we try." The chief sounded worried.

The carrier had to have transited the Straits barely two hours ago. If the submarine had intended to make a run on her, that would have been the time to do so. So what was she doing lying in wait by the Straits instead of tracking the carrier?

Just then, the lines on the sonar began to shift. New frequencies appeared, digitized, processed, and labeled with the sonar's best guess as to source. "She's on the move," Renny said. "Heading for the straits."

"How long until she gets there?"

"About fifteen minutes. It's like she's been waiting for something, sir," Renny added.

The captain looked at him slightly askance. Sure, the sonar technician had a keen grasp acoustically of what a submarine looked like, but speculating on tactical decisions at this level was a little bit out of his league. Still, he glanced up and saw the chief nodding as well.

"Talk to me—let's think this out." the captain said.

"No doubt," Renny said without hesitation. "If it's not the carrier, it's the Straits themselves. Captain, I think—"

Just then, a broad swath of noise shot across the display. Even the captain knew what it was. "Compressed air. But no torpedo." The captain felt a sick feeling starting in his gut.

There were only a few reasons for a submarine to be shooting compressed air out of her tubes. First, to launch a torpedo, but had she launched a torpedo, it would have been immediately evident on the screen. Second, she could be dumping garbage. Not likely during daylight hours. She could also be launching a special device to determine the sound velocity profile of the water, or a message buoy. But the final possibility, the captain knew instinctively was the right one.

Mines. The submarine was launching mines. He saw agreement in the sonarman's eyes.

"But why? The carrier's already in the Gulf. Who's he trying to keep from getting in?"

"Maybe he's not trying to keep anyone from getting in, sir," Renny said slowly. He pointed to the green lines on the screen that were the carrier's acoustic signature. "Maybe he's trying to keep us from getting out."

TFCC
0700 local (GMT +3)

"They're *what*?" Batman roared. "The hell you say—is Bellisanus certain?"

"Yes, sir. It's a single line across the Straits. He's requesting orders, Admiral," the TAO said. He held out the scribbled message they'd just received from the satellite.

"Take it out," Batman said unhesitatingly. "Take it out now." He turned to survey the tactical plot. "And I'll deal with the rest of it. I want everything we've got in the air. First priority—deal with those Iranian F-14s and give us night air superiority. It's gonna go downhill from there for them. Real downhill—and fast. Now do it *now*!"

Almost before he'd finished speaking, the low howl of Tomcats spooling up rattled overhead. Twenty minutes later, virtually the entire airwing was airborne and headed for the coast of Iran.

Sick Bay

Rat was the first one out of bed, but Fastball wasn't far behind her. They were pulling on their uniforms before the corpsman could even get to them, and by the time he'd found Bernie, they were already headed for the door.

"Where do you think you're going?" the doctor demanded. "Back in bed—both of you!"

"Not a chance," Rat said tartly. She pointed at the overhead. "You hear that? They're launching everything we've got onboard. We're fine and you know it. And I'm not about to let an aircraft sit on the deck for lack of an aircrew, even if I have to fly with this idiot."

"Yeah," Fastball said, not entirely comfortable with agreeing that he was an idiot, but figuring that he'd settle that later with Rat. "We're out of here, Doc."

Bernie regarded them for a moment, and saw the determination on both faces. Really, there was no medical reason they couldn't fly right now, although he would have been far happier keeping an eye on both of them for another couple of days just to be certain. But if there's one place that you can't wait around for certainty, it's on an aircraft carrier.

"Go," he said finally. "No punching out."

Rat and Fastball grinned and sprinted out of the sick bay. Five minutes later, after wangling permission from a harried CAG who barely seemed to remember who they were, they were walking to the paraloft to get their gear.

TWENTY-FOUR

Tomcat 102
Friday, May 7
1000 local (GMT +3)

Fastball leaned back in his seat for a moment, trying to ease the nervousness that filled his body. He was flying a northeasterly course over the Persian Gulf. His section was at about 10,000 feet. His RIO had been quiet for some time, no doubt setting up her LANTIRN and readying the two huge 2,000 lb.GBU-24 Paveway III laser-guided bombs his bird carried. They were meant for one of the hardened aircraft shelters at the MiG base near Bandar Lengeh.

He adjusted his night-vision goggles. This "strike stuff" was still new to him. He had always been a fan of the Tomcat's air-to-air prowess and had selected the Tomcat community because of its primary fighter mission. But the events of the last few years, with the addition of the LANTIRN and the shortage of strike aircraft due to downsizing, had forced the Tomcat community to take a lead role in strike warfare. Now, because of its vastly superior FLIR over that carried by the Hornet, the Tomcat was considered the air wing's preeminent strike platform.

Fastball was damned glad that he had an experienced RIO in his backseat. If Rat was anything, she was a good RIO. She was quiet and difficult to get to know, but she was one of the best RIOs in the squadron. Strike was her bag at the RAG and her specialty at TOPGUN. Some joked that she could find a cigarette on a busy street with her LANTIRN.

Fastball returned his attention to the flight. Glancing to his right, he saw Rat's FLIR display on his TSD. She was quietly looking over an Iranian oil platform. Probably taking a GPS fix, he told himself. A quick glance outside his cockpit revealed an empty, black sky, tinted only by the greenish cast given by the night-vision goggles.

He reconfigured his display screen and checked his time. He still had a minute-thirty to reach his next way-point—right on time. So far everything checked out. This mission was key to the *Jefferson*'s ability to obtain air superiority over the Iranian coastal areas. The goal was to hit the air base with a combination of Tomahawk cruise missiles and strike aircraft from *Jefferson*. The first barrage of cruise missiles would hit the control tower and a few of the smaller structures. Hopefully, the explosions would cause the aircrews and maintenance personnel to rush to ready their MiGs to scramble. The second, albeit smaller, wave of cruise missiles would then hit, exploding their submunitions over the tarmac, tattering planes and men. The Tomcats would then strike the hardened shelters with their 2,000 lb. bunker-busters.

A similar strike was planned for the MiG base near Chah Bahar. If these strikes succeeded, they could well destroy the vast majority of MiG-29s, which would leave Iran with no credible night-capable fighters and give the U.S. air superiority for at least a portion of the day.

"Coming up on way-point four," Rat said calmly. "Turn left, heading three-three-five. Mark."

"Copy," Fastball responded, banking his plane slightly for the turn.

"Start your descent to angels eight." Rat changed her display. "We are fifty-five miles from the target. Confirm weapons armed."

"Confirmed."

"Come to course three-one-five. Feet dry."

"Knocker's up" she called, meaning that she was switching her focus from air-to-air to her attack mission.

Hornet 406

"Football, Packers, we are blank," radioed Lieutenant Tom "Lyfa" Riley, one of the F/A-18 Hornet pilots flying SEAD. A "blank" call meant that the suppression of enemy defenses (SEAD) aircraft did not detect any emitters of interest. Riley's APG-73 radar scanned ahead in ground-mapping mode, his ESM gear listening for the telltale signs of air defense radars that might spring to life.

Tomcat 102

Fastball steadied his stick and throttle, settling into the designated speed and angle of attack. A blip now appeared on their radar fifty miles to the northeast of their position. A soft chirp also registered on their RWR. The Iranian Tomcats were out again, collecting airborne early warning data. Even though they were flown by considerably less capable pilots than those whom he had fought back in the States, Fastball was glad the Tomcats were staying clear of the fray. The Phoenix was still deadly, even in the hands of a green pilot.

Johnnie checked her radar predictions, comparing her

hand-drawn maps against her FLIR picture. She could see the base of a few hills, a small cluster of buildings, and . . . *there!* "I've got the airport." Rat's thin voice interrupted. They were now at thirty miles. She slewed her crosshairs over the second hanger, locked, then sweetened the fix with her thumb switch. "Captured. Designating the northern hangar." Rat clicked open her tactical mike. "Two captured."

Hornet 406

Three search radars suddenly appeared on Riley's radar screen just south of the airfield. The Iranians were certain to know that something was en route. *May be that's good,* Riley thought. More people would be in the open when the TLAMs hit. And if they were really lucky, some of them would be MiG pilots.

Tomcat 102

Johnnie checked the flight path against the mask curve on her screen. It looked fine, she thought. Fastball was flying right on course. She gave a quick check of her kneeboard card, which outlined the prebriefed release point, then depressed the hand-controller trigger, beginning the illumination. Unlike the smaller GBU-series bombs, the GBU-24's release point had yet to be programed into the Tomcat's computers, with the end result being that the bombs had to be released manually, based on visual and geographic cues. Johnnie began her range countdown, "three . . . two . . . one . . . *pickle!*"

Fastball triggered the first, then, on cue, the second GBU-24. The two bombs dropped from the Tomcat's undercarriage with a noticeable thump, then deployed their glide wings.

Morrow angled his fighter away from the target to his left, giving the LANTIRN's laser-designator its maximum unmasked field-of-view. Both crew members watched the display for a moment, seeing the men on the tarmac around the hanger scrambling about in reaction to the TLAM strikes. The brightness of the flash on their NVGs made them squint.

Johnnie had just switched back to air-to-air and was about to call the Hawkeye for a "picture" when a sharp *deedle deedle deedle* rang out over the RWR gear. Her eyes darted to her circular RWR display. "SAM launch. One o'clock. SA-2."

"I've got it."

"Music on. Packers, Steelers Two, SAM, north Bullseye at fifteen."

"Breaking right," Morrow called. "Watch our mask."

Hornet 406

"Copy, downtown." Riley loosed one HARM at the missile's source, then a second. The missiles zoomed off his bird and sped away at nearly Mach 5. Riley loved the SEAD role. It reminded him of the Shrike-armed Iron Hand missions his father flew in his A-4 over the skies of North Vietnam. But the HARM was vastly superior, he thought. It could remember where the site was even if it shut down.

Tomcat 102

"Looking good." Johnnie watched the bombs track and the LANTIRN's mask or blind spot. "Come left!"

"Boom boom!" Rat hollered as the two bombs crashed into the hanger. "Free to maneuver."

"Second launch!" Morrow slid into afterburner and banked into the SAM before rolling inverted and pulling toward the ground. Johnnie punched three clouds of chaff, just enough to confuse the guidance radar.

But the two HARMS loosed by Riley smashed into the SA-2's Fan Song fire control radar, destroying the unit and sending the SAMs ballistic.

Hawkeye 703

"Football, Talon, picture, two groups. Southeast, Bullseye for fifteen. East Bullseye for twenty. East group are Tomcats."

"Copy your call," came the response from each element.

"Steelers, eastern group. Packers, southeastern group."

Tomcat 111

"Steelers One, copy your call." Lieutenant Commander Steve "Jolly" Rogers quickly evaluated the developing scene. "Send Two after the AEW. Have Three-join on our wing."

"Roger that," his RIO acknowledged, then called the plan.

Tomcat 102

"Okay, Rat. Let's get us a Tomcat."

Johnnie studied the JTIDS picture on her TID. The two AEW birds were circling in a long, racetrack pattern at about twenty thousand feet and forty miles out. Either these two crews had yet to detect their Tomcat, or else there were other fighters in the area masked in the valleys of the coastal mountain range. Or, there was a SAM trap.

"Fastball, this bothers me. Something's not right." She glanced out her right then left side.

"Come on, Rat. We've got two sitting ducks straight ahead and you want to play war college tactician. I'm going to get me a Tomcat. Get some balls, girl. Switch to Phoenix!"

"Will you listen to me! Look at those guys. They're just waiting. I'm telling you, we aren't alone!" She waited for a response that never came.

"Phoenix selected, your dot."

"Fox Three on the westbound Tomcat, angels two-zero at twenty-five." The AIM-54C dropped momentarily, then raced ahead toward its victim.

"As soon as it's active, we're bugging," Rat called.

Fastball's fixation on the departing Phoenix was short-lived. Suddenly, his RWR chirped and showed two AIM-7 Sparrow missiles inbound off his port wing. "Rat, incoming. At our nine o'clock." He jerked his Tomcat into the missiles, then angled them back on his right side, trying to force the missile's gimbal to the extreme and break the radar's lock.

Johnnie flipped the switch, sending the signal for the Phoenix to go active. "Counter measures," she called. "Pumping chaff!"

One of the Sparrows shot over the canopy, failing to detonate.

"Geez that was close!"

A second exploded into one the chaff clouds.

"Two more! I've got two more! Three o'clock. Break right!"

Fastball broke into the missile and yanked his Tomcat down, just as the third Sparrow homed onto another chaff cloud. He brought his nose up, looking in the direction of the last missile.

"Where are they?" Johnnie's head spun from side to side. "Where are they?"

"Phantom! Eleven o'clock. Heading across . . . he's turning away!" The Iranian F-4E pulled a hard left slice turn, putting its hot pipes in Fastball's face. He snaked around, angling his Tomcat for the kill.

"Switching to heat."

"Watch for the second one. There's always a second one!" Morrow swung out wide to the right then used his rudders to swing his tail around. His Sidewinders screamed at him, locking on the red-orange plumes of the Phantom's J79 engines. "Tone! Fox Two!" He loosed a Sidewinder.

The F-4E exploded in a ball of fire, temporarily blinding the Tomcat crew. The fire lit the sky for miles as the debris cascaded to the ground. There was no way that there could have been a shot. It happened so fast.

"I've got two. He's at our six." Johnnie called. She was cranked around to her left, holding the turn bar with her right hand. "Swinging out to our right." She flipped around.

Morrow pulled up and tried to angle back.

"He's slowing. Must be GCI." The F-4s lacked night gear and were undoubtedly being guided by a ground controller or the Tomcats. "Dive . . . burner out. Get below the mountains."

Fastball reluctantly complied, tugging his throttles into idle and nosing over toward the desert below.

A flash appeared from the Phantom's left wing.

"Launch! Break right!" She popped a string of flares. The maneuver jerked her to one side, throwing her against the cockpit instruments.

The Sidewinder raced harmlessly past the Tomcat after one of the flares. She was damned glad these were older modeled Ps. *The Mikes,* she thought, *wouldn't be so easily fooled.*

"Missed!" shouted Fastball.

"We're pulling away. He's losing us. Come right . . . overshoot! There . . . at our eleven. Forty degrees high."

Fastball jerked his nose up and shoved into afterburner, powering toward the confused Phantom with a vengeance. "Make it count!" he cried, punching his last heat-seeker at the twin plumes. *"Fox Two!"*

"It's tracking!"

"Splash one Phantom!"

Johnnic looked away, then refocused her eyes on her radar. It took a second, but she noticed that one of the Tomcats that had been circling to the east was gone.

"Fastball, we got one of the F-14s! *It's gone!"*

TWENTY-FIVE

Iranian submarine
Friday, May 7
1200 local (GMT +3)

"That's the last of them, sir." The captain breathed a sigh of relief as the sonarman made his report that the last mine had been deployed. With each one now tethered to the bottom with a weight and mooring cable, he was free to leave the area and return to port.

The mines he had deployed across the Straits were not the most advanced models available in the world. They were activated by both contact and magnetic influence. They possessed no capability, as many more advanced models did, of distinguishing between large ships and small ships. Nor did they have a "counter" that would tell them to detonate on the fourth or fifth target they encountered, nor did they have the acoustic classification capabilities and processors that would have told them the difference between the U.S. Carrier and any other large ship.

But their disadvantages were outweighed by the fact that that they were cheap, plentiful, and that the submarine had the technology to accurately deploy them. And, of courses, they were exceptionally effective.

The captain consulted his chart, then said, "Come left to course 350. Five knots. What is the weather predicted for tonight?"

The navigator spoke up. "Partly cloudy, with a three quarter moon."

The captain grimaced. Far from ideal conditions. When the submarine came shallow to snorkel, she would prefer a completely black night. Rain was also good, as it helped mask the submarine's profile while shallow.

Still, it was not as though they would have to do this many times. One day at most, and they'd be back in home port. Certainly, a submarine was more vulnerable tied to a pier than submerged and underway, but despite his chosen profession, the captain had always viewed sailing beneath the surface of water as slightly unnatural. For a submariner, he was not as comfortable under water as he should've been. As his counterparts were.

Perhaps that was the result of having spent most of his career in shallow water. Maybe the ability to transit in the deeps, to know that he was acoustically and magnetically undetectable, would have given him a greater sense of security. But here in the Gulf, in the shallow, hot water, he had all the disadvantages of a submarine and none of the advantages.

On impulse, he pushed the bitch box button and contacted the chief engineer. "If we had to, could we make port without recharging?"

"Yes. But I wouldn't want to chance it, Captain. We'd be dangerously low on battery charge, down to reserves. And if anything went wrong, we would have no reserves to maneuver."

It was as he thought. Well, the decision would not have to be made now. He could reserve for later tonight, perhaps picking a moment when clouds were thick overhead to obscure visibility. But it was good to know that if he had to, he could get home without recharging.

And was five knots the right speed? Perhaps slow to two or three. Battery endurance was logarithmically proportional to speed, and he'd use far less than half of the same battery power at three knots than he would at five. He weighed that against the lure of being back on solid land and decided to stay at five knots. Allah willing, they would be home by the next morning.

USS Seawolf
local (GMT +3)

The *Seawolf* moved through the water, completely silent. No one moved more than was absolutely necessary. Commands that might be barked out at other times were whispered, passed from man to man quickly down the length of the ship.

"Conn, sonar. I have a firing solution." Renny's voice was low. Even with part of his conformal array degraded, he was certain he had a solid lock on the other submarine.

"Sonar, acknowledged. Hold fire for now." The captain looked at the chart for a moment, wondering what it was that made him hesitate. Deploying mines was most certainly an act of war.

Not that the Iranians agreed, of course. They claimed the entire Gulf as well as the Straits as their territorial waters, to do with as they pleased.

But international law and the agreement of most nations felt that there was an inherent right of free passage. To acknowledge that the Iranians owned those waters would be to allow them to impose taxes, duties, and all sorts of other onerous restrictions that would unfairly affect trade. So, the captain concluded, he was well within his rights to execute an immediate attack upon the submarine.

But still, there was the bigger question of what the battle group was actually up to. His last communication with them had been broken off just as they had entered the Straits, when they dived below by the attack. It could be that the tactical situation right now was even more precarious than it had been before.

There were no certainties, not even if he came up to confer with Admiral Wayne. And this was what he was paid to do, what he'd trained to do for decades—make the tough calls when he was alone—and make the right decision. The captain made his decision.

"Take us in close and hold us there. Maintain firing solution at all times—manual plot as well as the computer-generated solution. We're going to take this bastard now."

Even as he prepared to destroy the Iranian submarine, the larger question still loomed in the captain's mind. What was the battle group going to do about the mines themselves?

Should he could come shallow to communications depth and let the carrier know that the Straits had been mined. That would make *Seawolf* an easy target complicating the problem of cleaning the area. It would put the ship at serious risk. And maybe it wasn't necessary. He considered the alternative distasteful. There was every chance that one of the heavily laden merchant ships transiting the Straits would make the danger abundantly clear to the carrier very shortly. Once the carrier heard the distress calls and saw the ship listing in the water, it would be obvious what had happened. But as dramatic as a sinking merchant might be as a warning, that would not tell the carrier where the mines were or that the entire Straits were mined.

Bellisanus decided that notifying the carrier would have to wait until *Seawolf* had destroyed the other submarine. If a merchant struck a mine and alerted the carrier first, so be it. The *Seawolf* would hear the explostion and at least know that the carrier had been alerted. For now *Seawolf*'s only priorities were to destroy the sub and any other mines she carried and to survive executing the attack.

Iranian submarine
1400 Local (GMT +3)

Had the Iranian sonarmen been trained in the United
States in the last twenty years, they would have known
that the acoustic signature of the U.S. submarine had
changed radically during those times. They would also
have known that acoustic quieting and shock mounting
had reduced the amount of noise radiating to almost undetectable levels, vulnerable only to the most advanced
passive systems. Even their vulnerability to active sonar
systems had been reduced, with anechoic tiles on their
hulls, a new, smooth hull shape, and, in some cases,
soundwave cancellation electronics.

But the crew onboard the Iranian submarine wasn't
aware of those advances, nor were they really conscious
of how outdated their own equipment was. Certainly
they knew the technical specifications, but none of them
had really had it brought home to them just how antique
the sonar systems they were operating were, particularly
on the passive side of the house. Nor were they particularly familiar with the sort of blow tones the *Seawolf's*
damaged sonar dome was generating.

Since they intended to remain undetected by the remainder of the American forces, the captain was not
inclined to use the active sonar. Instead, he relied on the
assurances of his sonarmen, who were growing increasingly confident, as they assured him that they were alone
undersea.

That was the captain's first mistake.

The peculiar buzz line of a torpedo cut through the
submarine like a knife. Each sailor, without exception,
felt his gut twist and his blood run cold as the unmis-
takable sound reverberated throughout their boat.

In shallow water, there was little the captain could do
about it. Certainly he could increase speed, maneuver,
and eject decoys in an attempt to confuse it. His other
primary option was to conduct an emergency blow and

surface his submarine, open the hatches, and try to save as many people as he could.

But the captain, aware of the reception that would await him in Iran if he simply gave up, chose the first alternative.

That was his second mistake. And his last.

The smaller submarine accelerated to flank speed in a matter of minutes, and the captain immediately ordered a hard turn to starboard. He then ejected every noise-maker in his arsenal, hoping to confuse the torpedo into attacking a false target. He even amplified the output of his acoustic transmitter, on the possibility that the torpedo would home in on that fifty yards astern rather than on the submarine itself.

All to no avail. The U.S. torpedo was massively and inestimably smarter than the captain thought it was. It analyzed, classified, and immediately rejected each noise-maker. The mass of air bubbles churned up by the submarine's sudden turn was also easily recognized for what it was. The acoustic augmenter trailing the submarine confused it for just a few seconds, but then it detected the warm, roiling wake spewing out behind the real submarine as its propellers turned. The torpedo turned and unerringly followed the wake.

The captain, realizing his sin of pride in the last moments, ordered an emergency blow in a desperate attempt to save his men. But it was too late. In addition to being much smarter than he'd thought, the torpedo was also faster. It found the delectable propellers with their swirling troughs of air bubbles, and detonated.

The initial impact severed the propeller shaft and tore it loose from its thrust bearings. As the shock traveled through the ship, old seams sprang leaks, and then completely parted.

Under pressure, the streams of water rushing into the submarine were like sledgehammers. They smashed sailors against steel bulkheads, killing many of them before they could drown. As the bulk of water increased, it quickly flooded the battery compartment. The combination of seawater and battery acid yielded chlorine gas, and those that were not smashed, or drown, died of chlorine gas poisoning.

The captain had the presence of mind to order the watertight doors between the forward and aft portions of the submarine shut. Sailors frantic to escape the carnage astern surged forward, and the sailors in the forward compartments had to use their combined strength to slam the hatches even though arms or legs were still in the way. The steel hatches severed the bones, but the remaining flesh and blood fouled the seals and compromised the watertight integrity.

The captain also ordered the ventilation secured, thus slowing the spread of the chlorine gas. The sailors that survived rushed for the emergency breathing devices that were used to egress a submarine at depth. They fumbled with the straps and fasteners, the lessons not repeated often enough to become reflex.

As one by one they struggled to put them on, the submarine suddenly went hard down at the bow, throwing them all against the aft bulkhead. Two more died from the impact.

The awkward angle of the submarine, fifty degrees, nose down, made it virtually impossible to climb into the emergency escape hatch, but still some managed. They crammed too many people into it, and were unable to secure the hatch behind that would allow them to flood and escape after equalizing pressure. Not one of them was willing to leave and go with the second group. Finally, the largest sailor among them simply clubbed a smaller sailor over the head, and tossed him down into the control room below. They pulled the hatch shut and equalized the pressure.

Most sailors in the egress tube had donned their escape devices improperly. As a result, as the seawater flooded in, they drowned. The remaining sailors waited, panicking, as the water rose over their heads until pressure was equalized. They then left the lockout hatch, breathing out as they rose to keep their lungs from rupturing and let the buoyancy of their escape hoods take them to the surface.

Unfortunately, the submarine had been especially sloppy about discharging its garbage and food waste. As a result, a small school of sharks had taken to following immediately in her wake, and they found still-living flesh far more tasty than the remains of the crews' meals.

The sharks munched their way through the first egress groups, until satiated, and then left the second group alone. The captain was part of that group as the last man to leave the ship.

USS Seawolf
1403 local (GMT +3)

The captain turned on the speaker to allow the sounds of the other submarine breaking up to fill the ship. It was not some gruesome ritual, but a simple reminder of the reality of what they did for a living. Each man thought he was alone when he felt a sweep of sympathy and despair for the other submariners, yet not one of them would have traded places with them. They might regret killing other men but under the same circumstances they would do it again. After all, if the submarine's mines found their targets, far more men would die.

Finally, when the last creak and groan of mental stress died down, the captain said, "Communications depth. Are the mine positions ready to go into the Link?"

"Yes, Captain, they are."

"Very well. What to do about them is the carrier's problem, not ours." He turned to his XO. "How is Harding doing?"

"Doc says he's as stable as he's going to get. If you

can arrange the transport, Doc thinks he can withstand it."

The captain took a deep breath and shook off the tension and fear of the last several minutes. It was time to refocus.

"Admiral, I need a medical evacuation from my ship to the carrier." He recounted the details of Harding's injuries, concluding with, "When can I expect the helo?"

TWENTY-SIX

USS Jefferson
Friday, May 7
1430 local (GMT +3)

Batman turned to his air operations officer. Captain Bill "Copycat" Hart was a Tomcat driver himself, a post command senior aviator who knew how to take care of his people. Over the course of the cruise, Batman had developed the utmost respect for him. "Copycat, this whole thing stinks. Tell the helo squadron commander that I want a helo overhead that submarine within the next five minutes. Peel off a couple of our Tomcats as an escort." Batman's voice took on a peculiarly gentle note. "If that sub skipper is willing to risk his ass to talk to us about it, then I'm sure as hell going to get his boy out of there."

It took a little longer than five minutes—more like seven—but a helo loaded with a doctor, two corpsmen, and life-support equipment was en route to the submarine immediately. And the skipper of the helo squadron took the mission himself, with his XO in the copilot's seat. Between them, they had almost four decades of aviation experience.

A metal frame structure was attached to their hatch,

and once overhead, it was lowered to the surface, now broached by *Seawolf*. The submarine officer on the deck held up a grounding wire to discharge the static electricity, and pulled the structure down to the conning tower. Moments later, the injured sailor was strapped in, hoisted up, and on his way to the carrier.

USS Lake Champlain
1500 local (GMT +3)

Petty Officer Apples gently slid the last electronic card home, and gave it a gentle pat. He refastened the cover plate for the data processor, then turned to look up at his chief. "If this doesn't do it, I don't know what will."

Chief Clark looked down on him with approval. "I'll tell the captain that we're ready to go online.

Chief Clark found the captain on the bridge, making the conning officer nervous as he observed his station-keeping. "Captain, sir, ready to try it out."

"It'd better work."

"I can't promise anything, sir. We swapped out every piece of every component we had. We should be able to bring up a good enough resolution off the radar for fire control, but the IFF is definitely shot."

The captain grunted. "The aviators will just have to stay in their return corridors, then. Go on, light it off. We'll deal with any problems as they arise."

Chief Clark went back down to the data control center, and nodded at his petty officer. "Put her online."

Fingers trembling, Apple toggled on the power switch. He let the components warm up, then energized the antenna. Slowly, he increased rotation speed until it was at max. Then he put it online.

In combat, the radar screens flash on with a salt-and-pepper clutter on every bearing. The pixels wavered on and off, creating a blurry, grainy pattern. As he watched,

Chief Clark groaned. All those hours, all the time—dammit, where was the problem? Just as he started to despair, the radar picture snapped into sharp, clear resolution, and a computer began assigning identification tags to the contacts.

Chief Clark breathed a sigh of relief. He turned to tell the captain, only to find he was already standing behind him. There was a light of approval in the man's eyes that did not show in his voice. "Excellent work. Tell Apple." Saying no more, the captain picked up the tactical mike. "*Jefferson*, this is *Lake Champlain*. All systems online, standing by for orders."

Iranian Shore Station
1610 local (GMT +3)

Wadi looked at the assembled pilots. They were the cream of the crop, the best that Iran had to offer. "I will lead the flight myself," he said. "And now, let us go. It is time for us to retake our rightful place in the world."

With a loud cheer, the pilots broke formation and raced to their aircraft. As their last duties, the Russians had been required to fuel the aircraft and have them ready for launch. After a quick preflight, the pilots scrambled up boarding ladders, assisted by plane captains, and strapped themselves in.

Tomcat 104
Persian Gulf

Rat studied the picture developing on her F-14's TIDs and didn't like what she was seeing at all: three large groups of blips inching their way toward the carrier battle group from Iraq. One of the early warning E-2C

Hawkeyes had detected a flight of twelve Tu-22M Backfire-B bombers approaching at a range of 350 miles.

The Backfire was a Russian-built swing-wing bomber capable of carrying two AS-4 air-to-surface missiles. The AS-4, code-named "Kitchen" in NATO nomenclature, yielded a 2,205 pound warhead and had a maximum range of 450 miles, which meant it was already within range of striking *Jefferson*. Another group was forming over Iran while a third was taking shape over the U.A.E.

"Looks like they're heading straight for the *Jefferson* Rat," Fastball said to his RIO over the ICS as he glanced at his own TSD display. This was the strike that Intel had been predicting. The all-out attempt to get *Jefferson* before it could escape the Gulf. "See any fighters?"

"Negative on that." Rat switched her radar from Range-While-Scan mode to Track-While-Scan and guided her targeting brackets to the lead Tu-22M. After hooking, then designating it, she allotted the remainder of her Phoenix missiles. The plan called for the three division wings to target the bomber formations, while the lead, flown by Lobo would hold her Phoenix in reserve in case any of the bombers launched on Jefferson.

"Fastball," Davis said. "I've targeted the lead elements of the eastern group. They're at one hundred miles and closing. It's your dot."

Morrow watched the flight of Backfires on his Tomcat's Television Camera System (TCS) with great concern. The TCS, mounted under the Tomcat's nose, provided passive target acquisition and identification at ranges far beyond the naked eye. At this range, they were nothing more than a small dot. But given the distance, Morrow was sure that what he was seeing was an enemy bomber of some sort.

"Roger, Rat. Let's go to work."

"Viper One, Two, we are Fox Three on the eastern lead. Fox Three!" Fastball triggered each of the Tomcat's four AIM-54Cs then watched as each darted into the distance after their targets.

"Roger, Three's Fox Three on the main group."

"Four's got the western group."

"Tracking," she said, watching the missiles on her TID. "Going active . . ." She counted softly to herself then out loud. "Contact in six . . . five . . . four . . . three . . . two . . . one . . . *Shit hot!* Splash one!" she hollered as the first Phoenix hit its mark. Then the second, then the third. "Damn it! One missed!"

"Red Crown, Viper Two, splash three bandits. Repeat, splash *three* bandits." The other two Tomcats called similar hits. Now only six Backfires remained. Too many for Lobo's load of Phoenix. The rest would have to be handled by Chancellorville's Aegis system.

Tomcat 110
Southern Gulf

Bird Dog relaxed his grip on his control stick and steadied his throttles as his Tomcat rolled wings level. A second Tomcat took up position off his port wing, in a combat spread, with two F/A-18 Hornets flying two miles to his southeast. The two sections were part of an eight-plane Combat Air Patrol orbiting to the southeast of *Jefferson* and about sixty miles due west of the Straits of Hormuz. Tonight, under the cover of darkness, *Jefferson* and her battle group would make their run to break out of the Gulf.

But there were still two hours until nightfall. Intel had warned of a probable attack and the activity up north seemed to already confirm this as more than simply a "probable." Bird Dog looked out his side window at the Gulf shores that surrounded him. Right now, he thought, darkness sounds better than a date with Lobo. Skirmishing with the ill-trained Iranian and Iraqi Air Forces was one thing, but to be trapped in the Gulf and limited in number of available fighters was another story altogether.

Music stopped his weapons status review when he saw a faint return at the edge of his scope. Adjusting his APG-71 radar to reach out to eighty miles, he waited a moment, then switched into Track-While-Scan mode. "Bird Dog, I'm picking up something. Looks like two heavy groups. Crossing the coastline . . . now. Heading for us at four hundred knots."

"We were expecting something to happen." Fastball reconfigured his TSD to reproduce Music's radar scope, studying it for a moment. The two groups were attack aircraft headed for the *Jefferson*: one of MiG-23 Floggers and the second of the older, less-capable Su-22 Fitters. Neither were a match for Hornets or Tomcats, and that worried Bird Dog. *There must be some fighters somewhere? But where?*

"Dixie Flight, hold your course," Music called. "We're swinging right to get more separation."

"Copy your call."

Tomcat 104
Northern Gulf

"Fastball, we have a problem," Rat called over the ICS, her voice picking up in pace with excitement. "I've got a new group of contacts, fast movers. Three-three-seven, seventy-five miles at angels ten, five hundred knots. Heading one-five-seven," Johnnie called using the F-14 community's bearing, range, altitude, speed, and heading, BRASH brevity code.

"Must be the fighter cover," Morrow cursed. "Is there any backup? Radio the—"

Johnnie interrupted. "I've got a launch . . . multiple launches from the Backfires! Mother Goose, Viper

Two," she called the *Jefferson* by her call-sign. "Missile launch! We have incoming missiles at home plate. Request backup be dispatched at once. We have fighter escorts—"

A sharp *deedle deedle deedle* rang over her headset as a yellow light labeled LOCK flashed, signifying that radar somewhere had locked onto their aircraft.

"Where's it at, Rat? Where's it at?" Morrow's head wrenched from side to side until he saw the two light gray shapes of MiG-29s Fulcrums closing on his rear. "*Bandits! Bandits! Bandits!* At our seven."

"Got 'em, Fastball. Come left. Come left."

Morrow pushed his stick hard to port and sliced the nose down trying to pick up speed. The two MiGs hung in tight formation angling toward the Tomcat.

"One, Two has bandits on our six. Get over here, fast!" she screamed at her lead. But Lobo and her RIO were still a mile and a half to the east.

"Roger, Rat, visual. We're on him in ten seconds," answered Lobo's RIO.

Morrow shoved his throttles to the stops and held his turn as Rat glued her eyes on the fast-approaching MiGs. One of the MiGs started to climb while the second held a tight fix on her Tomcat.

"*Launch!*" screamed Rat, seeing a fire flash from under the MiG's wing. "Launch at our six! It's a heater."

"Hang on, Rat." Morrow held his grip and rolled his Tomcat inverted then pulled back on the stick, jerking both the pilot and RIO violently. Angling down toward the ocean, the F-14 released a steady stream of hot flares. The missile's heat-seeking warhead tracked, then locked on to the burning magnesium and exploded well behind the Tomcat.

"*It missed!*"

"Where'd he go? Where is he?" she hollered, rolling her head from side to side. "Damn!"

"He's in front! Switching to heat. *Fox Two! Fox Two!*" Morrow yelled. The AIM-9M Sidewinder ripped

off his port wing mount and raced after the Fulcrum.
The MiG had overshot and was now drifting out in front
of his F-14. Morrow quickly released a second then
watched as the two missiles exploded into the Iraqi MiG.

"MiG! MiG!" Johnnie yelled as tracers ricocheted off
the Tomcat's right wing then danced across the aircraft's
canopy. "Break left!" Glass shattered and Morrow felt
his aircraft shudder as his Tomcat rolled left then rolled
inverted out of control. Applying opposite rudder, he
leveled his plane and fought with all his strength to keep
it in the air.

"We're hit!"

"Fastball!" she shouted. "I've got a warning light on
our . . ." There was a loud bang and Morrow felt his
Tomcat shudder again as more rounds from the MiG's
laser-guided 30mm gun tore into his fuselage. *Thud . . .
thud . . . thud* they rang out as they walked along his
starboard side. Morrow pulled his F-14D into a tight
turn, causing the MiG to temporarily lose the Tomcat in
his sites. Then the young pilot heard a groan from his
backseat.

"Johnnie!" he shouted.

There was no response. "Talk to me, Rat!"

Looking around his Tomcat's interior, he saw his engine pressure gauge read low. A red warning light
flashed on his starboard engine. Morrow opened the tactical frequency and called to his lead. "Lobo, get this
guy off me. I've lost an engine."

"We're on him, Fastball. He's locked. Hold on!"

At that instant, he heard his radar warning device signal a lock. Now he was in trouble. The next sound would
be a launch warning. *If Lobo would just—*

"Fox One on the MiG, break right. *Two. Now!"* he
heard over his headset. Morrow complied and dove toward the ocean, now only a few thousand feet below.
He prayed his damaged Tomcat would hold together.
Looking back over his shoulder, he caught a glimpse
of the Iranian MiG seconds before Lobo's Sparrow

slammed into the Fulcrum's left fuselage and exploded. The MiG wobbled, then veered off toward the coast trailing black smoke.

Tomcat 110
Southern Gulf

"Eagle, Dixie Flight committing on the eastern group." Music confirmed the intercept called from the E-2C. Yankee Flight consisting of the remaining four F/A-18s, were tackling the westernmost group. The E-2 Controller guessed that group was made up of Su-22 Fitters and probably carried a shorter-ranged weapon than the Floggers.

"Floggers at forty and closing. Targeting western group. Two, target eastern group."

"Copy."

Music completed his switchology then hooked and designated the last MiG-23 in his formation before passing the dot to his pilot. The two Tomcats carried just enough AIM-54C between them to stop the entire raid. That is, if all worked properly. If not, the Hornets would clean up with their AIM-120s.

"Fox Three on lead MiG, angels seven, eastern group," Bird Dog called the first shot, then "Fox Three on—"

"*Bandits!* Tally, four o'clock low. They're climbing to us."

"Can you make them?"

"Damn small. Look like F-5s."

"Dixie Flight, One, Tally four F-5s at four o'clock," Music called. "Range seven miles. Three and Four, stay after the strikers."

"Three, copy." The two Hornets banked northeast and slid into burners, speeding toward the approaching MiG-23s.

Deedle deedle deedle rang the RWR. "I've got a spike!" The F-5's APQ-159 radar was sorting the American formation. Bird Dog was wide to the right and his wingman was low off his port.

"Missile inbound." Bird Dog saw its plum of smoke.

Tomcat 104

Rat leaned forward in her seat fighting the pain in her arm and chest. It was a tremendous pain unlike anything she had ever experienced. She looked down at her right arm, which was covered with blood and twitching. Shrapnel from the MiG had slammed into her right elbow and a bone protruded through her flight suit. She felt dizzy and sick. For a moment, she looked up at the shattered glass in her cockpit. Cold air was rushing everywhere around her. Most of her controls were smashed.

"Brad," she spoke in a faint voice. "It hurts . . . hurts real bad."

"Hold on, Johnnie. We're heading back to the boat. Hang on!"

He heard a few faint murmurs followed by a throaty cough.

"I'm not going home, Brad," she forced her words. "I'm so cold. . . ."

Her head bobbed again and her vision blurred. *This is it. It's over.* In the last seconds before blackness closed in. In a split second, she thought of her husband and her daughter.

Tomcats 110 & 100
Southern Gulf

Two of the Iranian F-5s detected the Hornets breaking for the Floggers and disengaged the Tomcats, leaving a classic 2v2 engagement. But two still bore down on Bird Dog and his wing. The Iranian Sparrows fired by the F-5s had just missed both Tomcats, resulting in the two aircraft having become separated. Bird Dog was to the north and his wing was heading due south, swinging out to meet one of the F-5s that appeared to be setting up a "hook."

Tomcat 110

"He's closing fast, Music. Coming down our port side low."

"I've got him locked. Let's keep him guessing." Music knew that the closure was too extreme for a Sparrow shot, but also knew that the tone over the F-5 driver's headset would make him nervous and might cause him to make a fatal mistake.

ZOOM! Bird Dog's head snapped back to his left as the jet whizzed by and started a turn into him.

"Got 'em!" Music hollered. "Coming around right. He's climbing some."

Bird Dog started a hard high-G left turn, then nosed up about ten degrees before dropping his nose down below the horizon. "Keep your eye on him!" If this worked, the two fighters would end up head-to-head. It was a classic two-circle fight where both fighters executed hard lead turns into one another at the merge. The trick was who could bring his nose around faster to place a heat-seeker on the other. Bird Dog was gambling that he would emerge first. But if he didn't, his second bet was that the F-5s pilot, like many American pilots in the early days of Vietnam War, didn't fully understand his missile's envelope. In either case, Bird Dog would gun him with his superior all-aspect AIM-9M Sidewinder.

"Tally" called Bird Dog. "Switching to heat." The F-5 was still pulling out of its turn when Bird Dog's Tomcat nosed around. The warble of the Sidewinder's seeker screamed in his headset, meaning a good lock. "Fox Two on the northern F-5."

The missile loosed from the rail seconds before one sprang from the bottom of the F-5. Both raced after each other's host, snaking across the sky. Bird Dog was first to react, jinking his Tomcat left, than right, while his RIO popped streams of phosphorous flares.

"Missed! Missile's vertical." Music called.

Bird Dog's missile exploded on the starboard wing intake of the F-5, sending the plane into a slow right turn back toward the U.A.E.

"We hit him, but he's still flying. He's heading home." Bird Dog recovered and entered a hard left slice turn, quickly setting up another shot on the F-5. "Fox Two!" The F-5 had little chance. The Sidewinder ran right up its port tailpipe, bisecting the plane in a fireball.

"Good kill!"

Tomcat 100
Five miles south of Bird Dog

"We missed!" the Rio called, still watching his Sparrow head aimlessly toward the U.A.E. The F-5 had managed to defeat it, through maneuvering and chaff, but had now decided to head home, no match for the better-trained Americans.

The Pilot pulled his Tomcat's nose up and pressed his throttles through to afterburner. "Let's get this bastard. He's not getting away that easy."

"Sparrow, your dot."

"Fox One, southbound F-5. Switching to heat." The P3 thumbed his selector. "Fox Two."

Both missiles raced toward the F-5 just seconds apart. The pilot detected the incoming Sparrow and ejected, leaving his empty plane without a chance. The Sparrow hit first, ripping the F-5s right wing from the fuselage, followed moments later by the Sidewinder tearing through the port engine. The F-5 crumbled, then began to roll before disintegrating.

"Splash One F-5, southbound, angels eight."

Tomcat 104
30 miles from Jefferson

Morrow looked at his displays. He was still too far for her in this condition.

"Lobo," he called over the tactical. "Move in and check out Rat. She's not responding."

"Roger, be there in a flash."

Morrow clicked his mike again. "Come on, girl. Talk to me."

"Tell Doug, I . . tell him . . . I . . . Hanna . . ." Her head fell against the headrest then hung off her left shoulder.

"*Johnnie! Johnnie! Respond!*" Morrow closed his eyes.

Tomcat 104
Flight Deck of Jefferson

Morrow shut down his remaining engine and hit the canopy release button, then started to loosen his restraints. He had to see what was wrong with his RIO. Lobo had said that the back canopy was shattered and that she could see splotches of red on the instrument console. In her estimation, Rat was either unconscious or dead.

Fastball managed to escape just as one of the flight surgeons scaled the right side of his Tomcat and peered into the backseat. "She's alive—for now," the flight surgeon shouted down at the corpsmen following him up the bounding ladder. "Come on, people—move! I want her in surgery in the next three minutes. Tell the orthopedic surgeon and neurologist to stand by. If we move fast enough, we may be able to save this arm!"

Morrow leaned back into his cockpit and lowered his head. His squadron had lost two aviators—would Rat make it three? Taking a deep breath, he fought the urge to throw up. Was it his fault? Should he have seen those MiGs or at least anticipated that they would be there? The long-range contacts had been a mere diversion for the MiGs on the deck.

"Damn it," he swore and punched the side of his Tomcat. Rat couldn't die—she just couldn't.

He turned his gaze toward Iran. The gray-blue waters of the Persian Gulf were rough tonight, the big warship rising and falling in the swells. Somewhere out there, he thought, an Iranian pilot is telling his squadron mates about the "great shot" he had gotten on an American Tomcat. A good shot, they'd say, but "not a kill." How ironic.

Iranian Tomcat

Wadi glanced at his fuel gauge, and saw how critically low he was. The last stretch of afterburner had done him in. He had forgotten how easy it was to lose track of time and expend fuel.

No matter, the second wave was launching now. As he had planned, the initial strike would return to base, refuel, and then relieve the second wave. They could keep this up almost indefinitely, until the American aircraft carrier and cruiser were worn down.

Reluctantly, he turned away from the fur ball of aircraft radar contacts. He clicked on his mike. "First flight, bingo." One by one, the aircraft broke off from their engagements and turned back for the base.

As he came in, he saw the fuel trucks lined up, waiting to begin the refueling. He taxied into position next to the first one, eager to be off the ground and back in the air.

While the refueling truck positioned itself, a technician scurried up the boarding ladder and offered him a high sugar, high protein snack and a drink of water. He gulped both down. Then he glanced over at his wing. Two of the refueling technicians were poking uncertainly at the fueling port, a look of concern on their faces. Fury boiled over in him. After all he had done, to be stymied by incompetence on the ground was too much to bear. He stood up, leaned out of the cockpit, and said, "You'll fuel this aircraft or you will die. You understand that?" He was so angry he almost leaped out onto the wing to complete the refueling himself.

The technicians drew back. Fear flooded their faces.

"What is wrong with you?" he screamed, now almost oblivious to everything around him. "Refuel my aircraft!"

Finally, one of them spoke, his voice trembling. "We . . . we cannot, sir. The fuel pump ports . . . they're welded shut."

Wadi took his pistol out of his survival and shot the man. Then he turned the second. "Refuel my aircraft."

The technician shuddered, aware that he would die within the next five minutes. "It is . . . it is impossible, sir." He shut his eyes and composed himself for death.

Wadi put pressure on the trigger again, then a sick feeling of horror swept over him. Those bastard Russians—had they dared? He scrambled out of the aircraft onto the wing, shoving the dead technician out of the way. He put his hand into the fueling port himself, and his fingers scrabbled against a mass of immovable metal.

Up and down the flight line, the other pilots were encountering the same problem. And he knew with a cold, dreadful certainty that every aircraft now in the air, all of his second precious flight, would also have fuel ports welded shut. They could sustain the battle for another fifteen minutes, but after that, it would be impossible.

TWENTY-SEVEN

After only two days of being accompanied by body-guards everywhere she went, Ambassador Wexler was already seriously tired of it. At Brad's insistence, the men followed her everywhere, and it seemed she could do nothing to countermand his orders. For the millionth time since she had called Brad from the restaurant, she wondered what it was in his background that gave him so much power. More and more every day, it was becoming clear that Brad was not exactly who she had thought he was.

Oh, he was still the perfect aide. There was still fresh tea brewed, insightful comments on current affairs. But lately she had begun to notice a hardness in his eyes when he thought she wasn't looking. And the man who accompanied her everywhere belonged to him.

Brad had also nixed dinner at any of her favorite restaurants, and so she and T'ing had taken to dining at each other's homes. He proved to be an excellent cook with a fondness for French cuisine and the tact to express appreciation for the deli sandwiches she usually produced.

This evening, dinner was at his townhouse located in a fashionable section of Manhattan. While she tried to mask her irritation at the security measures, she knew he could tell that something was on her mind. Finally, she told him what was bothering her.

He listened to her rant, saying nothing and showing no indication of understanding. When she'd finished, he said "You who are so perceptive in so many matters are so naive in others. Can you imagine that your government would acquiesce to your preferences about your personal safety? You gave up that freedom when you accepted this post, Sarah. You are now part of a greater purpose, with greater responsibilities. And these are not your choices alone to make."

Sarah's jaw dropped. "Maybe in your country, but not in mine," she said firmly. She said it with more force than she intended, and when she thought about it, the reason for that was anger. Anger, because at some level she suspected T'ing was right. She took another bite of her salad, and made a show of selecting just the right morsels as she considered her next move. "And who does he report to, do you think?"

"Secret Service, on temporary loan to the CIA," T'ing supplied immediately.

Wexler kept her face impassive. "How do you know this?"

T'ing shrugged. "You depend on your government's investigation, as it is reported to you. Not so with us. We know who Brad Carter is—we have known for some time." Seeing the anger start in her face, he raised one hand. "Our friendship aside, Sarah, surely you must understand that if your own government is lying to you, it is not my place to correct that. Indeed, would you even have believed me? And furthermore, I have always disapproved of your decisions in this matter. That you have been protected, even though you do not wish to be, has been of some . . . of some comfort . . . to me." He dabbed delicately at the corners of his mouth.

Just then, one of T'ing's guards appeared in the doorway. He spoke rapidly in their language, then disappeared again. T'ing grew very still. Then he stood abruptly, came to her side of the table, and tendered her his arm. "Come. We must go. You're not safe here."

"I'm not going anywhere," she said firmly. "My men are—"

"—already dead," he finished. "I have just been so informed."

Wexler reeled in horror. Although she had come to detest their presence, the fact that they had been killed shook her profoundly. "Why? Where?"

T'ing's grasp on her arm tightened. He effortlessly pulled her to her feet, though she tried to resist. They proceeded to the back of his townhouse to a closet. He opened the door, then popped a side panel. She saw a stairway leading down. "Come on." Still holding her elbow, he escorted her forward and led the way down the stairs.

The stairs terminated in a garage, but not his garage. It was, she surmised, the one for the townhouse that backed up to his. And in it was a Mercedes, black, with no trace of diplomatic tags or insignia on it.

One of T'ing's bodyguards was already there, standing by the door. Another was behind the wheel of the Mercedes. T'ing opened the back door, and handed her into the car behind the driver. He reached over her, fastened her restraint harness, and walked around to get in on the other side. He spoke in his own language, and the driver replied. The garage door began lifting. Two more bodyguards were outside, evidently having completed a search of the area. One of them slipped into the front passenger seat, and without further ado, the driver took off. Almost immediately, the radio crackled. T'ing turned her. "We are being followed. Please, hold on to the armrest and do not be alarmed."

Almost before he finished speaking, the Mercedes slewed violently across two lanes of traffic, over the median, and begin heading back in the opposite direction. A matching Mercedes fell in behind them, and she saw one three cars ahead. The sheer precision and planning for this contingency astounded her. Had T'ing taken the threats far more seriously that she had? Evidently so.

"What the hell is going on?" she demanded, choosing anger over fear. "Quickly, drive to the police station. I want those men—"

T'ing interrupted her. "It would be of no use. And it does not matter whether they seek you or me, though I suspect the latter. Whoever they are, they killed your bodyguards, which makes me believe that you are the target. But," he said, with a delicate shrug, "either is certainly a possibility."

She twisted around to look behind. "Are they still there?"

"No."

"Then where are we going?" she asked, doubts assailing her now. What if this was all some subtle plot, everything from their developing friendship leading up into the events of tonight? Had she been foolish, thinking him a friend? Was it even possible?

As though he could read her mind, T'ing looked over, his face grave. "We are going to the United Nations," he said. "The security forces there have been alerted. You'll see them appear as we approach. You understand?"

She nodded, satisfied, and leaned back against the seat for a moment.

"Down!" T'ing snapped suddenly, and he thrust her down across the seat and covered her body with his. The back window shattered, cascading glass fragments down them. Wexler stifled the scream that started in her throat.

T'ing muttered something that sounded like a profanity, and snapped out another command. Then he said, "Chinatown."

Wexler started to protest, then realized she had no better plan of action. The exit was immediately ahead, and evading whoever was behind them would be far easier in Chinatown than on the interstate. She shivered, the nearness of her escape coming home to her.

Why? Was it the Iranians, indignant over her treatment of their ambassador on the floor of United Nations? Or some disgruntled radical group who disagreed with her position? She debated a for moment asking T'ing, then realized it didn't matter. Safety first—then she would deal with everything else.

Chinatown

Wexler thought she knew Chinatown, but the one she dined in, shopped in, and toured was clearly not the same entity T'ing was familiar with. They were quickly off the main tourist venue and into the very heart of the neighborhood, winding down dark, crowded streets with exotic smells wafting past them. She and T'ing were flanked by his bodyguards and the crowd gave way easily before them. She noticed that T'ing nodded every so often to someone, and acknowledged an occasional hand raised in greeting. Just how deep did his roots run in this part of New York City?

The men led her to a restaurant whose name was shown only in Chinese characters. It was small, but the air-conditioning was brutally cold when she stepped through the door. A hostess stepped forward, clad in traditional garb, but the manager or owner saw them and rushed forward to displace her. He and T'ing exchanged a few words, then they were led immediately to the back, past the rest rooms and kitchens and out through a back door. The room behind the restaurant was about the same size as the main room but she noticed it had a steel security door at one end, all the windows were barred and shuttered, and there was a faint odor of disuse about it. Some restaurant supplies were piled in a corner on pallets, so she surmised this must be a storage room of some sort. But it was clearly not like any storage room she had encountered before.

In one corner, a couch and a few chairs were haphazardly arranged. T'ing led her there and said, "Now we wait."

The couch looked clean and serviceable, so she sat down. "Wait for what?"

"More men. Here, we're relatively safe. It is a controlled area, surrounded by . . ." For a moment he hesitated, as though wondering how much to tell her . . . "friends," he concluded finally. "People I can trust.

"But trust to do what?" she asked. This was all proceeding with the dizzying speed of Alice bolting down the rabbit hole.

Suddenly, the room they had just left, the restaurant, exploded with gunfire. She heard screams and the stutter of automatic weapons. Before she could fully absorb what had happened, T'ing and his men pulled her up off the couch and rushed her toward the back door. They bolted out of it into a dark, grimy alley, and T'ing dragged her along as he ran toward one end.

"What's happening?" she asked, aware that this was really no time to be asking questions but unable to resist the temptation. "Where are we going?"

No one bothered to answer.

Behind them, doors popped open as occupants' heads popped out to see what was happening, and then slammed hastily. One door stayed open, and they ran to it. Once inside, a steel door was bolted shut behind them.

More gunfire, and she noticed that they were down to three bodyguards instead of four.

T'ing held his finger to his lips, gesturing to be quiet. She almost held her breath.

Just as suddenly as it started, the gunfire ceased. An eerie silence settled over the area, as though every living thing had bolted into a hidey-hole. She suspected that was in fact the case.

Acting on some unknown signal, one of the men opened the door and looked out. He turned to gesture to T'ing, who pulled her forward. "Let's go."

She stepped out into the alley and was surprised to see, despite the silence, that it was crowded with people. They were moving quietly, barely seeming to touch the ground. Most of them bore weapons—knives, guns, and a variety of Chinese close-in fighting weapons. She shuddered when she saw those—not much of a match for automatic weapons, but the men carrying them didn't seem concerned.

Their car appeared at one end of the alley, and they ran for it, Wexler again cursing the fashionable high heels she wore as she stumbled over some trash and almost fell. T'ing caught her as she went down.

They practically fell into the back of the car, which took off before they'd even had a chance to strap in. As they pulled out onto the main thoroughfare, T'ing said, "We'll try to make it to the United Nations now. But if they're following, it may be difficult.

Was the United Nations security force capable of dealing with whomever was following them? She wasn't sure. On the surface, you normally just saw civil servants with badges and handguns, manning the entrances with their floruoscopes and metal detectors. But when it came down to men armed with automatic weapons, she suspected they might not be much use.

But then again, in the last decade, the UN's consciousness of international terrorism and the dangers thereof had moved more and more to the forefront. She tried to recall the briefings she had heard, the contingency plans, and realized that there would probably be additional security forces at the UN that she'd never seen.

"Are you certain?" she asked.

T'ing nodded. "In the end, this will have to be stopped where it started. And that means the United Nations."

TWENTY-EIGHT

CVIC
USS Jefferson
Friday, May 7
1700 local (GMT +3)

"That does it," Batman announced as the last of his air-wing broke off and began returning to the carrier. "It just goes to show, they don't have the will to fight."

"Wonder why they all broke off at once like that?" his air operations officer mused. "I know what people say about them, but I would have thought the fighter community would have stuck it out. I know they were tough when we used to train them back in the seventies."

Batman shrugged. "I don't know and I don't care. They're out of my airspace—that's all I care about. Now all we have to do is figure a way to get past that line of mines."

"The helos have been reconfigured for minesweeping," the TAO announced. "They're ready to commence sweeping immediately."

"Give them the go-ahead—and keep a close eye on them," Batman answered. "But until you find a sweep CO who will give me his personal assurance that the

water in front of me is spotless, I'm still going to set
zebra below the waterline." Setting zebra referred to
closing every watertight hatch and fitting that would be
secured during general quarters. It was used to ensure
maximum structural integrity when transiting a suspected minefield.

Four hours later, the helos had towed their massive
minesweeping frames through the suspected minefield,
and snipers had detonated the mines that were detected.
A narrow swept channel was laid out on Batman's tactical plot. Everyone who'd looked at it, including Batman and Lab Rat, had made every suggestion that they
could think of. There was nothing left to do except trust
that the helos' gear had worked as advertised.

"Maybe we should just wait for the minesweeps to
arrive," Lab Rat's chief said. "I'd feel better if we did."

"Me, too. But we can't, Chief. The rest of the world
is watching."

"They watched us knock everything they could throw
at us out of the air," the chief said.

"Yeah, that's true. But in the end, if they can keep us
locked in the Gulf, they win. We can't let them get away
with it—we can't." Lab Rat studied the chart one last
time, looked at the overlapping swaths of supposedly
clear water, and finally put his pencil down. "Sooner or
later, you got to take the risk."

The chief grunted. "Yes, sir. But I don't expect you'll
have a lot of heartache about it if I stay above the waterline for the next couple of hours."

"Nope. I'll be in TFCC if you need me."

Lab Rat settled into a back corner of the crowded compartment as the carrier started her approach on the swept
channel. It seemed that they'd done everything they
could, but as good as that might be, sometimes it wasn't
enough.

The edge of the flight deck was ringed with lookouts,
all carefully checking small sectors of water for potential

hazards, especially unexploded mines. Each lookout was equipped with a flotation device and a pair of binoculars. Lab Rat was willing to lay odds that they'd formed a betting pool before they'd reported for their assignment, wagering on which one of them would be the first to sight a mine.

Every so often, interspersed between the enlisted men and women, Lab Rat saw the glint of metal on a collar. There were not nearly as many officers as enlisted men and women volunteering for lookout duty, but there were enough to show the troops just how critically important their jobs were. The admiral hadn't had to make assignments—there'd been more than enough volunteers. Lab Rat himself had put his name on the list, only to be told that he was needed in TFCC instead.

The air operations officer had one last suggestion. "Let's send the cruiser through ahead of us, Admiral. She can post lookouts closer to the waterline—they'd have a better chance of seeing anything the sweeps missed."

Batman considered it for a moment, then pointed at the cruiser's track history on the screen. "See that? She's got minimal control over her rudder right now—looks like a drunk trying to walk home. Yeah, her lookouts might see something, but there's no way we can follow exactly in her wake. It's too erratic, too narrow, and the *Jefferson* isn't nearly as nimble. Besides, she's taken enough damage already. No, we'll go first. Put lookouts up everywhere we can, and get the helos out in front of us. If they've done their job, we'll be fine."

The first fifteen minutes of the swept channel transit passed with excruciating slowness. The plot showed their progress through the swept channel and the TAO made periodic announcements of the time remaining.

Four minutes before they were to clear the minefield, the monitor showed a group of lookouts break away from the edge of the ship and start running for the center of the flight deck. A massive thrumming rang through the ship, and Lab Rat knew immediately what was happening, even before the collision alarm started, even before the bridge could make the announcement on the 1MC.

The carrier slammed violently to the left, then went hard down at the bow. The angle on the deck was two degrees initially, then quickly increased to five degrees. Damage control teams were called away and the 1MC began to carry the litany associated with controlling flooding.

Batman paced the compartment furiously, signing emergency messages out, talking to Fifth Fleet on the radio, watching the ship's progress through the minefield and waiting for another detonation. Lab Rat stood back out of the way, helpless to assist him in any way.

Finally, when the chaos was just starting to die down, six short blasts sounded on the ship's whistle. Lab Rat felt a cold shudder run through him.

Six blasts. Man overboard. And given what they'd just been through, it clearly wasn't a drill.

The muster reports poured into the admiral far faster than they ever did during drills. One by one, the ship's major departments accounted for all their personnel and reported that fact to the ship's captain, who kept a running tally going in TFCC. For a few minutes, it looked like it has indeed been unnecessary. But two names repeatedly rang out over the 1MC, the Officer of the Deck's voice increasingly pleading as he ordered the two to report to their muster stations.

Each time Lab Rat heard the names, it felt like a physical blow. And finally, an hour after they'd hit the mine, with the flooding still out of control on the starboard bow and the two people still missing, Lab Rat admitted the awful truth to himself. He looked over at Batman, and saw tears on the admiral's cheeks.

TWENTY-NINE

Office of the Chief of Naval Operations
The Pentagon
Friday, May 7
1800 local (GMT −5)

Tombstone planted his hands on his uncle's desk and leaned across toward the older man. "I don't think you understand—I have to get out there."

His uncle watched impassively for a moment, then slowly shook his head. "I meant what I said, Stony. Batman's on his own—he can handle it."

"It's not that I think he can't handle it. It's just that—dammit, you said it yourself. This is the sort of thing I was born for. I have to get back out there, Uncle. Besides, Tomboy is out there."

His uncle slammed his fist down the desk. "Don't try to make me believe that's what this is about, Stony. Because you know it's not. You're aching for one last shot at this, and you are not going to get it. You're staying here—and that's final."

"At least let me get a message to Batman. He's trapped in there—it's *Jefferson*, Uncle. *My Jefferson*."

"Batman's *Jefferson*. And no—no messages. And

don't make me implement security measures to keep you from bullying your way out there, Stony. You know I will—don't make me. Because all you'll do is end up looking foolish. You got that?"

Tombstone drew himself up straight. His mind raced furiously, trying to find some loophole in his uncle's reasoning, some reason and train of thought that would convince his uncle how important it was. But try as he might, he kept coming back to one conclusion.

His uncle was right.

The reality of the situation started to sink in and Tombstone slumped into the chair in front his uncle's desk. "It's really going to happen, isn't it?"

His uncle nodded. "Yes, Stony. It is."

Just as Tombstone opened his mouth to apologize, to explain what he meant, there was a sharp rap on the door. The admiral's chief of staff stepped into the room. He held a message in one hand. "Admiral—this just came in, sir. *Jefferson*—she's hit, sir. Hit bad."

"What?" Tombstone and his uncle exclaimed simultaneously. Tombstone reached for the message, but the chief of staff kept it out of his reach and handed it to the chief of naval operations, who suddenly looked ten years older than he had just moments before. He took the message and started scanning, but did not object when Tombstone walked around behind the desk to read over his shoulder.

The cold details, devoid of all emotion, made *Jefferson*'s circumstances iminently clear.

The minesweeper had done the best it could, but they missed one. *Jefferson*, with *Lake Champlain* following in her wake, had hit a mine. It detonated just under her forward bow. Seven percent of her forward compartments were flooded, and she had a five-degree list she couldn't correct. Damage control teams had stopped the progression of the flooding and dewatering was in progress now. Batman concluded with, "Whether or not flight operations can be resumed will depend on shipyard-level repairs."

Shipyard level—not something they could handle on their own. Batman was telling them that the carrier was not currently capable of flight operations—and might never be again.

"It would have happened whether you'd been there or not, Stony. Batman made the same decisions you would have."

"No, he didn't." Tombstone's voice was filled with fury. "Damaged or not, I would have had that cruiser in front of us. The submarine, too, if I had to. Without the carrier, there is no battle group. None."

"There's the *United States*," his uncle said.

For a moment, Tombstone didn't understand what he was saying. Then it hit him—his uncle meant to replace *Jefferson* with the new carrier. Just like that, without even seeing *Jefferson* himself, without pulling out all the stops at the shipyard.

Tombstone turned on him. "You're going to give up on her? Just like that. After all *Jefferson* has been through, I think she deserves a little more consideration than that."

"No, she doesn't. The ship isn't the battle group— neither are the aircraft. It's the men and women who sail in her, the ones who make the tough decisions just like Batman made."

"We don't yet know how bad it is. We won't know until we get back to the states."

"Yes, we do. Read it again. You know what Batman's saying."

Tombstone scanned the message again, and saw that's exactly what Batman was recommending. It was unthinkable—the ship he'd spent most of his career on, now mortally wounded. He longed to be at sea with her, as if somehow his very presence could hold back the future he saw rushing inexorably toward her.

How many battle groups had she carried to every part

of the world, how many countless times had she gone
into harm's way to protect their national interests? It
couldn't be that serious . . . it couldn't, it simply
couldn't.

"Sir." There was another rap on the door, and a radioman chief came in, holding another message. "The
casualty list, sir."

Casualties—of course, there would be casualties. Men
and women trapped in compartments below the waterline, those thrown overboard by the impact, mostly enlisted technicians serving their time in the Navy deep
below the surface of the ocean. How could he have forgotten them, even with the excuse that he'd been concentrating on *Jefferson*'s fate?

His uncle took the message, scanned the pages, and
his face turned pale. He tried to speak, but no words
came out.

Tombstone felt a new surge of horror. He reached for
the message, but his uncle held it away. It was someone
they knew—it had to be.

"Who is it?" Tombstone demanded. "Who?"

"Sit down, Stony," his uncle said, his voice thick.

And in that instant Tombstone knew. Knew irrevo-
cably, knew it as certainly as though his own arm had
been severed.

"It's Tomboy . . . she's dead."

THIRTY

United Nations
New York
Friday, May 7
2000 local (GMT −5)

Even before they pulled up to the private entrance to the United Nations, Wexler could see that chaos reigned on the sidewalk outside. Perhaps two dozen men clad in nondescript clothes were moving about purposefully. They had no particular uniform. Some were in conservative suits, others wore blue jeans and T-shirts. They had one thing in common, however—a purposeful look in their eyes that kept everyone away from them.

And weapons. Their choices seem to be about equally divided between automatic weapons and handguns. There was an air of menace around them, and for just a moment she quailed. Had they come this far only to be trapped right outside their own building?

Then she saw that Brad was right in the thick of it, clearly in charge. She breathed a sigh of relief.

T'ing shot her a thoughtful look. "He is very well-organized," was all he said.

As their car approached the area, they were immediately surrounded by the armed men. Sarah rolled down the window, and Brad rushed over. "You're okay?" he asked, a hard note in his voice.

"Yes. It has been . . . it has been interesting." She laid one hand on his forearm. "But my friend took care of things." She saw the light of slight surprise in T'ing's eyes, as though he had not expected her to publicly acknowledge what he'd done.

A group of men quickly formed up behind him, and Brad helped her out of the car. She was immediately surrounded by them, shielded completely by their bodies. She turned back to the car. "Are you coming?"

"Madam Ambassador, we don't have—" Brad started.

She cut him off. "The ambassador has been most generous with his resources. We will reciprocate." There was steel in her voice, and she noticed Brad blinked.

"Of course." He made a motion, and additional men formed a separate protective group.

T'ing waved them off. "Thank you. I appreciate very much the offer of assistance. However, given the events of the last few hours, I suspect that I have some matters to resolve." A brief, but bloodthirsty look flashed in his eyes. "I will call upon you when I return, if I may."

"What are you going to do?" she demanded. "Who were they, and what did they want with me?"

But T'ing only shook his head. "I'm sure you can answer part of that—and as for the final act in this sequence of events, I must decline to share the details with you. Perhaps some later date." The window rolled up, T'ing spoke quietly to the driver, and the car pulled away.

"Now, Madam Ambassador," Brad said firmly, and it was clear from his voice that he would brook no further delays. "I want to get you to a place of safety immediately." She had a suspicion that whatever T'ing planned to do would accomplish more toward that end than surrounding her with armed guards.

She let Brad's men sweep her into the building, forming a solid shield of human flesh around her. When they reached the elevators, another group had already secured them, and no one else was allowed on. She crowded in with six of Brad's men and they went to her floor.

Never had she been so grateful as she was at that moment to walk into her office. The secretarial administrative staff, as well as the two assistants, all had a shocked, stunned look on their faces. They rushed to her immediately.

Brad waved them off. "The ambassador has had a difficult day. Later, please." With that, he ushered her into her own office and shut the door behind them.

Wexler sat on the couch, leaned back against the armrest, swung her feet up on the couch, and kicked off her heels. She cut her eyes toward Brad, then let them drift closed. "I suppose tea is out of the question."

For moment, she saw a flash of her old aide, the cheerful, genial, confident man who kept things running so smoothly. Then it disappeared, replaced by the new, harder man. "Of course it's not out of the question," he said easily. "I still remember how to make it."

He left for a few minutes to go make it.

Finally alone, a new weariness came over her. Brad— CIA, FBI, or what? It would have to be resolved, and immediately. How dare they . . . ?

Is this perhaps your own fault? A small voice asked. *Is it so wrong to expect some degree of contact with your office? After all, you're all after the same thing— protecting U.S. interests, right? And you must admit, there were times when assistance from the CIA would have made your job easier. Like with Wells—some hard data on who and what he is would have made the job of figuring out what he was up to much more simple.*

Have I been so blind? she wondered. *Have I actually damaged national interests in my efforts to keep a wall up between this office and other U.S. agencies? Their methods are distasteful, the goals and objectives inconsistent with what I believe is important in the world. But*

*we all work for the same man—have I been too hard-
headed about this?*

Brad came back in, bearing her tea service. He poured
her a cup, and slid it across the coffee table to her. Without getting up, she picked it up, and took two sips. The
warm, faintly orange-scented fluid had an immediately
restorative effect. She let it trickle down her throat, then
said, "So tell me everything. From the beginning."

"There's not much to tell. The contingency plan
was—"

She cut him off with a gesture. "Don't even try. I
mean the real story. Who are you—who do you work
for?"

"You have my real name," he began, and for some
reason that didn't reassure her. "Before coming to your
office, I was employed by the FBI."

"That was after the CIA, was it?" she asked. "Or do
they have some sort arrangement that allows you to
work for both at the same time?"

A longer silence this time, and she could see conflict-
ing emotions warring on Brad's face. Finally, he said,
"There are some things I can't tell you. I'm sorry, Ma-
dame Ambassador, but I simply can't. They're mostly
things that would endanger programs now in place, or
people in particular situations. But what I can tell you,
I will."

Wexler took another sip of tea, buying herself some
time. Exactly how much did she want to know? How
much did she need to know? She had already decided
that it was partially her fault that the CIA had been
pushed to these measures, but she wasn't going to tell
Brad that. No, whatever her sins had been, the agencies'
had been worse.

"Tell me what you can . . . I'll decide if it's enough."

"For starters, I'll answer your first question Yes. I
have at some point been employed by the CIA. I still
have many contacts there, but I don't report to them
anymore. The FBI is my only other master. And as to

why—well, I think you can figure that out." He leaned forward, his voice intent. "Domestic terrorism is becoming an increasingly critical problem. The lines between CIA and FBI responsibilities are more blurred than they have ever been before. And I suspect the boundaries between diplomatic and intelligence office functions are going that way as well." He splayed his hands in a placating gesture. "I wanted to work for you—I asked to be allowed to apply here. My request was granted. And although you haven't asked, I'll tell you that I have tried to do my best for you, and this hasn't been a comfortable dichotomy for me. But I believe in what I've been doing—I want you to know that."

"And what do we do when my wishes conflict with the FBI's?" she asked softly. "What have you told them?"

"I have told them what they needed to know in order to do their job. No more." There was a trace of steel in his voice now that matched her own. "I regret that it has come to this, but I'm profoundly grateful that my connections with the FBI—and yes, those were FBI agents supplementing the UN security force—have kept you safe. I only wish I'd sent more men immediately to the restaurant."

She shook her head, tired of it all. The job at the Red Cross was looking more appealing by the minute. "We can't continue like this," she said slowly. "I should be very sad to lose you, Brad. But I must know that your sole and complete loyalty is to me—to this office."

"I understand." He stood, and made as if to leave. She ignored him. "For that reason, I shall require an immediate meeting between the three of us—you, me, and the head of the FBI. If you're both agreeable, we'll hammer out a working arrangement. I will insist that he sign documents indicating that my wishes take preference over his." Seeing his look of protest, she continued, "But I shall also make every effort to develop a close professional working relationship with them. Keep in mind that I do not agree with your assumption that the lines between diplomacy and intelligence are quite so vague. Indeed, I feel it is our obligation to maintain those boundaries. How are our allies and the unaligned nations to deal with us if they suspect that every casual conversation goes immediately into intelligence files?"

"Every other nation operates in that fashion," he said quietly. "It is the American naivete—and most of them find it very foolish—this dream that men and women of goodwill can find solutions to the world's problems in an aboveboard and honest fashion. You will not find that feeling shared anywhere else."

"I serve the president," she said. "Of course I shall discuss this with him—he knows about it, doesn't he?" she asked with a sudden flash of insight.

Of course he does. He had to have known—known and approved the arrangement. She felt a wave of disappointment that he felt that was necessary, that he could not have come to her directly. "Don't answer that—I'll asked the president myself."

"The question is, do you wish to continue as my aide? And," she said, "with a collateral duty as my liaison to the intelligence community."

"How can you doubt that I would want to stay? It's taken me years to learn how to brew tea properly—I'm not about to teach someone else how to do it. Besides, it's not such a transferable skill within the intelligence community—there's very little call for it."

"Well, then." She moved her feet down to the floor, suddenly feeling refreshed. "The question is what do we do now. So tell me—who was behind this afternoon?"

"As near as we can tell, it was Iran," he said immediately. "Our sources inside the country—and no, I can't tell you anything about them—indicate that the government is becoming increasingly uncomfortable with having to deal with a woman. They made this point forcefully to the president two weeks ago, and his reaction was about what you'd expect: He rebuffed them completely. Since then, agitators have been stirring things up, calling you, and I quote, an abomination. I'm certain that the government itself will take the same stance on this that they did on the attack on the cruiser if the connection is ever revealed. 'A violent separatist group, not acting on behalf of the government,' they'll say. How much we believe of that is up to us."

"There's more, isn't there?" she asked. He nodded.

"They are especially uneasy because of your relationship with the Chinese ambassador. Inside Iran, within the inner circles, they make jokes about it. Obscene jokes. And yet they are concerned that this signifies a plot between the U.S. and China to force additional economic measures on the Middle East. And they're not the only ones." Seeing her look of surprise, he shrugged. "You wouldn't expect it, but the British are concerned as well. For decades China was her own private preserve, and they have never really gotten over the dissolution of the British Empire."

"Ambassador Wells?" she asked.

He nodded. "His roots go back decades in China, for generations of his family. It was thought that if anyone could glean insights into your relationship with T'ing, as well as perhaps sabotage it, he would be the one. In fact, at one time, it was suggested that he attempt to replace the Chinese ambassador in your affections." Seeing her look, he had the decency to blush. He held up one hand in protest. "Don't shoot the messenger—I'm just telling you what I know."

Sarah Wexler laughed out loud. "They told the British ambassador to seduce me?"

"In so many words."

She leaned forward, too amused by the idea to be angry. "Oh, this is just too delicious. Please tell me how he was to accomplish this." And as Brad continued his story, she felt her spirits growing increasingly light. She had never known that intelligence work could be quite so much fun.

• • •

Wexler saw Wells when she was still forty feet away from him. Accompanied by her security man on one side and Brad on the other, she moved quickly to catch up with him.

"Ambassador Wells," she called out, her voice high and girlish. "Please, wait up."

The British ambassador turn to face her and she saw a puzzled look on his face, replaced immediately by warm smile. "Why, Ambassador Wexler. How pleasant to see you."

She hurried up to him and caught his elbow. "I was wondering if you might be free for dinner this evening— in the executive dining room, of course. It's so much more secure, isn't it?"

"Of course, of course. I must say, my dear woman, we were all terribly horrified by your adventure yester-day. That a member of the diplomatic corps should be subjected to such things . . . well, it simply boggles the imagination, does it not?"

"It certainly does," she agreed. "A simply horrifying experience, I assure you. But it's over now, and I have decided to follow your example," she said, cutting her eyes toward Brad and the security man. "So intrusive, but the things we do for our nations . . . Of course, you would know more about that than I would."

She felt him stiffen slightly. "Of course, there are cer-tain sacrifices that must be made," he agreed. "But you seem to have something specific in mind, madam."

Wexler laughed. "Oh, come now, my friend. You know exactly what I'm talking about. I must say, I'm flattered, and indeed, I was tempted to simply say noth-ing and see how matters progressed." She leaned toward him until her chest brushed against his arm, her voice low, "The rumors I hear about you are simply astound-ing. In this country, we'd call you a stud. Actually, I was rather looking forward to—"

Ambassador Wells pulled away. "Madam! I certainly

don't know what has gotten into you today."

She sniggered. "The question is what *hasn't* gotten into me, I suspect." She smiled, and ran her tongue over her lips in a deliberately erotic manner. Brad and her security guard pretended not notice, but she could see the ambassador's men were just as stunned as he was. "As you said, the sacrifices one makes for one's nation."

The British ambassador turned a brilliant shade of red. He drew himself up to his full height, and threw a foul glance at Brad. Did everyone in the world know more about her aide than she did?

Suddenly, Wexler dropped all pretext. "Get rid of your people for a few moments, Wells. We're safe here—they can go play patty-cake with mine for all I care." There was a note of tempered steel in her voice as well as in the glare she leveled at him.

Drawing on some inner resource, the British ambassador composed himself, as British aristocracy had been able to do for centuries. He made a short, dismissive gesture with his hand, and his men drew back. "Now. Exactly what is this about?" All traces of the bumbling fool were gone, and she faced a man who had the blood of kings and queens running in his veins.

But her ancestors were just as illustrious, if for decidedly different reasons. They had fought their way up as immigrants, learning a new language with a new way of life in America, and building astounding lives in their adopted homeland. Just two generations ago, graduating from high school had been considered a major achievement.

And now, standing on the progress they'd made, Sarah Wexler walked these halls as though she owned them—which in fact, she did. So she met him on an equal footing, as fully confident of her background and heritage as he was.

"We both know what I'm talking about," she said. "So let's dropped all the nonsense, Wells. America and Britain stand together against the rest of the world. A small part of that relationship is built here—but not all of it. We go back centuries, sir. We have so much in common, a common view of the world—there is a strength to our alliance that is like no other. Even the Middle Eastern nations, which have so much in common, cannot rival the bond we have managed to forge across the oceans. So I ask you now—can we put aside the nonsense that has gone before and begin again? Because the issues that face us are far too serious for these games we play."

He considered her for a moment, as though deciding who she really was. Finally, he held that his hand. "Very well, Madam Ambassador. Without admitting culpability in any acts that sparked your . . . *errr* . . . rather remarkable performance just now, I apologize for what has gone before. Yes, we shall begin anew, starting right this moment."

She took his hand and exerted firm pressure as she shook it. A smile crossed her face. "And I was serious about dinner," she said. "Because there is something I desperately need to talk over with you, something I will need your help with. But I simply cannot abide the stuffy environment here one second longer. So how do you feel about pastrami sandwiches?"

THIRTY-ONE

United Nations
New York
Saturday, May 8
1000 local (GMT 5)

Ambassador Wexler stood, glanced around the room, and met the gaze of Ambassador Wells. She nodded slightly. Everything would go as they discussed, no surprises. With a deep breath, she asked for recognition from the Secretary General.

"Mr. Secretary General, members of the assembly, Thank you for attending this weekend session. My aides are passing out briefing sheets to you as I speak, and I believe you will see the necessity for extending our work week. In the folders, you'll find full and complete documentation of the charges I am bringing today. I hope to answer any questions you may have in the short address.

"Most of you have heard of the events of the previous days, of the unexpected adventure that the ambassador from China and I were subjected to. The perpetrators of the attacks have not yet been caught—" A slight lie, she realized, as she suspected that T'ing had taken care of them. "—but we have hopes that they soon will be. In any event, I level this charge now—the country of Iran is behind everything that has happened, both to me personally and to America's military forces. I ask for immediate sanctions from the assembly, as well as a resolution condemning this. We expect reparations, both compensatory and punitive. And finally, we wish the leaders of Iran to understand that this is not how civilized nations conduct business. The despicable treatment of women inside your own borders is abhorrent to civilized nations. But when you attempt the political assassination of a diplomatic representative simply on the basis of gender, you have gone too far."

She paused for a moment, and let the angry rumble in the assembly build. "You will apologize, on behalf of your country for this manner. Publicly and fully, accepting complete responsibility for both the attempted assassination and the attack on our forces. Or I shall promise you, sir," she continued, stabbing one finger in the direction of the ambassador from Iran, "that your country will experience immediate and irrevocable consequences. Yes, we know what is behind the recent maneuvers. Let me assure you that the American battle group you intended to trap in international waters is no longer held captive. She remains in the Gulf under the president's orders, acting on authority of a resolution from this very body, and she is poised to inflict a damaging surgical strike on key military installations."

Wexler stopped, took a sip of water and for a brief, irrelevant moment wished that it were orange oolong tea. What she was about to say went against every fiber of her being, but there was no backing down now. "I've been given to understand that you station civilian women and children at key military installations for the very purpose of deterring retaliation. We cannot tell you how despicable this is, but the fact remains that should harm befall them, their blood will be on your hands. A country must care for her own individual citizens—that you have elected to use your citizens in this fashion does nothing but bring scorn from the international community down on you. And if you believe the sanctions you've experienced in the last five years have worked a hardship upon you, let me promise you that is nothing compared to what is to come. Now apologize, or face the consequences."

All around the chamber, the delegates stirred, looking uneasily at one another. All, except those from the Middle East. They sat frozen in position, as though waiting for a signal. And Ambassador Sarah Wexler, representative of the most powerful nation on Earth, realized with a sinking heart that the lessons she'd learned so many years ago still held true. The floor of the UN was not the place to resolve these matters. No, the deals were always made in the back rooms. She resisted the impulse to glance across to T'ing.

The seconds ticked by, and Wexler fought to not let the tension show in her face or demeanor. She remained standing, projecting confidence and determination, waiting. Ambassador Wells made a movement as though to stand, then stayed in his seat. She knew now that he, too, understood how things worked.

Finally, the utter stillness broke. In one smooth motion, the ambassador from Iran stood. Without looking at the rest of his allies, without saying a word, he turned and left the room.

The silence continued long enough for his first footsteps on the tiled area to be heard, the rustle of his garments, the small noises that people make when they walk. But then chaos erupted, several nations screaming for immediate recognition. Ambassador Wexler stood silent and implacable as she watched the rest of the Middle Eastern delegates walk out.

This battle had been won. The question remained who would win the war.

THIRTY-TWO

Flight Deck
USS **United States**
Saturday, August 8
1330 local (GMT −5)

Tombstone snapped up a salute as the band began playing *Hail to the Chief*. It was a cool fall day in Norfolk, Virginia, the kind of day that gave Virginia its reputation as a place for lovers. The last warmth of summer baked into the flight deck and he felt the familiar discomfort in his feet.

He glanced down at the nonskid, sucked down the rich smell of it into his lungs. Would this be the last time he stood on a flight deck, felt the heat radiate up through his shoes?

And the flight deck itself—so pristine, the gritty feel of the nonskid not yet worn down by the controlled crashes that constituted carrier landings. There was not a trace of oil, fuel, or any other foreign substance on it, no sign that it had ever been even walked on. Everything on the ship was like that—just as it had left the craftsman's hand, not yet marked by the crew that would someday sail in her. It made the massive aircraft carrier feel a little bit like a model home . . . perfect, yet not yet inhabited.

Suddenly, the president was standing in front of him. The band still played, blaring out the exuberant notes. The president studied his face for a moment, then glanced pointedly at the empty chair at Tombstone's side. Despite the standing room only crowd, Tombstone had insisted on it—it was only right to save the seat next to him for the only person he wanted there that he couldn't have. Although people had flown in from all around the world to be at his retirement ceremony, there was a massive, aching hole in his heart.

The president returned Tombstone's salute then held out his hand. Tombstone dropped his salute to take it.

"How are you doing, Admiral? Really, I mean—not what you tell the rest of the world."

Tombstone started to temper his answer, to let fall the words he'd learned to say so easily over the last month and a half. But gazing into the president's deep blue eyes, he realized it wouldn't wash. But if he started talking, started telling the president how he was really doing, he knew he would never be able to make it through the ceremony.

As though he were reading his mind, the president's gaze softened. "We'll talk later. Whatever I say in public, know this—your service to this nation has been beyond measure. And I'm for one profoundly grateful for it. Now, let's get on with this before these old farts start dropping their salutes out of sheer boredom."

The president turn to the crowd as *Hail to the Chief* ended and returned their salute. Tombstone's uncle stepped forward to introduce the president, but the president waved him back. With his voice pitched to reach the open the microphone, he said, "They all know who I am, Admiral. And it's not me they're here to see."

The president's protocol officer turned pale, as did the chief of naval operations. But when the president wants to speak first at military ceremony, there's not much anyone can do about it.

The president approached the lectern. He paused, giving the crowd a chance to settle down. "I would give anything if the circumstances were different," he said simply. He looked back at Tombstone and said, "We're assembled here today to observe the retirement of a great naval officer—and a great man. At some point in the program, we'll go over the exact details of his career. You probably already know them as well as I do. But as I reviewed Admiral Magruder's record, I found myself repeating one word—and perhaps some of you can guess what it was.

"Patriot. Admiral Magruder has been on the front lines of every conflict this nation has faced for the last several decades, putting his life on the line to protect our way of life. And, perhaps more difficult—as the admiral will tell you himself—he has had to make decisions that affected the lives of others. I can tell you from personal experience that while the danger may be less immediate, there's no more difficult agony that one faces. And in the end, his sacrifices have been greater than those most of us have been called upon to make. And yet here he stands—a patriot. I think that's not too strong a word.

"I could go on for hours, you know. Members of Congress tell me I often do." There was a small, appreciative chuckle from the crowd at that. "But this is his ceremony, and I'd rather hear what Admiral "Tombstone" Magruder has to say, as I'm sure you would. Admiral?" The president stepped back from the lectern.

His uncle nudged him. "Go ahead, Stony. It's all yours." Tombstone stood, and found that his knees were trembling slightly. He called upon every ounce of iron will that he possessed and forced himself to walk to the lectern.

Not like this, oh not like this—not alone again. I never knew how much I needed her until she was gone. And now . . . I don't know if I can face what is coming. To lose Tomboy, and now to lose the only other thing that ever mattered in my life . . .

He gazed out over the front row, and saw a drawn, pale Batman sitting there in the midst of the other admirals. If there was one person who understood the agony coursing through him, it was Batman. His best friend had not yet been able to speak a full sentence to him, his voice growing thick and harsh every time he tried. Tombstone knew that his old friend held himself personally responsible for Tomboy's death.

It was only at Tomboy's memorial service two weeks ago that Batman had finally been able to look in his eyes. Gazing at the torture there, Tombstone had felt his own loss recede just the slightest bit. Tomboy was gone—nothing would bring her back. And not even having a body to bury made closure even more difficult. Tomboy was officially MIA—missing in action—rather than KTA, but it was only a matter of a few weeks before she would be officially declared dead.

But the survivors had to go on, one way or the other, as they had before.

Tombstone had pulled Batman into a hard hug, and the rest of the crowd had drawn away for a few moments to give them the privacy they needed to each express his own grief.

"You never think this day will come," Tombstone began, surprised to find this voice sounded steady. "Those long hours you spend pulling alert-five, the countless days spent sitting in the Ready Room, studying, hammering facts and data and emergency procedures into your head, the midwatches you stand . . . time seems to stand still, you watch the minute hand barely moving on your watch, but in the back of your mind you know that it's only a matter of time until you walk down that flight deck and climb up into the most powerful fighter in the world. And that thought, that's what keeps you going. That, and thinking of the people that you're protecting every time you put on your flight suit, every time you fly a boring mission. And when you're just starting out, it seems that it will last forever. That's always who you'll be, a fighter pilot."

He paused for a moment and gazed out over the crowd. Some of the older men and women had a look of recognition on their faces, but most of them seemed a bit baffled. What was it he'd heard last cruise—that the average age of a sailor onboard *Jefferson* was only twenty years old? Few people appreciated the sheer numbers of young people that were the backbone of every military force, yet looking out over the crowd, he was struck by how much older he was than most of them.

He didn't feel old, dammit. Okay, maybe a few aches and pains, but he wasn't *old*.

But in this community, he was. A sudden peace settled over him. Yes, this was the right thing to do. Step aside, make room for those moving up. And go on to build a second career, one that thank god still involved flying, but apart and separate from the military.

I'll always be a fighter pilot, he thought, with a rush of insight. *Always. Even after I'm too old to crawl down the tarmac and strap my ass into an aircraft, it won't matter. I was born to be a fighter pilot and that's who I'll be until the day I die. So let this new assignment bring what it will—it won't change who I am, who I've always been.*

"I'm leaving you a Navy facing increasing commitments around the globe," he continued. "You've got some powerful new weapons to use—like this aircraft carrier we're on. But it won't be enough—it never is. And although I haven't asked him, I think perhaps my uncle wouldn't mind if I told you what he told me a few months ago.

"The battle group's not the aircraft carrier. It's not the airwing or the combatants that protect her. It's not the mass of metal or the spare parts or even the submarine that goes with us.

"The battle group is you. All of you. It's your dedication, your commitment, your courage and your steadfastness that makes this Navy what it is. And I know you've got what it takes—I've served with too many of you not to know that this is the finest fighting force in the world."

Tombstone paused again, not sure he could continue. But he would. He owed them that much. "So. It's yours now. The battle group, the people, all of it. Treasure it, and use it wisely to defend this nation. As I have tried to do. Now, with my thanks to each and every one of you, I bid you farewell."

Tombstone snapped off a salute, held it for a long moment, then turned and walked away from the podium.

GLOSSARY

O-3 LEVEL: The third deck above the main deck. Designations for decks above the main deck (also known as the damage control deck) begin with zero, e.g. 0–3. The zero is pronounced as "oh" in conversation. Decks below the main deck do not have the initial zero, and are numbered down from the main deck, e.g. deck 11 is below deck 3. Deck 0–7 is above deck 0–3.

1MC: The general announcing system on a ship or submarine. Every ship has many different interior communications system, most of them linking parts of the ship for a specific purpose. Most operate off sound-powered phones. The circuit designators consist of a number followed by two letters that indicate the specific purpose of the circuit. 2AS, for instance, might be an antisubmarine warfare circuit that connects the sonar supervisor, the USW watch officer, and the sailor at the torpedo launched.

C-2 GREYHOUND: Also known as the COD, Carrier Onboard Delivery. The COD carries cargo and passengers from shore to ship. It is capable of carrier landings. Sometimes assigned directly to the air wing, it also operates in coordination with CVBGs from a sore squadron.

AIR BOSS: A senior commander or captain assigned to the aircraft carrier, in charge of flight operations. The "Boss" is assisted by the Mini-Boss in Pri-Fly, located in the tower onboard the carrier. The air boss is always in the tower during flight operations, overseeing the launch and recovery cycles, declaring a green deck, and monitoring the safe approach of aircraft to the carrier.

AIR WING: Composed of the aircraft squadrons assigned to the battle group. The individual squadron commanding officers report to the air wing commander, who reports to the admiral.

AIRDALE: Slang for an officer or enlisted person in the aviation fields. Includes pilots, NFOs, aviation intelligence officers and maintenance officers and the enlisted technicians who support aviation. The antithesis of an airdale is a "shoe."

AKULA: Late model Russian-built attack nuclear submarine, an SSN. Fast, deadly, and deep diving.

ALR-67: Detects, analyzes, and evaluates electromagnetic signals, emits a warning signal if the parameters are compatible with an immediate threat to the aircraft, e.g. seeker head on an antiair missile. Can also detect an enemy radar in either a search or a targeting mode.

ALTITUDE: Is safety. With enough air space under the wings, a pilot can solve any problem.

AMRAAM: Advanced Medium Range Anti Air Missile.

ANGELS: Thousands of feet over ground. Angels twenty is 20,000 feet. Cherubs indicates hundreds of feet, e.g. cherubs five = five hundred feet.

ASW: Antisubmarine Warfare, recently renamed Undersea Warfare for some reason.

AVIONICS: Black boxes and systems that comprise an aircraft's combat systems.

AW: Aviation antisubmarine warfare technician, the enlisted specialist flying in an S-3, P-3 or helo USW aircraft. As this book goes to press, there is discussion of renaming the specialty.

AWACS: An aircraft entirely too good for the Air Force, the Advanced Warning Aviation Control System. Long-range command and control and electronic intercept bird with superb capabilities.

AWG-9: Pronounced "awg nine," the primary search and fire control radar on a Tomcat.

BACKSEATER: Also known as the GIB, the guy in back. Nonpilot aviator available in several flavors: BN (bombardier/navigator), RIO (radar intercept operator), and TACCO (Tactical Control Officer) among others. Usually wear glasses and are smart.

BEAR: Russian maritime patrol aircraft, the equivalent in rough terms of a US P-3. Variants have primary missions in command and control, submarine hunting, and electronic intercepts. Big, slow, good targets.

BITCH BOX: One interior communications system on a ship. So named because it's normally used to bitch at another watch station.

BLUE ON BLUE: Fratricide. U.S. forces are normally indicated in blue on tactical displays, and this terms refers to an attack on a friendly by another friendly.

BLUE WATER NAVY: Outside the unrefueled range of the air wing. When a carrier enters blue water ops, aircraft must get on board, e.g. land, and cannot divert to land if the pilot gets the shakes.

BOOMER: Slang for a ballistic missile submarine.

BOQ: Bachelor Officer Quarters—a Motel Six for single officers or those traveling without family. The Air Force also has VOQ, Visiting Officer Quarters.

BUSTER: As fast as you can, i.e. bust yer ass getting here.

CAG: Carrier Air Group Commander, normally a senior Navy captain aviator. Technically, an obsolete term, since the air wing rather than an air group is now deployed on the carrier. However, everyone thought CAW sounded stupid, so CAG was retained as slang for the Carrier Air Wing Commander.

CAP: Combat Air Patrol, a mission executed by fighters to protect the carrier and battle group from enemy air and missiles.

CARRIER BATTLE GROUP: A combination of ships, air wing, and submarine assigned under the command of a one-star admiral.

CARRIER BATTLE GROUP 14: The battle group normally embarked on *Jefferson*.

CBG: *See Carrier Battle Group.*

CDC: Combat Direction Center—modernly, replaced CIC, or Combat Information Center, as the heart of a ship. All sensor information is fed into CDC and the battle is coordinated by a Tactical Action Officer on watch there.

CG: Abbreviation for a cruiser.

CHIEF: The backbone of the Navy. E-7, 8, and 9 enlisted paygrades, known as chief, senior chief, and master chief. The transition from petty officer ranks to the chief's mess is a major event in a sailor's career. Onboard ship, the chiefs have separate eating and berthing facilities. Chiefs wear khakis, as opposed to dungarees for the less senior enlisted ratings.

CHIEF OF STAFF: Not to be confused with a chief, the COS in a battle group staff is normally a senior Navy captain who acts as the admiral's XO and deputy.

CIA: Christians in Action. The civilian agency charged with intelligence operations outside the continental United States.

CIWS: Close-In Weapons System, pronounced "see-whiz." Gatling gun with built-in radar that tracks and fires on inbound missiles. If you have to use it, you're dead.

COD: *See C-2 Greyhound.*

COLLAR COUNT: Traditional method of determining the winner of a disagreement. A survey is taken of the opponents collar devices. The senior person wins. Always.

COMMODORE: Formerly the junior-most admiral rank, now used to designate a senior Navy captain in charge of a bunch of like units. A destroyer commodore commands several destroyers, a sea control commodore the S-3 squadrons on that coast. In contrast to the CAG, who owns a number of dissimilar units, e.g. a couple of Tomcat squadrons, some Hornets, and some E-2s and helos.

COMPARTMENT: Navy talk for a room on a ship.

CONDITION TWO: One step down from General Quarters, which is Condition One. Condition Five is tied up at the pier in a friendly country.

CRYPTO: Short for some variation of cryptological, the magic set of codes that makes a circuit impossible for anyone else to understand.

CV, CVN: Abbreviation for an aircraft carrier, conventional and nuclear.

CVIC: Carrier Intelligence Center. Located down the passageway (the hall) from the flag spaces.

DATA LINK, THE LINK: The secure circuit that links all units in a battle group or in an area. Targets and contacts are transmitted over the LINK to all ships. The data is processed by the ship designated as Net Control, and common contacts are correlated. The system also transmits data from each ship and aircraft's weapons systems, e.g. a missile firing. All services use the LINK.

DESK JOCKEY: Nonflyer, one who drives a computer instead of an aircraft.

DESRON: Destroyer Commander.

DICASS: An active sonobuoy.

DICK STEPPING: Something to be avoided. While anatomically impossible in today's gender-integrated services, in an amazing display of good sense, it has been decided that women do this as well.

DDG: Guided missile destroyer.

DOPPLER: Acoustic phenomena caused by relative motion between a sound source and a receiver that results in an apparent change in frequency of the sound. The classic example is a train going past and the decrease in pitch of its whistle. When a submarine changes its course or speed in relation to a sonobuoy, the event shows up as a change in the frequency of the sound source.

DOUBLE NUTS: Zero zero on the tail of an aircraft.

E-2 HAWKEYE: Command and control and surveillance aircraft. Turboprop rather than jet, and unarmed. Smaller version of an AWACS, in practical terms, but carrier-based.

ELF: Extremely Low Frequency, a method of communicating with submarines at sea. Signals are transmitted via a miles-long antenna and are the only way of reaching a deep-submerged submarine.

ENVELOPE: What you're supposed to fly inside of if you want to take all the fun out of naval aviation.

EWs: Electronic warfare technicians, the enlisted sailors that man the gear that detects, analyzes, and displays electromagnetic signals. Highly classified stuff.

F/A-18 Hornets: The inadequate, fuel-hungry intended replacement for the aging but still kick-your-ass potent Tomcat. Flown by Marines and Navy.

FAMILYGRAM: Short messages from submarine sailors' families to their deployed sailors. Often the only contact with the outside world that a submarine sailor on deployment has.

FF/FFG: Abbreviation for a fast frigate (no, there aren't slow frigates) and a guided missile fast frigate.

FLAG OFFICER: In the Navy and Coast Guard, an admiral. In the other services, a general.

FLAG PASSAGEWAY: The portion of the aircraft carrier that houses the admiral's staff working spaces. Includes the flag mess and the admiral's cabin. Normally separated from the rest of the ship by heavy plastic curtains, and designated by blue tile on the deck instead of white.

FLIGHT QUARTERS: A condition set onboard a ship preparing to launch or recover aircraft. All unnecessary personnel are required to stay inside the skin of the ship and remain clear of the flight deck area.

FLIGHT SUIT: The highest form of Navy couture. The perfect choice of apparel for any occasion—indeed, the only uniform an aviator ought to be required to own.

FOD: Stands for Foreign Object Damage, but the term is used to indicate any loose gear that could cause damage to an aircraft. During flight operations, aircraft generate a tremendous amount of air flowing across the deck. Loose objects—including people and nuts and bolts—can be sucked into the intake and discharged through the outlet from the jet engine. FOD damages the jet's impellers and doesn't do much for the people sucked in, either. FOD walkdown is conducted at least one a day onboard an aircraft carrier. Everyone not otherwise engaged stands shoulder-to-shoulder on the flight deck and slowly walks from one end of the flight deck to the other, searching for FOD.

FOX: Tactical shorthand for a missile firing. Fox one indicates a heat-seeking missile, Fox two an infrared missile, and Fox three a radar guided missile.

GCI: Ground Control Intercept, a procedure used in the Soviet air forces. Primary control for vectoring the aircraft in on enemy targets and other fighters is vested in a guy on the ground, rather than in the cockpit where it belongs.

GIB: *See backseater.*

GMT: Greenwich Mean Time.

GREEN SHIRTS: *See shirts.*

HANDLER: Officer located on the flight deck level responsible for ensuring that aircraft are correctly positioned, "spotted," on the flight deck. Coordinates the movements of aircraft with yellow gear (small tractors that tow aircraft and other related gear) from maintenance areas to catapults and from the flight deck to the hangar bar via the elevators. Speaks frequently with the Air Boss. *See also bitch box.*

HARMS: Antiradiation missiles that home in on radar sites.

HOME PLATE: Tactical call sign for the *Jefferson.*

HOT: In reference to a sonobuoy, holding enemy contact.

HUFFER: Yellow gear located on the flight deck that generates compressed air to start jet engines. Most Navy aircraft do not need a huffer to start engines, but it can be used in emergencies or for maintenance.

HUNTER: Call sign for the S-3 squadron embarked on the *Jefferson.*

ICS: Interior Communications System. The private link between a pilot and a RIO, or the telephone system internal to a ship.

INCHOPPED: Navy talk for a ship entering a defined area of water, e.g. inchopped the Med.

IR: Infrared, a method of missile homing.

ISOTHERMAL: A layer of water that has a constant temperature with increasing depth. Located below the thermocline, where increase in depth correlates to decrease in temperature. In the isothermal layer, the primary factor affecting the speed of sound in water is the increase in pressure with depth.

JBD: Jet Blast Deflector. Panels that pop up from the flight deck to block the exhaust emitted by aircraft.

USS JEFFERSON: The star nuclear aircraft carrier in the U.S. Navy.

LEADING PETTY OFFICER: The senior petty officer in a workcenter, division, or department, responsible to the leading chief petty officer for the performance of the rest of the group.

LINK: *See data link*

LOFARGRAM: Low Frequency Analyzing and Recording display. Consists of lines arrayed by frequency on the horizontal axis and time on the vertical axis. Displays sound signals in the water in a graphic fashion for analysis by ASW technicians.

LONG GREEN TABLE: A formal inquiry board. It's better to be judged by six than carried by six.

MACHINISTS MATE: Enlisted technician that runs and repairs most engineering equipment onboard a ship. Abbreviated as "MM" e.g. MM1 Sailor is a Petty Officer First Class Machinists Mate.

MDI: Mess Decks Intelligence. The heartbeat of the rumor mill onboard a ship and the definitive source for all information.

MEZ: Missile Engagement Zone. Any hostile contacts that make it into the MEZ are engaged only with missiles. Friendly aircraft must stay clear in order to avoid a blue on blue engagement, i.e. fratricide.

MIG: A production line of aircraft manufactured by Mikoyan in Russia. MiG fighters are owned by many nations around the world.

MURPHY, LAW OF: The factor most often not considered sufficiently in military planning. If something can go wrong, it will. Naval corollary: shit happens.

NATIONAL ASSETS: Surveillance and reconnaissance resources of the most sensitive nature, e.g. satellites.

NATOPS: The bible for operating a particular aircraft. *See envelopes.*

NFO: Naval Flight Officer.

NOBRAINER: Contrary to what copy editors believe, this is one word. Used to signify an evolution or decision that should require absolutely no significant intellectual capabilities beyond that of a paramecium.

NOMEX: Fire-resistant fabric used to make "shirts." *See shirts.*

NSA: National Security Agency. Primarily responsible for evaluating electronic intercepts and sensitive intelligence.

OOD: Officer of the Day, in charge of the safe handling and maneuvering of the ship. Supervises the conning officer and other underway watchstanders. Ashore, the

OOD may be responsible for a shore station after normal working hours.

OPERATIONS SPECIALIST: Formerly radar operators, back in the old days. Enlisted technicians who operate combat detection, tracking, and engagement systems, except for sonar. Abbreviated OS.

OTH: Over the horizon, usually used to refer to shooting something you can't see.

P-3'S: Shore-based antisubmarine warfare and surface surveillance long-range aircraft. The closest you can get to being in the Air Force while still being in the Navy.

PHOENIX: Long range antiair missile carried by U.S. fighters.

PIPELINE: Navy term used to describe a series of training commands, schools, or necessary education for a particular specialty. The fighter pipeline, for example, includes Basic Flight then fighter training at the RAG (Replacement Air Group), a training squadron.

PUNCHING OUT: Ejecting from an aircraft.

PURPLE SHIRTS: *See shirts.*

PXO: Prospective Executive Officer—the officer ordered into a command as the relief for the current XO. In most squadrons, the XO eventually "fleets up" to become the commanding officer of the squadron, an excellent system that maintains continuity within an operational command—and a system the surface Navy does not use.

RACK: A bed. A rack-monster is a sailor who sports pillow burns and spends entirely too much time asleep while his or her shipmates are working.

RED SHIRTS: *See shirts.*

RHIP: Rank Hath Its Privileges. *See collar count.*

RIO: Radar Intercept Officer. *See NFO.*

RTB: Return to base.

S-3: Command and control aircraft sold to the Navy as an antisubmarine aircraft. Good at that, too. Within the last several years, redesignated as "sea control" aircraft, with individual squadrons referred to as torpedo-bombers. Ah, the search for a mission goes on. But still a damned fine aircraft.

SAM: Surface to Air missile, e.g. the standard missile fired by most cruisers. Also indicates a land-based site.

SAR: Sea-Air Rescue.

SCIF: Specially Compartmented Information. Onboard a carrier, used to designated the highly classified compartment immediately next to TFCC.

SEAWOLF: Newest version of Navy fast attack submarine.

SERE: Survival, Evasion, Rescue, Escape; required school in pipeline for aviators.

SHIRTS: Color-coded Nomex pullovers used by flight deck and aviation personnel for rapid identification of a sailor's job. Green: maintenance technicians. Brown: plane captains. White: safety and medical. Red: ordnance. Purple: Fuel. Yellow: flight deck supervisors and handlers.

SHOE: A black shoe, slang for a surface sailor or officer. Modernly, hard to say since the day that brown shoes were authorized for wear by black shoes. No one knows why. Wing envy is the best guess.

SIDEWINDER: Antiair missile carried by U.S. fighters.

SIERRA: A subsurface contact.

SONOBUOYS: Acoustic listening devices dropped in the water by ASW or USW aircraft.

SPARROW: Antiair missile carried by U.S. fighters.

SPETZNAZ: The Russian version of SEALS, although the term encompasses a number of different specialties.

SPOOKS: Slang for intelligence officers and enlisted sailors working in highly classified areas.

SUBLANT: Administrative command of all Atlantic submarine forces. On the West Coast, SUBPAC.

SWEET: When used in reference to a sonobuoy, indicates that the buoy is functioning properly, although not necessarily holding any contacts.

TACCO: Tactical Control Office: the NFO in an S-3.

TACTICAL CIRCUIT: A term used in these books that encompasses a wide range of actual circuits used on-board a carrier. There are a variety of C&R circuits (coordination and reporting) and occasionally for simplicity sake and to avoid classified material, I just use the word "tactical."

TANKED, TANKER: Navy aircraft have the ability to re-fuel from a tanker, either Air Force or Navy, while airborne. One of the most terrifying routine evolutions a pilot performs.

TFCC: Tactical Flag Command Center. A compartment in flag spaces from which the CVBG admiral controls the battle. Located immediately forward of the carrier's CDC.

TOMBSTONE: Nickname given to Magruder.

TOP GUN: Advanced fighter training command.

UA: Unauthorized Absence, the modern term for AWOL.

UNDERSEA WARFARE COMMANDER: In a CVBG, normally the DESRON embarked on the carrier. Formerly called the ASW commander.

VDL: Video Downlink. Transmission of targeting data from an aircraft to a submarine with OTH capabilities.

VF-95: Fighter squadron assigned to Airwing 14, normally embarked on USS *Jefferson*. The first two letters of a squadron designation reflect the type of aircraft flown. VF = fighters. VFA = Hornets. VS = S-3, etc.

VICTOR: Aging Russian fast-attack submarine, still a potent threat.

VS-29: S-3 squadron assigned to Airwing 14, embarked on USS *Jefferson*.

VX-1: Test pilot squadron that develops envelopes after Pax River evaluates aerodynamic characteristics of new aircraft. *See envelopes.*

WHITE SHIRT: *See shirts.*

WILCO: Short for Will comply. Used only by the aviator in command of the mission.

WINCHESTER: In aviation, it means out of weapons. A Winchester aircraft must normally RTB.

XO: Executive officer, the second in command.

YELLOW SHIRT: *See shirts.*